AMERICA
PACIFICA

AMERICA PACIFICA

ANNA NORTH

virago

VIRAGO

First published in Great Britain as a paperback original in 2011 by Virago

First published in the United States of America in 2011 by Reagan Arthur Books,
an imprint of Little, Brown and Company

Copyright © 2011 Anna North

The moral right of the author has been asserted.

*All characters and events in this publication, other than those
clearly in the public domain, are fictitious and any resemblance
to real persons, living or dead, is purely coincidental.*

All rights reserved.
No part of this publication may be reproduced, stored in a
retrieval system, or transmitted, in any form or by any means, without
the prior permission in writing of the publisher, nor be otherwise circulated
in any form of binding or cover other than that in which it is published
and without a similar condition including this condition being
imposed on the subsequent purchaser.

A CIP catalogue record for this book
is available from the British Library.

ISBN 978-1-84408-696-2

Printed and bound in Great Britain by
Clays Ltd, St Ives plc

Virago
An imprint of
Little, Brown Book Group
100 Victoria Embankment
London EC4Y 0DY

An Hachette UK Company
www.hachette.co.uk

www.littlebrown.co.uk

For my family

RENFREWSHIRE COUNCIL	
180292721	
Bertrams	22/08/2011
	£12.99
CEN	

AMERICA
PACIFICA

I

The trouble started when the woman with the shaking hands came to the apartment. Her face was small but fleshy, with a little puffy mouth. She was dressed in shabby, slightly strange clothes— a magenta skirt a little too short for her age, a T-shirt with home-stenciled snowflakes—and her skin was a weird sallow color like she had just fainted or was just about to faint. She said she was a friend of Darcy's mother, but Darcy's mother didn't have friends.

"You're all I need," Sarah would say as she combed the knots out of Darcy's hair.

Darcy didn't like the woman's hands. The rest of her was long and skinny, but those hands were so plump they were almost knuckleless, and they quivered like dreaming dogs. Hard-core solvent-heads shook like that, but this woman's pupils were normal, and she didn't smell like a huffer or twitch and scratch like a snorter. If she wasn't high she was sick or scared, and they didn't need any extra illness or worry.

Darcy started to say that her mother was out and would be out for a while, but then Sarah came down the hall from the bathroom carrying their toothbrush and looking at the woman the way you look at someone you've been expecting to see. She had changed out of her wet diving suit and into an old Seafiber jumpsuit with holes in the knees. She was little and hard, like a knife. The woman's shaky hands were opening and closing.

"Darcy," her mother said, in a voice that sounded like it came from a time before all the tenderness and bitterness and songs and rhymes and whispers and private names that had grown between them in the eighteen years of Darcy's life. "Can you give us a minute?"

Darcy didn't like it. The woman's eyes were moving all over the hallway like they were expecting something to come charging through the wall.

"What's this about?" Darcy asked.

The woman looked at Darcy's mother and Darcy's mother looked at Darcy with an expression she had seen on the other mothers but almost never on her own, an expression that said, *Please do this and don't ask me why.*

Darcy obeyed. She left the apartment and the woman walked in. They shut the door and Darcy was alone in the hallway. A wad of underwear lay against the far wall. She walked toward it so they would hear her footsteps. Then she tiptoed back. She knelt by the door of the apartment and pressed her ear against it. The door was made of cheap Seaboard—it smelled like the dirty ocean after a long rain, and if you scratched it, it flaked away under your fingernails. Through it she could make out the women's whispers, like dishwater swishing in a tub.

"I *swish* your note," the woman was saying. "I never *swish* it would happen again. I wasn't ready."

"Will you go?" her mother said. "I *swish swish swish*, but I just can't do it."

Darcy tried to hear the emotion in her mother's voice, but she was still speaking strangely, as though all along her voice had contained another voice and she was just now unwrapping it.

"I'll talk to *swish swish*," the woman said. "We're going to need money, though."

Then her voice went so low that Darcy couldn't hear it. Darcy pulled her necklace up around her chin and tucked the charm into her mouth, an old nervous habit. The charm was silver, a small scaly bullet-shape that her mother had explained was called a pinecone. Darcy had found it folded into Sarah's oldest, most threadbare shirt when she was doing laundry by herself for the first time, five or six years ago. All Sarah would say was that it had belonged to Darcy's grandmother and that pinecones grew on trees on the mainland.

"You can have it if you want," she had said. "I don't care about it."

For several years after that Darcy had imagined pinecones were fruit and wondered what they tasted like. The charm itself tasted familiar and foreign, like Darcy's own teeth and like some far-off salty earth, and sucking on it gave her a furtive, inward pleasure.

"Okay," she heard her mother say.

Their footfalls approached the door, and Darcy jumped up and ran into the bathroom. It was dark and swampy. All three stalls were occupied: a set of feet beneath each door shifted slightly. A large flat glossy cockroach glided across the floor. The bathroom hadn't been cleaned in weeks; old human smells lay thickly one on top of the other, piss and shit and menstrual blood and paper towels so sodden with these things that they became almost human themselves. Liberty Ramirez was in the middle stall with one of his pornoflyers—the soft sounds of his masturbation stopped when he heard her come in. Darcy stood against the stained sink and waited for footsteps in the hallway. She heard several minutes of silence. Then the bathroom door opened and the woman came in. Under the fluorescent light, her skin was fish-belly green.

"You have a nice apartment," she said.

Darcy stared.

"Are you joking?" she asked.

The woman smiled. Her teeth slanted inward in the front, like an arrow pointing down her throat. She turned the tap on and jumped back a little when the pipes coughed. Then she stuck her fat shivery hands under the lukewarm water and wiped them on her face.

"What were you talking to my mom about?" Darcy asked.

"Oh, just catching up."

The woman looked around the bathroom.

"We don't have paper towels," Darcy said. "You have to use toilet paper. Catching up on what?"

"You know, old times."

She lifted the hem of her T-shirt—cheap Seafiber, stained in several places—and dabbed at her face with it.

"I have to go," she said. "It was nice talking to you."

"Hold on," Darcy said, but the woman turned and walked out the door without looking back.

When Darcy came back to the apartment, Sarah was cleaning. The bed was made, their few spare T-shirts were piled in a corner. Sarah was scraping the dried bits of beef food off the hot plate.

"What did she want?" Darcy asked.

Sarah looked up, eyes wide with innocence.

"Who?"

"You know who. That woman."

Sarah laughed, a little high tight laugh that usually meant she was overtired or about to cry.

"Oh, her," she said. "She's crazy."

"How do you know her?"

Sarah turned her back to Darcy and began scraping again. When she answered, she spoke quickly, giving each word as little weight as possible.

"I used to hang around with her when I was younger."

Darcy knew this was a bad sign. Her mother never talked about the mainland, or about coming to Pacifica, or about what it was like to live on the island before it was overcrowded and overbuilt and falling apart at the edges, when it was still an exciting new escape from the frozen, used-up hulk of North America. Darcy knew Sarah had lived in a co-op in Seattle, that she'd come to the island on the first boat when she was just ten years old, that she'd done odd jobs until she got pregnant, when she became a pearl diver, that Darcy's father's name was Alejandro, and that he was dead. Everything else that happened to Sarah before Darcy's birth was off-limits, and Sarah didn't even get satisfyingly angry when Darcy asked about it. She just put on her faraway face, her face that said, *Even though I know everything there is to know about you, there are things about me that you will never know,* and gave Darcy the only piece of advice she ever gave: "Don't get stuck in the past." Since Darcy had no past beyond a few years of school, a few nights spent huffing cheap solvent out of paper bags, and many boring days of mixing jellyfish powder and spice into imitations of mainland food, she didn't have much to do with this advice. She'd stopped asking questions that might elicit it. Still, she didn't like the woman with the shaking hands, and she wasn't quite ready to let it drop.

"What did she want?" Darcy asked.

Sarah stopped scraping and stood still for a moment with the scouring pad hovering in the air. When she turned she wore an expression of nonchalance that looked like it had taken effort to compose.

"She has this get-rich-quick scheme. Get this: I just put up a hundred dollars, and in the next year a hundred people each send me a hundred dollars."

"How come I've never seen her before?" Darcy asked.

"I told her, first of all, does it look like I have a hundred dollars, and second of all, do you think I don't know what a pyramid scheme is?"

Sarah finished scraping the hot plate, then opened the window and put the scrapings on the sill. A soot-stained parrot flapped down, made the sound of a bus horn, and began chewing them.

"That's all it was?" Darcy asked.

"Yes, what did you think? Some kind of a drug deal? Or maybe she was coming to tell us we'd won a million dollars from the Board of Trustees in some kind of sweepstakes? If we had a million dollars, the first thing I'd do is knock down this entire building and replace it with a giant urinal, because that's what it smells like anyway. What about you?"

Sarah often sounded childlike, especially at the end of a long day, but now she was talking too fast, and her eyes danced with excitement or anxiety. The woman's sallow face and little pursed mouth chafed at Darcy like sand under fingernails.

"Do you *promise* that's what you were talking about?"

Sarah put her hands on her hips and made her parody-of-an-exasperated-mother face. Usually this face was a joke—Darcy and Sarah were rarely at cross-purposes, and Sarah was rarely the kind of mother to tell Darcy what to do. But when Sarah spoke, her voice had an edge to it.

"What is with you?" she said. "Yes, I promise. Now come sit with me. If you give me a foot rub I'll sing you a song."

Darcy took off her mother's socks and laid them damp and stinking on the windowsill to air. She stuck her head out the window and smelled the hot wet briny breath of the sea, a mile away to the west. The wind was changing; the rains would be coming soon. On the ceiling, last season's leaks lay dark and spongy, ready to seep like sores again when the weather turned.

One year the leaks had gotten so bad that the whole ceiling streamed rusty water, like an enormous showerhead, and they had to move all their clothes and Darcy's makeshift toys to the top of the bed and sleep under a canopy made of garbage bags. The next day the edges of the blanket were slurping up water, and the apartment was oozing into the hallway, and Augusta Beltran came by to ask if they wanted to stay with her. But Sarah put her arm around Darcy's shoulder, like a wing, and said they didn't need any help, and that night and the next night and the next they ate their cheese food and seaweed crackers on the inundated bed, and pretended they were sailing on the ocean. They were happy, except for the time that Sarah asked, "We're fine, aren't we?" and Darcy knew she had to say yes.

Sarah's feet were long and thin, her toes all huddled together. Even in the steaming heat they never got warm. Darcy rubbed her mother's cracked heels, her blue-veined insteps, the crumpled scar where she'd lost her little toe to frostbite thirty years ago. Her mother's feet always made her jealous; they had seen her mother through the secret years before Darcy was born. They had shivered in the snow on the mainland, slapped against the deck of the first boat as it crossed the Pacific, scrambled over the sand of the island when it was unbuilt and undirtied and new. They had rubbed against the feet of Darcy's father, dark and broad and snub-toed like hers, before he died and took half of Darcy's provenance out of the world.

Sarah was singing now. It was a song Darcy had never heard before, a song about sunshine. Her mother knew so many songs.

Darcy couldn't sing any of them. She could hear the music in her mind, but it came out of her mouth all thinned and flattened and wrong.

Sarah shut her eyes; she was sliding out of the room, away into a place she kept for herself in her mind. Darcy rubbed the fine, thin tendons on the tops of her feet. She wished her mother were something she could keep in a closed fist, like a coin.

" 'Cause if I never saw the sunshine, baby, then maybe" — she opened her eyes and looked at Darcy like she was someone else — "I wouldn't mind the rain."

Darcy sat in her usual seat on the number 9 bus to Floridatown, next to the green-jumpsuited woman with the small solvent burn on her neck. Usually they didn't speak, but this morning the woman turned to her, a copy of the news flyer in her hand.

"You see this?" she asked.

The printing was cheap, doubled like drunk vision, but today's headline was a screamer: SEAGUARDS THWART HAWAIIAN ATTACK. Below it was a line drawing — the few working cameras on the island had rotted into hunks of scrap long ago — of a ship with enormous guns jutting from its sides. Twice before in Darcy's memory they had shot down invader ships, destroyers coming west from Hawaii. The last time had been ten years ago — Darcy was eight, and for weeks all the kids talked about nothing but boats and torpedoes and wars. Then the threat dimmed, and the western settlements became what they'd always been — far-off enemies, featureless and vaguely fearsome, a role to force the uncool kids to play in games of make-believe. Some of the kids in Darcy's high school even claimed that all the westerners had died, that a hot ocean current had fried them just like the cold had frozen America. You got in trouble if your teacher heard you say so, but more and more in recent years Darcy had seen underground flyers posted around Little Los Angeles, their blurry type proclaiming, HAWAIIANS DEAD! FIRE THE SEAGUARDS! They were never up for more than a day.

"This happened yesterday?" Darcy asked.

The woman nodded. Darcy had never really looked at her face before. Her skin was coffee-colored, and lines sprouted from her eyes. She was still pretty. Darcy gazed into her lap at Founder Tyson's morning column, all the way on the right edge of the flyer, above the baseball scores. Tyson's face at the top was as avuncular and strong-jawed as ever. It was the face on the banners that hung across the Avenida, and across Wabash Avenue in Chicagoland, and across every other street big enough to make room for them. It was totally unlike the ancient, sunken face that made its way down from the northern tip of the island for each year's Founder's Day parade, turning slightly from side to side, smiling its fixed smile.

"This weekend's attack shows us that the Hawaiian threat is still very real," Tyson's column read, "and we must maintain vigilance. And yet, this is also a time to remember the blessings of our island, the things that make it worth protecting. As of today, Manhattanville has gone two full months without a cave-in, and although minor cave-ins did occur this week on the western edge of Little Los Angeles, they are being swiftly and diligently repaired."

Darcy let her eyes wander; she had never cared much about the news. The bus began to climb the northern hill, and Little Los Angeles fell away around them. Smog lay thick as pudding along the eastern mountains and between the towers of the refinery. Cars crushed together in the teeming flats; the first weak bits of sun clung to the soiled old Hollywood sign. The New Library

Tower, still unfinished, stretched its vacant spire up through the haze. On the sidewalk, a girl fought with a boy on a lowrider bicycle. Both were covered in thick winter sweat. The girl kept tugging up her yellow tube top. She looked young and ugly and tired.

"You know what this means, don't you?" the woman asked.

"What does it mean?" asked Darcy. She was still half-asleep. The attack seemed far away from her. It seemed unreal.

"The Board elections. It means the incumbents will talk up island defense, and they'll just win again. I've voted for Lisabeta Moreno five times now, and not once has she even made the runoff."

The bus stopped at Figueroa and two blue-suited men got out, heading for the Seaboard plant. Then the engine choked on a salt chunk and made an ugly noise like a sick baby. The driver cursed and pounded the bypass button with her fist. The woman next to Darcy had her cheap wristwatch on; Darcy tried to look at the time without letting her see. It was 5:45 a.m.; she had fifteen minutes.

"When are the elections again?" Darcy asked. She was more worried about getting to work on time than about voting.

"January fifth," the woman said. "Not that it matters, since it's the same people every time."

"So?" Darcy asked.

The woman shrugged, her face bitter.

"So, we keep getting cave-ins, Seaguard taxes, same shit as always. And all the GreenValley and Pacifica Flyers execs keep sitting pretty. Sweet deal for them, I guess."

The elections happened every six years, and everyone on the Board had to stand except for Tyson, who had been elected to a special twenty-year term when Darcy was a kid. She was technically eligible to vote this year, but she hadn't thought much about it. She wasn't sure the elections would change anything on the island, no matter who won. And even though she didn't know anyone who had gone from a Little Los Angeles childhood to a GreenValley office, she still thought maybe it was possible. There might be some combination of luck and persistence that could bounce her off the track of buses and hairnets and cheese food on seaweed crackers; she just wasn't sure what it was yet.

As they crested the hill and rolled down through Sonoma, Darcy watched the pink and blue stucco buildings with their little climbing grapevines. No big bras and boxers hanging out to dry here — they must all have working dryers in their clean, dry basements. And no fans clattering in the windows either, because these people had air-conditioning. On sleepless nights when her mother's breathing was loud as an alarm bell in her brain, when every catch or pause in that breathing forced her into sudden vigilance, she would play over in her mind the images of clean and quiet apartments in Sonoma. She would imagine going to sleep by herself in one of them, and waking up by herself, without the smell of her mother's sweat on her skin. She wasn't dumb enough to think that everyone on America Pacifica would ever have their own house, but if she could live like the people in Sonoma one day, she wouldn't worry about anyone else.

"If somebody can give me the money to move out of my shitty apartment," she said to the woman, "I'll vote for him. If not, I don't really care."

The woman made a huffing noise in her throat and turned away. The bus turned off the Avenida onto Waterfront, and had to stop for a cave-in crew. The cave-in was at the Arizona Project, a block west of Waterfront. In the faux-sandstone facade of the project complex was a hole, like a gap in teeth. A family stood around the hole, still in their nightclothes, staring. Cave-ins happened every week, but still they looked surprised. Behind them was the orangey murk of the sea, the bits of Seaboard bobbing on its surface already beginning to dissolve. Farther out, where the water was less solvent-poisoned, a jellyfish trawler hauled in its morning catch. And farther still, on the horizon, the dark guard boats squatted against the bluing sky. Darcy supposed she should feel grateful to them, but all she felt was jealous of how much money their crews made. The bus engine hacked and stalled again. She tried to sneak another look at her seatmate's watch, but the woman lifted her wrist away from Darcy and smoothed her sparse hair. Darcy bit her fingernails one after the other.

They got under way again, turned east to cross the Florida border. The bus grumbled down Palm Beach Avenue, past the pink and teal apartment buildings, built before Darcy was born and pocked now with monsoon damage. Some of the worst scars were covered over with gray asphalt paste, waiting for a team from the Pacifica Aesthetic Company to come paint over them. You got in trouble for painting yourself here, or for doing anything that violated the neighborhood's theme. Once a high wind had blown the Seaboard flamingos out of the World Experiences lawn, and a guard had arrived with an injunction to replace them. It was important, he said, to maintain the neighborhood's ancestral character. The guards didn't bother too much about graffiti or paint jobs in Little Los Angeles, though. Some neighborhoods were too cheap for ancestral character. After the apartments came the first of the nursing homes, big gloomy Eden Acres. The woman let her wrist fall into Darcy's view—5:54. The bus hit a red light at Palm Beach and Tampa, just before Darcy's stop. She bit down hard on her thumb and tasted blood.

Then they were at her stop and Darcy charged out. She ran past the Paradise Valley Assisted Living Center and the Graceful Living Retirement Home, past the medical-supply store and the mortuary, past the long pale polished stairway and the World Experiences Mature Community sign, around the side of the building, and into the little mouse-colored door marked SERVICE. Then down the low beige hallway, in and out between the jugs of cooking oil and boxes of dried jellyfish, over the pile of discarded seaweed cans, through the second door, and into the steamy smelly kitchen. The clock on the wall read 5:59.

"You hear about the attack?" she asked Trish as they pulled on their hairnets.

"Yeah," Trish said. "Somebody told me the Hawaiians got frozen out years ago. Guess they were wrong."

"I heard they had crazy glass-domed cities," said Win, firing up the griddle. "And boats with built-in grenade launchers. I heard they're sending a whole fleet for, like, revenge."

Trish rolled her eyes. Win was known for his solvent habit and his alarmism.

"Whatever," she said. "You hear about this?"

She pointed at the blackboard where their boss Marcelle had written the day's menu. It read:

BREAKFAST: hash browns, jellyfish sausage, scrambled egg product
LUNCH: turkey (jellyfish) sandwich, seaweed salad
DINNER: seaweed salad, mashed potato product, T-bone steak

In Darcy's two years at World Experiences, T-bone steak day had occurred only twice. They served Salisbury steak every other Friday, but that they could make out of jellyfish and beef flavor and texturizer; T-bone had to be mostly real. They got it from the one stockyard on the island, in Texas Town, and one steak cost more than Darcy made in a month. Breakfast and lunch were a blur of anticipation. Darcy and the rest of the kitchen staff bolted their break-time protein bars without tasting them. They barely talked about the attack. Their minds were all on how to steal some meat.

Trish's method was the simplest—she cut a small piece off every fifth steak as she was plating it, then shoved it in her mouth. Trish was a year younger than Darcy but she'd been working twice as long. She'd gotten a waiver from the Pacifica Board of Trustees because she had so many brothers and sisters. Her youngest brother was her favorite because he was smart; Trish said he was going to get a scholarship to go to the University someday and study marine engineering. Every year there were fewer scholarships—fewer bright, hopeful names published in the April news flyers—but still every smart kid on the island dreamt of them at night. If you went to the University you were basically guaranteed a good job, something where you sat at a desk all day and didn't get your hands dirty. Something that would pay for a full apartment with its own toilet and shower. Most of the kids who went to the University were born rich, but for those very few scholarship kids it was a way to make money, a way to bounce yourself out. Darcy had always been an inattentive and indifferent student, so she'd never had a shot at this kind of escape. But before she dropped out, she remembered the older kids coming back from scholarship qualifying exams, looking uneasy and confused. Nobody would ever say what was on the exams; supposedly you'd get arrested if you told. And Darcy had never known anyone who'd passed.

Win's method was the grossest. He plucked each steak off the plate and licked it before adding scoops of potato food and seaweed salad. Darcy had bigger plans. She wanted to steal a whole steak. Her job was to trim the gristle off the meat and lay it on the griddle. When she got an especially big steak, she let the knife swing wide, until she had four gristly pieces to lay on the griddle in the rough shape of an actual steak.

"I'm not plating that," Trish said. "It looks stupid."

"You just have to make sure Megan Kramer gets it. Or that Emily woman with the one eye. They won't be able to see the difference."

"Oh right, so I'm just supposed to tell Stella to give this one to a blindie? What if she asks why? How come you can't just sneak pieces like a normal person?"

"Because I want a real steak dinner for my mom and me. With the bone in it."

She slipped a rare steak off the griddle, wrapped it in two layers of Seafiber napkin, and stuffed it down the front of her jumpsuit.

"Just hand it to Stella last," she said. "The blindies always come in late anyway. It'll be fine."

Trish shrugged and snuck another bite.

"It's gonna taste like your sweaty tits," she said.

Darcy smacked her in the arm. The birdsong tape started playing in the dining room, and the residents began drifting in. Darcy peeked out the serving window—as usual, the youngest and most able residents were arriving first. The dining room was prairie themed. Someone in the early days of World Experiences had sponge-painted a golden grassland across the walls. In the corner near the kitchen, a family of prairie dogs stuck their pointed noses and giant cartoon eyes up out of the grass. On the opposite wall three wild horses, slender and bright red, drank from a blurry stream. Next to the entrance, and farthest from the kitchen, a milky-skinned girl in a blue dress stood at the doorway of a thatch-roofed cottage, perpetually waving good-bye. The girl

17

had made Darcy laugh when she first got to World Experiences—it had been a good fifty years since anyone could've gone outside on the mainland prairie in a dress that flimsy. Probably whoever painted it had never seen a mainland meadow that wasn't heavily lidded with snow. Darcy could've done just as good a job, even though she was island-born and the only dogs she'd ever seen were the ones that came over on the last boat with all the criminals and homeless people. She hadn't paid much attention in history class, but she knew people wanted to remember the mainland the way you remember a beloved dead person—pretty, and young, and happy, and always the same.

Win set the plates in the serving window and Stella, in her bright blue prairie-girl dress, set them before the women. The room filled quickly at first, then more slowly as the arrivals grew slower and lamer and blinder, pushing walkers before them and trailing IV bags behind them and moving laboriously through the gel that time becomes for the very old and sick. The people at World Experiences weren't very rich. They had more money than Darcy—the people in her building got old and died right there, not in homes with nurses and cooks and prairie girls on the walls. But the really rich people—old executives and Board members and higher-ups in the guards—went to Paradise Valley, where Darcy heard they got steak once a week and jellyfish powder was banned. Or their families hired service workers from Little Los Angeles or Lower Chicagoland to push their wheelchairs and spoon crushed-up real strawberries into their mouths. These jobs paid well, but Darcy hadn't been able to get one. You needed a smooth face, unpockmarked, and straight teeth—you had to be just like a rich person, except poor. The old men and women who hobbled in now couldn't afford servants, and they couldn't afford Paradise Valley. What their middling fortunes could buy was steak once a year and someone like Darcy to lie in wait and steal from them. Finally Emily Jones made her slow way in and sat in the back by the waterfall with Megan Kramer and Che Simpson, who could only say the word "kale."

"Okay—now," Darcy said. "Put it out now."

The fake steak lay between the potatoes and the seaweed, the edges of its component parts melted slightly together by the heat of the griddle. Trish placed it in the serving window and Stella took it. Then Trish said, "Shit."

"What?" Darcy looked up from a sink slowly filling with suds.

"Marcelle."

Darcy looked out and saw her boss, regal in her old-style skirt suit, broad-hipped, small-waisted, her eyes narrowed in constant, minute appraisal.

"It's fine," Darcy said. "They won't notice anything, she won't notice anything. It's fine."

Stella picked her way past canes and walkers and wheelchairs to the back of the room, where she set plates in front of Megan and Emily.

"See?" Darcy said. "We're fine."

Then the dining room door opened and in came Ramona Smith-Sanchez, graceful, loose-limbed, and sharp-eyed. Ramona did yoga every day. She still got the mystery flyers delivered to her room. Stella lifted the final plate and Darcy willed it to teeter, to flip, to splay its contents across the golden-brown prairie floor. But Stella conveyed it smoothly through the air and set it in front of Ramona.

She didn't look at her plate right away. First she made some joke to Stella, who gave an employee's polite laugh. Then she touched Megan on the arm and the two of them shared some kind of furtive, sympathetic communication. Then she looked at Stella again, and for a moment Darcy thought that time had become a circle, that they would be trapped forever in the minute and a half before Ramona touched her steak. Stella was laughing again. Ramona was laughing. Megan was quietly filling her mouth with food. Then Ramona picked up her fork and knife and cut herself a piece of meat. She put it between her lips. She chewed. She shut her eyes in pleasure like the woman on the GreenValley Foods flyers.

"Okay," Trish said, "you were right."

But Ramona was pausing with the second bite still on her fork. She was looking down at her plate with precise concentration. She was using a knife to pry the pieces of steak apart. She was calling for Stella, and they were both peering at the plate, and then Marcelle was stirring from her spot in the corner of the room, and she was gazing balefully at the mangled steak, and she was moving in the direction of the kitchen, the offending plate in her manicured hand.

"Look busy," Darcy hissed, and they all began showily scrubbing.

Darcy was shoving a stack of mixing bowls into scalding water when Marcelle came through the swinging doors. She stood in the center of the kitchen and seemed to pull the whole room toward her, like a weight in the center of a cloth. She held up the plate. The steak was spread apart, and its pink juices were staining the potatoes.

"What is this?" she asked.

Her anger always had pleasure at the edges of it, like it would bring her joy to be proved right about their uselessness. She was forty-five, high-cheekboned, handsome. In her office were drawings of her attractive, well-nourished children.

Darcy could feel the others silently willing her to confess. They would never say it, but they wanted her to step forward and bear the punishment alone. But she couldn't afford even a small pay cut right now, not with their rent due next week.

"It's a steak," she said.

"It is not a steak," Marcelle said. "A steak at World Experiences is a tasty, succulent piece of meat presented in an attractive fashion. Ms. Pern, does this object meet that definition of a steak?"

"No, but—"

"And why not?"

Before she dropped out of high school, when she hadn't studied for a test, she sometimes tried to open up her mind so that the universe could pour answers into it. She would shut her eyes, hold her breath, and imagine her brain as an open bowl into which inspiration could flow. It worked once—when the date of the island's founding, April 10, 2043, had fallen into her consciousness like a cube of glittering ice. She tried it now, but all that came were stupid ideas—a monkey came in and ate part of the steak, it was like that when we got it from the butcher, Ramona must've hidden a bone in her sweater. Darcy chose the least dumb of these ideas.

"That steak was supposed to be for Megan Kramer," she said.

Trish shot her an angry face.

"She asked us for one without the bone," Darcy went on. "She doesn't like the way it looks. But things just get so crazy in here, and we forgot to tell Stella."

"So if I were to ask Mrs. Kramer, she'd tell me she wanted a steak with no bone?"

"Not to be disrespectful," Darcy said, "but Mrs. Kramer isn't always the most consistent of our residents."

At first Marcelle seemed to be looking at Darcy with skepticism. Then Darcy saw it was confusion.

"Darcy," she asked, "what is on your jumpsuit?"

Darcy looked down. The steak juice had oozed through the Seafiber, making an angry red-brown stain on the left side of her belly. Trish's eyes burned at her. Standing behind Marcelle, Win pointed a finger gun to his temple and fired it. Darcy felt herself teetering forward into a future in which she confessed, pulled the steak out of her jumpsuit, lost her job, and walked out onto the street with no money and nowhere to be. The sensation was almost pleasurable. Then the idea she'd been waiting for came and knocked her back.

"I'm sorry," she said, "I'm so sorry."

Then she doubled over with fake tears.

"I thought it had stopped," she went on, gasping and covering her face with her hands.

"What on earth is wrong with you?" Marcelle asked.

"I had an operation. I didn't have the money for a hospital, so I went to someone I heard about. He didn't sew me up right, and now it keeps bleeding."

Something wavered in Marcelle's eyes. Darcy stepped up her sniffling. She told herself she was a truthful, pathetic, injured person who had every reason to cry.

"You know better than that, Darcy," Marcelle said. "Go clean yourself up. You're a health hazard."

Darcy nodded and wiped her eyes.

"And I'm going to garnish your wages to pay for that steak. I'm not going to reward this kind of behavior."

Darcy went to the staff restroom, a little Seaboard stall off the kitchen, and splashed cold water on the stain. She didn't know how she was going to make rent now, but she took the steak out of her jumpsuit and looked at it, and lifted it to her nose and smelled it, and felt a thief's pride.

★   ★   ★

When she got home it was dark, but still hot. The smell of rain was heavy as a lid on the air. A street show was going on outside her building. The players came to the Avenida on nights and weekends hoping for spare change, and they usually did one of three routines—girls getting their clothes accidentally torn off, a trained monkey in a business suit dancing around with a briefcase, or a group of men acting out life on the mainland and the origin of the island. This was the mainland show—the Mainland family were huddled together on the sidewalk, shivering. The North Wind was blowing all around them and scattering Seafiber snowflakes.

"What will we do?" asked Mrs. Mainland, a big man whose chest hair peeked out the neckline of his dress. "Our crops are dead and we're running out of cats to eat!"

Sarah wasn't back yet. Darcy let herself in and started getting dinner ready. She set the steak, still in its bloody napkins, on a stack of old romance flyers in the cool spot under the window. She plugged in the hot plate, then opened a can of chopped onion. In the mini fridge she found half a can of peas, not yet foul smelling. The pan was dirty. She took it to the bathroom to wash it in the sink. Augusta Beltran was there before her, mixing water with her baby's powdered formula. The baby himself was strapped to Augusta's chest—he looked at Darcy with his tiny alien eyes and began to wail.

"He's just hungry," Augusta said, and she shook the liquid until it went white. "My bus broke down and I had to walk back here from Chicagoland, and it took an hour and a half and I stepped in monkey shit, and he wouldn't eat when my mom tried to feed him, for whatever reason, so of course he's starving—"

Darcy gave her a polite smile and turned away. Augusta was lonely—she worked ten hours a day on a refrigerator assembly line where no one was allowed to talk, and her husband had gone insane and wandered up and down the Avenida talking about some kind of conspiracy, and if you stood next to her for any length of time she'd tell you a story so sad you didn't want to get out of bed anymore.

The plate was hot when Darcy got back. She set the clean pan down on it, and the water sizzled underneath.

"Mrs. Mainland," said Mr. Mainland outside Darcy's window, "I'm sorry that it's come to this, but we're going to have to eat the children."

Heavy boots clomped on the stairs; Verano Ortiz must be back from the refinery. Darcy heard his wife come out to kiss him. Sarah was late. Verano almost never got home before her. Maybe she had taken an extra dive. Darcy unplugged the hot plate. When her mother dove till dark in search of extra pearls, she came back looking like a sea creature—her eyes big and staring, her fingers long and white and cold like the clammy toes of some underwater salamander. Her hair and skin smelled like the ocean, and her speech was always vague and abstracted, and she forgot the names of things.

Darcy unfolded and refolded her mother's worn-out jumpsuit, her own old school uniform, her one extra T-shirt. She straightened her dolls—rocks with Seafiber skirts wrapped around them—and the cheese-food can cut into the shape of a crown that she'd worn for dress-up as a child. She wiped the dust off *An Animal Atlas of the West Coast,* the only possession her mother had saved from the mainland. Outside, Mr. Mainland was getting ready to butcher his children. He sharpened a big Seaboard knife on a chunk of rock. The children—two fat men in old-fashioned sailor suits—mewled and cried.

The alarm clock read 10 p.m. The electricity would be going out soon. Darcy lit the oil lamp—the sweet smell of solvent came crackling up. Then she plugged the hot plate back in and filled the pan with steak, onions, and peas. A prerational part of her brain was taking over, and it was telling her that Sarah was more likely to come when she was distracted. She stirred the onions and flipped the steak. She shook some cheese powder into the pan. She tried not to listen for footsteps on the stairs.

On the street below, Founder Tyson arrived at the Mainland family's house. Mr. Mainland was chasing the children around. The actor playing Tyson was wearing a red coat trimmed in fake white fur, high-heeled shoes, and white gloves. He put on a high, patrician voice.

"Oh dear! This riffraff is going to commit murder. Whatever shall I do?"

Two guards walked by and the actors froze. The guards' attitude toward the street shows was unpredictable. Usually they approved of references to mainland culture—cowboy bars and baseball teams and even Elvis impersonators supposedly got subsidies from the Board. But those were Old Mainland, before the ice—newer memories didn't get the same privileged status. Darcy had once seen a guard handcuff a player for making fun of Tyson, and shove him into the back of his shiny black-and-white car.

When the guards turned the corner onto Fifteenth Street, the Tyson actor gave his forehead an exaggerated wipe, then shifted back into character. One of the children stopped running and stood up to Mr. Mainland.

"Wait, Daddy," he said, "don't eat us. I have an idea. What if we make a boat and take it over the ocean to where it's warm outside? Then none of us will have to die."

"That's a grand idea," trilled Tyson, running into the scene.

"Let's tell everyone! And don't worry, young sir, you'll get all the credit. I won't take any of it at all."

The audience outside laughed, and then the electricity went out. Darcy sat in the folding chair in the waxy orange light of the oil lamp. Even if her mother had taken a dusk dive, she should be home by now. It was 10:45.

The latest Sarah had ever come home was 3 a.m. Darcy had been eight. Before that she had never worried about Sarah. But that night she had looked out onto the Avenida de la Reina and seen it riven with cracks, fissures her mother could slide through that would take her somewhere far away that Darcy could never reach. A bus could run her down, or the man selling solvent on the corner could shoot her with a gun. The two big boys in muscle shirts could kidnap her, the girl gang drinking beer in the alley could beat her up, the guard in his patrol car could arrest her for a made-up crime. Or her bus could explode, or she could drown during a dive, or—most disturbing of all—she could decide to walk away and never come home.

That night Darcy had gotten into their bed and pulled the blanket up around her and cursed all the people she could think of to curse. She cursed her father for dying before she was born and leaving only one person to take care of her, and her grandmother back on the mainland for abandoning her mother and disappearing down some frozen road instead of huddling around her, sag-breasted and wise, like other people's grandmothers. She cursed the kids at school for thinking she was weird, and the few kids who did play with her for being weird themselves and making her look weirder, and old Dolores Beltran for checking on her and bringing her *buñuelos* and making her feel like an orphan. And most of all she cursed her mother, for curling against her at night so that without her the bed felt empty, and for making a headdress of parrot feathers or a rock doll or a game with cheese-food cans on Sunday mornings so that Darcy never wanted to leave the apartment, never wanted to make another friend, because who would know her so well, who would pay so much attention to her, who would create a little sealed-off world inside the real world where they were the only people and theirs were the only laws?

That night ten years ago, Sarah had come back apologetic, saying she'd been with some friends. It didn't make sense to Darcy— her mother didn't have friends then either—and so Darcy had asked her who they were. Her mother had taken Darcy's hair in her hands and begun to braid it, but she kept dropping strands and having to start again.

"You know when you don't see someone for a long time," she had said, "and then when you do, you have a lot to talk about?"

"No," Darcy had answered.

"Well, one day you'll know what I mean, and then you'll understand why I was gone so long."

"No I won't," Darcy had said, very sure. "Who are you talking about? Why didn't they come here?"

But Sarah had only crawled into bed with Darcy and fed her arms under Darcy's armpits so they were like one two-headed, four-armed, four-legged animal, and whispered that Darcy shouldn't be afraid because it would never happen again. Still Darcy had been afraid all the rest of that night, and the next, and for a long time after, and she was afraid now.

She looked out the window and down the Avenida. She saw a small woman carrying a bag, and her belly fluttered with hope— then the woman turned onto Fifteenth Street, and the hope turned to acid in her throat. She uncovered the pan to look at their dinner—a little weak warmth came floating up. All the smells of the food had mixed up together, so instead of steak and

27

peas and onions, Darcy smelled a metallic, chemical funk. She knew she should eat her half now, while it was still a little warm. But her throat felt stopped up, like she couldn't put anything down it. The napkins from World Experiences were blood-soaked and useless now, so she got some toilet paper from the bathroom. Then she wrapped everything up into an oozy package and stuffed it in the fridge, closing the door fast so as not to let too much cold out. It would serve her mother right to come home to a dinner that looked like what rich people fed their cats. She hated that she had gotten her pay docked for a mess of lukewarm meat, and although she knew it was stupid, she thought that maybe stealing the steak had somehow made her mother late.

Outside, the player Tyson was rhapsodizing about his plans for the island.

"And everything will run on my wonderful new solvent invention," he said, "which is totally nontoxic and will under no circumstances leach into the ocean and cause the coastline to collapse."

Darcy got in bed. The sheets needed washing. They smelled like Sarah's sweat, a smell so familiar and predictable that it was like a time of day. She nestled in the midnight of her mother's sweat. If she could fall asleep, Darcy told herself, in the morning her mother would be back. She closed her eyes; the weight of the day pulled the lids tight. She thought of setting the alarm clock and decided her mother would set it when she came in. Setting it would be like willing her mother not to come back.

She turned to face away from the window. A woman's footsteps rang in the hallway. Darcy lifted her head. They died away; she lowered it again. She was listening to the people clapping for the mainland show, and listening to the hallway for the disturbance of a shoe, and then she was locked in her dream again, the dream where the real Tyson was going to give her a house with a hundred white-walled rooms. He was smiling over her, calm and good-looking, like in the news flyers, and all she had to do was sign the deed, but all that came from her pen were curse words, *cocksucker* and *shiteater* and *cuntface,* and no matter how much Tyson yelled or pleaded or threatened her with prison, her hand wouldn't even begin to form her own name.

The rain had started. The smell woke Darcy, all the stirred-up dirt and parrot shit, the rancid stink of wet trash, and, beneath everything, the sharp, savory smell of the sea.

"Time to get the bucket," Darcy said, but no one answered.

She turned. Beside her in the bed was a space for her mother, cool, sweat-smelling, and unused.

The air seemed to change color. Yellow walls of panic slid down between Darcy and the world. The splatter of the rain grew dim and Darcy was in a box, a yellow box with nothing inside it but her and the fact of her mother's absence. She jumped out of bed and the box followed. She ran down the hallway calling, and the box ran with her, and when Dolores Beltran opened her door and asked if everything was all right, her voice barely penetrated the box.

"Have you seen my mother?" Darcy asked.

Mrs. Beltran's face was yellow. Her loose Seafiber nightgown was yellow, and her teeth and tongue were yellow when she opened her mouth to say, "Not since yesterday morning. Is everything all right?"

The bathroom doors were yellow and the toilets were yellow like someone had pissed all over them, and Dici Quintero's penis was yellow when she walked in on him in a stall.

"Don't you knock?" he yelled at her, but she and the box were tearing down the stairs (yellow), out onto the wet sidewalk (yellow), and down the Avenida to the bus stop, where the bus (always yellow, now a sickening liverish brown like beef tea) was just rumbling into view.

On the number 3 bus Darcy realized how late it was. A man's yellow watch face peeked out of his jumpsuit sleeve; it read 9:15. Darcy remembered the alarm. She should have been at work three hours ago, and now she was on a bus going in the opposite direction. A calculating part of her brain fought its way through the yellow. The island was maybe six, seven miles thick down here, and she wasn't halfway across. If she got off now she could make it to World Experiences by 10:30, walking. She'd get a pay cut for sure—she was already on thin ice from yesterday—but then maybe her mother would be home when she got back and everything would be fine. But if Sarah wasn't back, then she'd have to go looking for her the next day, and every day she couldn't find her was not just another day of fear, but another without Sarah's wages and thus another fifty dollars they wouldn't have for rent. Darcy wondered what it was like to be rich and be afraid. Well-dressed, smooth-skinned Manhattanville mothers must get sick sometimes—did their children just fall back on the strong arms of their wealth, sure that the right amount could solve any problem? And if it couldn't, if their mothers grew thin and gray and faintly translucent as though edging their way out of the world, did the children sob and run in circles and scratch their legs bloody in terror? Or was it true, as Augusta Beltran had once suggested, that rich people didn't need feelings?

Darcy didn't get off the bus as it moved east toward the docks. Her calculating brain told her that she should, that there was no use wasting money until she was sure it was necessary. But her animal brain kept right on roiling—she imagined her mother's body in her slick diving suit, her lips blue, seaweed woven through her hair. To the animal brain this disappearance was the culmination of an old dread, older even than the night ten years ago when Sarah was so late, as old as the first question that Sarah had refused to answer. The animal brain whispered that Sarah had always had a secret place she was half-inside, and now she had gone all the way. Darcy chewed her fingernails as the bus plowed past the Hollywood sign and the Paramount Flyers building, past the Seaboard Sears Tower with the long fingers of parrot shit down its front, down the Strip, past the climate-controlled baseball stadium that cost a month of Darcy's wages just to get into, and then out onto the narrow road that ran along the eastern shore.

This was the restricted side — on the western beaches you could sunbathe and buy shaved ice and cut school to lie in the sand and huff solvent if you were lucky enough to still have school to cut. But on the east coast, for some reason that Darcy had never fully understood, the only civilians allowed were pearl divers and refinery workers. A retaining wall ran gray and solid along the edge of the road, crowned with barbed wire. Just beyond the wall, clinging to the beach on its constantly reinforced supports, was the southernmost of the solvent refineries. Even through the shut bus windows, Darcy could smell the hot stench of seaweed being converted into fuel, darker and brinier than that other stench, the one she used to smell back when Solve-head Sammy lived downstairs, of fuel being converted into drugs. Around the refinery, the sea was almost red, the solvent by-products turning salt water into a corrosive industrial blood. At least once a year, her mother said, one of the refinery workers fell in and got the flesh licked clean off his bones.

Strung out along the horizon, past the solvent stain, were the guard boats, their guns pointing ·east. In the ten years between attacks, the warning sirens had blared a handful of times, but they had always been drills, and people had begun to ignore them. Now the guard boats looked menacing again, and sunbathers on the western beaches would stampede inland at the next siren, trampling their towels and overturning the shaved-ice stands and shoving their elbows in one another's faces in the fear, and secretly the hope, that this was another real one.

Darcy got off the bus. She walked across the shoulder of the road—spongy seaweed-based asphalt, beginning to liquefy in the rain—to a gate in the seawall, where an old guard with bloodshot eyes looked wearily at her from underneath a gray umbrella.

"Where you headed?" he asked her.

"Persephone Pearls," she said, and pointed through the chain link of the gate at a squat Seaboard building looking out on a dock. She had never been there before—now she remembered that her mother needed a pass to get in.

"Don't recognize you," the guard said. "What's your business there?"

Darcy thought of saying she was a new diver, but probably he had some sort of ledger he could check, and if he caught her lying he'd never let her in.

"I'm looking for my mom," she said. Raindrops were collecting on her eyelashes.

"You got a pass?"

"No, but she works here, and she's missing, and I really need to find her."

"You got to have a pass." He took a step to the right and swayed a little—Darcy realized he might be high. She felt frustration whirring inside her like insects beneath her skin.

"How do I get one?" she asked.

"You got to request an application by mail. Then you fill it out, then they consider it for four to six weeks or so. Then they let you know."

"I don't have time for that. Isn't there a quicker way?"

The guard rubbed his eyes, then looked over his shoulder and held out his right hand. Darcy checked the pockets of her jumpsuit. All she found was five dollars, just enough for the bus ride home. If she gave it up she'd have to walk all the way back, and it would take her at least three hours. Still, she didn't know what else to do, so she offered him the money. The guard looked at her like she'd made an especially stupid joke. He pointed to her neck.

"What about that?" he asked.

Her hand went up reflexively to clutch the necklace. She hadn't thought about her attachment to it before—she hadn't known her grandmother, and her mother hadn't presented it to her as anything with any value. In fact she couldn't remember her mother saying anything about it, after the initial explanation. Her own feelings for it were nonverbal—she had a visceral desire not to give it up.

"I can get more money for you later," she said, "if you let me in now."

The guard didn't even bother to respond—he just raised an eyebrow to show he wasn't buying it.

Darcy held the charm in her hand. She resisted the urge to suck on it. What was she afraid of? She would find her mother soon, and they would laugh about it—her hesitation over something so silly. She unclasped the necklace and handed it to the guard—his fingers were clammy as they brushed along hers. He undid the rusty latch, and the gate swung open with a sound like crying.

The path to the building was made of ground-up mainland trash, leftovers from the landfill project that had built out the coastline when the first-boaters came. The pieces were timeworn and rain-winnowed, and they shifted under her feet like pebbles in a stream. Here and there she saw a red or bright blue flash, bits of pigment left over from a time when no one had yet imagined this place, this road.

The Persephone Pearls office was silent except for the breathing of a single woman sitting at a desk. On the wall hung a chart with names and tally marks—the number of pearls found that week maybe, or that month. Her mother had the most tally marks of anyone. Next to the chart was a window that looked out at the ocher sea. The patrol boats sat on the horizon, their outlines furred by the rain.

"I'm looking for Sarah Pern," Darcy said.

The woman didn't look at Darcy. She was staring at a map. Her desk also held a slide rule, a pencil, and a drawing of a broad-faced child. The woman made a mark on the map with the pencil. Then she looked up for a second.

"Sorry?" she said.

"I'm looking for Sarah Pern." Darcy started to explain why, but she felt tears roughening up her throat. "Did she come to work yesterday?"

The woman looked down at the map again. It showed the eastern coast, with a big orange area drawn around it—solvent contamination. The woman made another mark just outside this area.

"Excuse me," Darcy said.

"Just a minute," the woman answered. She stared at the orange area until Darcy couldn't believe she was still staring, until she felt like she had fallen down a hole in time at the bottom of which was this woman, ignoring her forever. Then she lifted the map, looked at a list underneath it, and said, "She was here yesterday."

She put the map back down, erased the second mark and made a new one slightly to the left.

"Do you know if her dives went okay?"

"No."

Panic poured from the edges of Darcy's brain into the center again.

"What happened?" she asked.

"No, I don't know if her dives went okay. I don't have that information available."

Darcy's hands were shaking. She felt the tears building behind her eyes.

"Well, could you check? It's important."

The woman was writing on the map again. Darcy wanted to hurt her. She wanted to open her lips and yank words out of her throat, like pieces of lodged food.

"Please?" she said.

"I don't have that information available."

A membrane broke inside Darcy and she began to sob. Her breath was shaking up through her throat and her eyes were running and the inside of her nose was getting wet. In school she had seen other girls cry and get what they wanted—a passing grade in the class, a citation for solvent huffing reluctantly torn up. They must have known some secret, some way to make sympathy where none existed before. This woman should want to help her, Darcy thought. She had to.

"Please," Darcy said again. "My mom is missing. I don't know where she is."

"Look," the woman said. "I have to code a hundred of these pearl maps every day, and if I'm even one short I get fired. I don't have time to talk to you, or anyone. Other people have problems too, okay?"

Darcy didn't move. She looked at the drawing of the child and knew that the woman probably had to work hard to feed him, but she didn't have any room to sympathize with anyone else. After she had stood in one spot crying long enough that she began to choke, the woman's face softened.

"Go ask the divers," she said. "They might know something."

Darcy walked out onto the dock. The Seaboard was soggy with rainwater and gave a little under her feet; she left half-inch-deep prints on the boards behind her. Four cleats, made of rusted salvage metal, poked out of the dock surface. On both sides of the dock lapped the burnt-orange, sour-smelling sea. About fifty feet out, where the waves turned blue and safe again, a little diving dinghy was anchored. A spotter in a yellow rain hat and slicker was crouching in the prow. Darcy waved at her, and she seemed to shade her eyes and look at Darcy through the rain, but then she turned away and the dinghy didn't move. Darcy shouted, and waved some more, and her shouts grew ragged and panicky, but the spotter showed her the back of her rain hat, and didn't budge.

Darcy sat down on the dock. Rain sluiced over the bridge of her nose and pooled in her lap. Her jumpsuit was completely waterlogged. Darcy wondered what it felt like when her mother wore her wet suit. Did it feel clammy like this? Or was it like being invincible, like walking through fire without getting burned? Was she wearing her wet suit now?

Then something moved close to the horizon, something at first like a bug crawling on the sea, and then like a mouse, and then fast and gray and oblong: another boat. It slowed as it passed the dinghy, and the man at the wheel seemed to speak with the spotter. Then it sped up again, and cut through the rain-pocked water, and pulled up to the dock in the middle of a phlegmy wake. It was a good boat, with a steering wheel and a Seaboard roof over the front. The man wore a green Seaguard's uniform. He was young, pale and pink-lipped. Darcy called out to him before he cut the motor, and she had to call again to make herself heard.

"Yeah, I know Sarah," he said. "She's practically the only diver who's ever nice to me."

He stepped out onto the dock and opened a green Seafiber umbrella over the two of them. Darcy felt the reprieve from rain like taking off an uncomfortable shirt.

"Did you see her yesterday?"

"Yesterday?" he said. "God, I can't remember. The last couple of days have been so crazy."

"Crazy how?"

He gave her a petulant look.

"The attack," he said, "obviously."

"Right, sorry."

"That is so typical," he said. "The one time—*the one time*—I actually do something, people just forget right away. You know what the divers call us? Fish-watchers! It's not even funny. It doesn't even make sense. They're the ones who are down there looking at fish. I'm trying to protect the island, and when I finally get a chance to show how totally necessary and important that is, people ignore it. Sarah's the only one who cares. Where is she, anyway? They said she's not diving today."

She was so happy to find someone who actually cared about her mother that she could overlook his whining, his insistence that people take him seriously for a job he did once every ten years. The Seaguards got paid more than any of the other guards—more even than the members of the personal force that guarded the wall between Tyson's headquarters and the north edge of Manhattanville.

"Actually, I'm trying to find her. She's my mom. Can you try to remember if you saw her yesterday?"

"Let's see," he said. "Usually I say hi to her when I'm done with my shift, around now, but when the attack happened, I didn't see anyone until almost dark, and all the divers were waiting for us on the dock—at least this one time they actually congratulated us, but you could tell they didn't like it. They were pissed that we were actually heroes. There was July, and Elena, and Lisbet, and the new one, Icestorm or something, I forget, and Sarah was there, she was asking me questions like always, she wanted to know what it was like. And I told her it was just like they said it would be in training, everything was just like that. Except the boat was maybe a little smaller than in the drawings. But it just came out of nowhere, going really fast. Or pretty fast anyway. The Japs probably wanted to surprise us by coming around and attacking the east side. But we were ready—before they even got a shot off it was 'Fire main torpedo, fire secondary torpedo, fire cluster bomb,' and they were *gone*. Nothing but scrap metal. It'll be another ten years before they try that again."

He paused for a moment, considering.

"Except you can never be sure, obviously. They could come again tomorrow, we don't know."

"Wait," Darcy said, "but that was two days ago. Did you see Sarah yesterday?"

"I'm *getting* to that," he said. "Ordinarily I come in at eight a.m., but yesterday we had a debriefing in the morning and I came in at ten a.m., and July and Elena ignored me as usual, like I didn't just save their asses the day before, and then, yeah, Sarah said hi to me as I was heading out, nothing big, but you could tell she was grateful."

"Did she say anything else?" Darcy asked. "Did she mention going anywhere?"

He put his hand to his chin, childlike.

"Nothing like that," he said, "but she did seem nervous. Or more like really energetic, like she was extra excited to be at work that day."

"Thanks," Darcy said. "If you think of anything else, will you send me a letter?"

"Sure," the guard said. "I hope she comes back soon. You should ask the land guards about her. They're not as smart as us, but they still might help you."

"You mean like the guy at the gate?" Darcy asked.

"No, that guy's a solve-head. Go to the Eighteenth and Avenida station. Some of the guys there are halfway decent."

He turned to walk down the dock.

"Wait," Darcy said, "do you have something to write down my address?"

"Don't worry," the guard said, "we have everyone's address. I can just look you up."

The guard station at Eighteenth and Avenida was next to a taco stand. Every time the wind changed, the gamy, artificial smell of imitation goat washed over the people squatting in the packed waiting room, and the women waved their hands in front of their faces and the children pinched their noses and the men looked out the little windows at the rushing late-afternoon street. Every few minutes someone new came in—occasionally a convict with plastic handcuffs and a guard at his back, but more often a visitor or supplicant like Darcy, face shivering with brittle hope, shoulders squared into a shape of long waiting. The line made space for each arrival—men scooted closer to one another along the mouse-gray Seaboard wall, women offered GreenValley Picante Snacks from yellow bags, children adjusted their play to the new shape of the crowd. Over and around Darcy ran the intertwining skeins of group conversation, a long braided murmur of worry. The walls of the room were covered with fresh Seafiber flyers explaining protocols for future attacks—evacuate the beaches, head for designated inland safe houses—but no one seemed to be talking about them. Most of these people were here about a son or daughter or sister or brother who had gotten into trouble, some young person stuck to the flypaper of the criminal justice system. Darcy had snorted solvent and stolen razor blades like any Little Los Angeles teenager, and she had even worked for a dealer for a little while, but she'd never been arrested. Once you were, even if they released you, you were never really out. You'd never get a legit job again, and the guards would haul you in every time anything bad happened in your neighborhood, whether you'd done anything or not.

A man in a blue land-guard uniform came down the line and all the people stopped their conversations and put on their official faces. He passed over an old lady with a small child, a man chewing seaweed tobacco, and a boy no older than twelve who began shouting about his sister. Then he motioned to Darcy to follow and she walked out of the waiting room. A collective grumble of injustice filled the space where she had been. The guard was young and broad and tall, with a smooth open face and wide hands. Darcy followed him down a narrow hallway with lots of doors. She heard a yelp like an animal being kicked. Then they went down a set of stairs, and another set of stairs, and the guard led her into a private room. He handed her a box of soft Seafiber tissues.

"Would you like coffee or anything?" he asked her.

He had a posh accent, second-boat lilt mixed with sharp Manhattanville consonants. Darcy imagined his family's nice apartment, the antique photos on the walls, the separate beds for everyone. The kids Darcy went to school with all said the guards were useless, preppy not-quite-rich kids who just wanted to bust you for solvent or keep you from hanging out in the nice neighborhoods. But she liked this man's easy calm. Someone with nothing will never help someone else with nothing, but he had money and power and information and security—surely he could spare some of that for her.

"No thanks," she said. "I just want to find out about my mom. Her name is Sarah Pern. Has anyone seen her?"

"I'm going to find that out for you," he said. "First we'll take your statement, then we'll cross-reference it with all the reports we've gotten since she went missing. We should have some information for you very soon."

He pulled out a folding chair for her at a little rickety table. The walls were lined with bookcases full of bound records. One small high window let in the view of the rain.

"Thanks," she said. "Nobody's really been able to help me."

"That's what we're here for." He smiled. He had nice, white teeth. "Now, can you tell me when your mother went missing?"

"She didn't come home last night. I woke up this morning and she wasn't there."

"And did she say anything? Anywhere she might've been going?"

"Nowhere," Darcy said. "Where would she go?"

He nodded seriously and wrote something down on a pad.

"Had she been behaving unusually lately? Any signs of depression?"

"What do you mean?" Darcy said. The yellow walls came down again. She had not noticed that they were gone. "Do you mean do I think she killed herself? She didn't kill herself."

"Of course not."

He shifted his chair closer to her and spoke in a lower voice.

"It's just important for us to know about any mood changes. It will help the investigation."

The yellow faded slightly. Darcy wondered if she would know if her mother was depressed. Sometimes she saw flyers at the bus stop, in English and Spanish, with a drawing of a sad woman in bluish ink, and a number you could call. But often the flyers had rude things scrawled on them, and Darcy didn't know anyone who had called the number. The only people she knew who even used the word "depressed" were the nurses at World Experiences, referring to the patients who stared at the wall all day—to earn the word, you had to be able to afford someone to look after you.

She did know people who had killed themselves—DJ Lopez had jumped out the window of his family's apartment building in eighth grade, while high on solvent, and Joelle Thompson, who had come to school with bruises all up and down her neck and face every week after she turned thirteen, had slit her wrists the following year. But Sarah didn't do solvent, and nobody was hitting her. And if the life seemed to leave her eyes sometimes and go somewhere Darcy couldn't reach, it always came back again.

"She seemed fine to me," Darcy said.

He wrote on the pad.

"Did anything unusual happen in the days before her disappearance?"

"Well, there was the attack I guess. And a woman came over," Darcy said. "I'd never seen her before."

The guard wrote several lines.

"That's very interesting," he said. "That will be very helpful. Now, the most important thing you can do is be calm. When something like this happens, people often feel very isolated, very alone. But we are here to help you. Just leave everything to us."

Darcy was confused. Why wasn't he asking her more about the woman? She wanted to spend hours here, telling him everything about her mother. She wanted to give him so much information that he couldn't help but find her.

"The woman had a round face," Darcy went on. "It looked kind of puffy. Her hands shook."

"Sure," the guard said, "just leave everything to us."

He was smiling, and past his shoulder Darcy saw a pair of shoes pass by the window; it must be just above the level of the street. Someone would have to lie down on the sidewalk to look in. The guard scooted closer to her and began rubbing her back with one of his large hands. Darcy looked at the pad in front of him and saw that it was full of doodles and squiggles, no writing at all. The yellow walls came down hard and she heard a ringing in her ears. He leaned over and began to kiss her. His mouth was smooth. His breath tasted like mint powder. He was trying to put his tongue between her lips. Her thoughts split apart and began to run along parallel tracks. One track wanted to push him away, wanted no one and nothing to touch her until she found her mother, and especially not this man, who should be helping her, who should not be invading the salty private space of her mouth with his slick mint tongue like a bar of soap.

The other track told her to kiss him back, because maybe if she gave him what he wanted, if she made herself soft and sweet for him, instead of a hard thin arrow pointed at her mother, then he would write real words down on his pad for her. Probably he had picked her out of the crowd because he liked her looks, and maybe he would pick her problem out of the great roiling swill of convictions and assaults and disappearances and deaths that poured through his station every day.

Then he put his hand on her left breast, and the second track snapped, and she ran along the first track all the way out of the guard station and onto the soggy street.

It was almost five by the time Darcy got back to her building. She was soaked and exhausted and her panic had turned into a hard heavy thing, like a tumor hanging in her guts. Jorge, the superintendent, was in the entryway, mopping up the asphalt that had melted in the rain and oozed through the front door. Every couple of months the news flyers claimed that a new type of asphalt was on the way, one made of some nonseaweed substance and impervious to rain, but no trucks ever came to lay it, and the street still turned to soup every time the monsoons came.

"Hey," he greeted her. "Crazy about the Hawaiians, right? You think they'll come back?"

Darcy gave a depleted shrug.

"I have no idea," she said. "You haven't seen my mom, have you?"

He shook his head. "Maybe she's visiting someone?"

Darcy sat on the stairs and put her head in her hands. Even though Jorge took money from her every month, more if it wasn't on time, she liked him. He worked for the management company and lived in a medium-sized apartment on the first floor. He didn't have kids, or a solvent habit, or any of the other things that made people so hungry for money they were willing to sell one another out to get it. He had his job, and she knew he would evict her if he had to, but there was none of the crazy desperate scraping between them that she heard about from Trish, whose landlord kept raising her rent to pay for her daughter's glaucoma treatments.

"She's not visiting someone. I went to the docks, I went to the guards. I don't know what else to do."

"She'll probably come back on her own," he said. "I wouldn't worry about it too much. Get some rest, maybe have a beer."

She couldn't imagine rest. At some point in the future she knew she'd sleep, but her sleep would be only a break between fear and anxiety, probably filled with fever dreams.

"I can't," she said. "How would you find someone, Jorge?"

He put the mop down and sat beside her on the step. He smelled like the disinfectant he used when somebody vomited in the hallway.

"I'd wait," he said, "and see if they came back."

"What if you couldn't wait?"

Jorge shrugged.

"I don't know."

They were silent for a moment. Dolores Beltran came in wearing her heavy rubber raincoat and carrying a bag of canned vegetables from the big GreenValley store on the Chicagoland border. Darcy avoided her eyes. The more people she told about her mother, the more her absence seemed to multiply, until there were five, ten, twenty versions of Sarah, all of them gone.

"This isn't really the same thing," Jorge said. "But my cousin's son got shot once. He was paralyzed from the waist down. The guards didn't do anything because it was gang on gang. So my cousin went to this guy, some kind of fixer or something, and he found out who shot her son."

"Who was the fixer?" Darcy asked.

"He had a weird name. Ansel. Ansel Martinez or Rodriguez or something. When she knew him he worked at the Big Top."

"And what happened with her son?"

Jorge stood up and began mopping again. The asphalt was drying on the entryway floor, making a blackish-green stain in the shape of a hammer.

"Oh, he's all right. Still paralyzed. I think he hands out flyers or something. My cousin found the guy who shot him and she went to his house. I told her not to go. She said she just wanted an apology. But I think she must have threatened him. She washed up a couple weeks later on the unrestricted beach."

"I'm sorry," she said.

"I didn't really know her that well. But that's why I say, just wait. Your mom will probably come back on her own."

As she opened the door to the apartment, Darcy let herself hope that her mother would look up at her, from the bed or from a perch on the windowsill, laughing, saying, "Have I got a story for you." The blanket was lumped up on the bed, and she rushed toward it, but when she laid her hand on empty cloth instead of her mother's skinny hip, she remembered that she and she alone had left it that way, and knew that if she slept at all tonight, she would sleep by herself beneath it. Her stomach gnawed, and so she opened the refrigerator. The steak smelled the way meat smells just before it starts to turn. She sat on the floor and ate it with her fingers, untasting, like a starving animal or a person without a brain.

2

To Darcy's right was the Las Vegas Las Vegas Hotel and Casino, its Seaboard facade of the old Vegas Strip lit by yellow solvent-burning kliegs. In front of its Romanesque entrance, a fountain spurted weak jets of semichoreographed water while a stuffed tiger looked on with a perpetually open maw. To the left was the Big Top, its Seafiber roof once red, blue, and yellow, now oxblood, gray, and beige. Posters on its wall recommended, "Experience an Alaskan Winter at THREE HUNDRED DEGREES BELOW ZERO," and, "See Real Live POLAR BEAR! From the Wilds of the Yukon! No Costumes, No Tricks!" Darcy had seen flyers for this show—the Big Top always had something "Alaskan" or "polar" going on this time of year, when the weather was especially hot. A barker at the entrance, bundled in a parka and visibly soaked with sweat, shivered and shouted, "Brrrrrr, it's so cold in here! Can you handle it? Can *you?*" Behind him stood three big bouncers with their arms crossed over their chests.

Just east of the Big Top were the porn hawkers and freelance freaks—a woman with a thumb growing out of her shoulder, a macaw that did impressions of passersby, the heavily advertised

Man with Projectile Sweat. East of them were the wedding chapels, their doorways belching forth floral scents and organ music,
and beyond those were the casinos, and beyond those the whore-
houses. Darcy had heard of girls being jumped into some of the
seedier ones, but surely her mother was too old, and surely those
stories were lies anyway, cooked up to keep girls from going out
by themselves at night. She walked up to the Big Top entrance.
The barker in the parka shouted "Brrrrrrr!" in her ear.

"Do you know an Ansel Martinez?" Darcy asked him. "Or
Rodriguez?"

She was aware of how stupid it sounded that she didn't even
know Ansel's full name, and the barker's blank stare was exactly
what she expected. Then one of the bouncers spoke up.

"I can take you to see Ansel," he said.

The other two bouncers stepped forward. They were big; their
bellies were bright in their striped shirts; they made a box around
Darcy. They bellied her past the main entrance, past the polar
bear poster, and through a side door into a long dim narrow room.
All along one wall were piled old-style black steamer trunks and
brown Seaboard boxes and dented birdcages, some with macaws
still squawking in them. Mirrors lined the other wall, hung with
feathered headdresses and cowboy hats and prairie bonnets and
fake beards. Three brown-skinned women were putting war paint
on one another in front of one mirror. At another, a man in the
bottom half of a wrinkled gray elephant suit smoked a seaweed
cigarette. At the end of the room was a curtain; from behind the
curtain, Darcy could hear cheering.

"Is Ansel in here?" Darcy asked.

"You'll see him," said the biggest of the men.

His shirt was striped red and yellow like peppered cheese food,
and his five o'clock shadow appeared to be painted on.

"Hey Sunshine," he called out. "We got a good one!"

A tall and skinny woman in a yellow flowered dress turned to look at Darcy. Her skin was brown and pockmarked and her hair was oily and her wrists stuck three inches out of her cuffs—she was the opposite of the little milky prairie girl on the World Experiences wall. Her mouth was painted orangey red. Her eyes were messily lined with black; they were small and proud and penetrating.

"She's too skinny, Tug," she said to the man in the striped shirt.

"Good one for what?" Darcy asked.

Sunshine rummaged in an overfilled trunk, then held a fur coat open in front of Darcy.

"Come on," she said.

"What is this?" Darcy asked. "I'm looking for Ansel."

"If you do this," Sunshine said, "I'll take you to him."

"Do what? I don't want to do anything."

"Look, either you leave now, or you put on the costume and do the Eskimo dance, and then you can meet Ansel."

The fur smelled like sweat and rancid cheese food, and Darcy didn't want to do any sort of dance in front of a bunch of people. She had no way of knowing if Ansel could even help her, but he was the only lead she had. If she gave up now, all she could do was go back to the apartment and wait, and the waiting would drive her insane. She slid her arms into the sleeves, pulled the hot hood up over her head. Then Sunshine handed her a pair of padded pants and heavy fur-lined boots with holes in the soles. Finally she shoved several pillows down the front of the coat to make Darcy look fat.

Loud tinny music came piercing through the curtain into the dressing room, along with the sound of applause.

"Time to go," said Sunshine. "Don't forget to shiver, like you're cold."

"If I was really an Eskimo, why would I be cold?"

Sunshine didn't answer. Instead she led Darcy past the elephant, past a girl in a cowboy hat practicing gun twirls, past a man with a fake beard trying to put a dress on a monkey, through an open curtain, and out into very bright light.

She knew she was onstage only because of the screaming. The white light shone straight into her eyes, and she could see nothing except the wisps of fur around her face. Next to her, Sunshine was calling, in a strange accent not her own, "Here she is, ladies and gentlemen! Inge, the real-life Eskimo!"

The crowd's voice rose up to meet Sunshine's. Whistles and whoops stuck up out of the general yowl. Someone yelled, "Take off the coat!"

Sunshine disappeared, and a man's voice from downstage shouted, "And now, Inge will perform a traditional dance from her home in the frozen north!"

Darcy's vision cleared enough for her to see a round, short man in suspenders and a weird long coat pointing up at her. She stood very still for a moment, vehemently not dancing, and then she ran to where she hoped the curtain was. The man Sunshine called Tug was standing there, his arms crossed over his chest. He gave her a simple warning look. She turned and ran across the stage in the other direction, ducked behind a Seaboard cutout of an igloo, and came up short against a wall. The crowd began to boo. Darcy heard something wet splatter on the stage.

"Looks like Inge's not in the mood for dancing tonight," said the man with the suspenders. "Let's give her a little incentive."

The crowd screamed again. Darcy wished she had something to throw back at them. She thought about killing the man with the suspenders. She thought about driving an ice pick down into his head. Instead she took the fur coat off and threw it into the crowd. The pillows slid away from her body and fell to the ground with a *shlump*. Then Tug opened the curtain and some smoke came out.

"Ladies and gentlemen," the man in suspenders began.

Something was moving in the smoke. It was moving slowly and making gurgling sounds. Tug reached back and hit it and then it was charging toward Darcy, snarling.

The man in suspenders shouted, "The famous polar bear!"

Darcy was running. She was running across the stage and the bear was running after her, its steps heavy, its claws clacking on the boards. She could smell its body—it smelled like jellyfish and urine. Its growl was higher and angrier than a dog's—it sounded like it was hurt somewhere inside, like it wanted to hurt someone else. She hid behind the igloo and then it came at her from around the side, and she saw that it was covered with white paint that had worn away in places, exposing the black fur underneath. She put her hands up in front of her face, and it stopped for a second, just inches from her. It made a sound in its throat that was not a growl. It was more like a sigh. She looked at the bear's eyes and saw dark ooze shining around them. This bear was sick, and it was tired, and it was trapped, and it was humiliated, and Darcy was not going to be like this bear. She ran again, but this time she ran straight forward, and jumped off the stage, and landed in a white pool of pure pain.

A second later she could see but she didn't want to see. She wanted to wrap her brain around her ankle like a warm cloth so that the pain could not get in. She thought of the pain as something coming into her from outside, from the floor, and so she kept trying to lift her ankle off the floor, but every shift made the pain feel worse until finally she curled up tight, like a grub, and sobbed.

She could hear voices around her, and voices on the stage, singing, distracting, and voices from the crowd booing and yelling, and then Sunshine's face swam forward into her eyes, and a pair of arms slid under her as though to lift her up.

"No!"

She was snarling like the bear. She was flailing her arms.

"Come on," Sunshine whispered. "You're hurt. I'm trying to help you."

Darcy writhed, and Sunshine took her chin between her thumb and forefinger and squeezed hard.

"Stop," she whispered.

Darcy stopped.

"Let me help you," she said, gesturing up at the stage, "or they're going to come down here and kick your stupid ass." More loudly, so the others could hear, she said, "And you better stay out!"

Darcy gave up and let herself be carried. Sunshine walked slowly, grunting with her weight. The man in the suspenders scolded the crowd in a scared, joking voice. The girl in the cowboy hat came onstage.

"The famous Annie Oakley!" the man in the suspenders yelled.

Then Sunshine pushed open a door under the stage and carried Darcy through a dark close place sliced through with beams, and then into an even darker place, with a smell of sawdust and rat poison and a sound of snoring. She laid Darcy down on something soft, like a blanket or a sleeping bag. She heard a rustle, then a man's voice in the dark.

"Who are you?" it asked.

"Ansel, meet—who are you exactly?"

"Darcy Pern."

"Darcy, meet Ansel. Now stay put. I'm going to get something for your leg."

Ansel was close enough that she could smell him—his unwashed hair, the private, meaty smell of sweat.

"What brings you here, Darcy?"

His voice was young to be so courtly, and high, with a crack running along it. When her eyes adjusted, she saw a long-nosed, high-domed, avian head, with thick dirty black hair and a nasty parrot-fever scar under the left eye.

"I was looking for you," she said. "Then I got my leg broken by your polar bear. He looks like he needs some medicine, by the way."

"He's a she," said Ansel. "And like most women, dangerous in ways you don't expect."

Footsteps broke into the darkness, and Sunshine was standing over them, smelling like sweat and paint and, strangely, apples, rustling and riffling in her incongruous prairie dress.

"I don't know why you were looking for this clown," she told Darcy. "But I wouldn't listen to him. He'll only get you in trouble."

"I am not a clown," Ansel protested. "I am merely an Eskimo on hiatus."

"Permanent hiatus, if I have anything to say about it," Sunshine said. "I wish they'd shoot that stupid bear."

"Now Auntie," Ansel said, "that would be violent. And you don't approve of violence, do you?"

"Shut up. You need your rest."

Sunshine knelt over Darcy and held something hard against her right leg. She began to wrap a cloth around it. Pain shone at the edges of Darcy's vision.

"I don't really know how to do this," she said, "so you should probably get a real doctor to redo it when you get out of here."

"You guys should pay for it. You tricked me!" Darcy shouted. "That bear could've killed me."

"Keep your voice down," Sunshine hissed. "Believe me, I know. We're struggling. We used to have a moose—it died. Same with the wolves. People want to see all the old animals, you know. Something from back home. But pretty soon all we'll have are monkeys and people in costumes."

"Polar bears aren't from back home, are they?"

Sunshine knotted the cloth around Darcy's calf.

"They're from the snow. It's close enough. Look, I'm fifty years old. I was born in the real Las Vegas. For me 'back home' means getting a rash in your crotch because there's no fruit and you got scurvy. Does that sound like a good circus to you?"

Ansel's laugh sounded like glass breaking.

"It's not funny," Sunshine said. "You weren't there, you don't know."

"That's true," Ansel said. "I don't know anything about deprivation. I've never gone without food because other people had to stuff themselves. I've never risked my life so other people could laugh."

Sunshine sighed. Darcy thought of her mother, how she would come home some nights so tired and hungry she didn't make sense, her body all light and empty like a balloon. She'd sing snatches of cowboy songs and tell broken jokes with no punch lines, and every five minutes she'd ask what time it was. "Let's dance," she'd say, and then she'd twirl once and fall into a chair, where Darcy would take her by the feet and twist her ankles back and forth until she laughed.

"Save it," Sunshine said to Ansel. "Darcy, you got what you

wanted. Here's Ansel. Say whatever you've got to say, but don't make a lot of noise. They catch you down here, you'll be sorry."

"Wait, Auntie," said Ansel, but Sunshine was already receding. Her body was a rough place in the smooth dark; then it was nothing. The circus was still going on above their heads. A loud, rhythmic thumping moved across the stage, like someone running or hopping in enormous shoes. Ansel's blankets rustled.

"You want to see something?" he asked.

"What is it?"

"It's a surprise."

Ansel sat up. Despite the heat, he was wearing a Seafiber trench-coat with long sleeves. He pushed the right sleeve up to reveal his arm, but Darcy saw no hand, no wrist, no forearm—nothing until the blunt end of an elbow. He turned the stump so she was looking down the barrel of it, and for a moment she stared transfixed at the wide, wet wound, soupy at the center, crinkled at the edges where it was trying to heal.

"What happened?" she asked him.

"I wasn't as lucky with Nanook as you were."

If Ansel could really find missing people, Darcy wondered why he had to resort to being chased by a bear.

"Did they trick you too?" she asked.

"Nah. I've been working here a while. Sunshine got me the job. I'm the reason they have to grab people off the street. Me and this stump here."

"I'm sorry," Darcy said. "But listen, somebody told me you could help me."

"Now who would've told you a thing like that?"

Sitting there in the dark, she almost wished no one had. What was this man who seemed to spend his days lying crippled under the Big Top going to do for her? She felt the decline of hope like a headache coming on.

"Jorge Barrera," she said. "He told me you helped him find his cousin."

She expected him to say he didn't know what she was talking about, but instead he laughed, a dry, unlovely sound that was older than his voice, and said, "So word of my exploits is getting around, is it? The Barrera kid was a nasty business, though—there are other things I'd rather be known for."

"But you do know how to find people?" Darcy asked. "That's something you do?"

"That depends," he said, "on who you want found."

A loud shapeless thud ricocheted around the dark. Darcy flinched. Ansel laughed.

"The curtain," he explained.

Darcy breathed. She'd come here to tell him her problem, but now it stuck on her tongue. All the time she was little, first grade, second grade, fifth grade, she ran home as quick as she could from the little squalid elementary school with the cheese food smeared on the windows so that she could lie on the floor and wait for the signature vibration of her mother's feet in the hall. This was before the pay cut, before Sarah had to dive long past dusk and come home pale and wrung out and alien. Then there was nothing she wanted more than to hear the first sound her mother made when she entered the building, to own every one of her familiar evening movements—the stretching of her arms and toes, the shucking off of her wet suit to reveal the tender bumps of her spine. Only when she got older did the other kids at school begin to hold allure for her, with their private jokes, their mean faces, their makeup stolen from their older sisters. Once in seventh grade she stayed late behind the science trailers with a girl named Cali, and they huffed cheap solvent from a bag and lay on their backs and told secrets. Cali's eyes grew wide as she was talking, her whole face became luminous, she made it seem like there was something wondrous behind gossip, something perfect and crystalline and rare that all their words were mere clumsy gestures toward. When Darcy came home late and still wobbly in the legs and hands, Sarah didn't ask her about the solvent.

"Who were you with?" she said instead.

"Just a girl," Darcy answered, and then, shyly, still wanting to let her mother in on her secrets, "She told me who she likes."

"Be careful," said Sarah. She was turned away from Darcy, picking at a stain on the wall. "You can't always trust people."

"She won't tell anything," Darcy said. "We swore."

Sarah turned around, and her eyes were fierce.

"I don't mean she's going to tell on you. What do you have to tell anyway?"

It knocked the wind out of Darcy. For a moment she stood in the center of the apartment holding her belly, like she'd been hit there. Then she yelled, "I hate you," the one and only time, and ran to hide in the bathroom, but not before she heard her mother say, "I mean that she could hurt you," in a little far-off voice.

After ten minutes Sarah came to find her, and smoothed her hair back, and kissed her eyelids, and let her eat a whole can of cheese food on pieces of square packaged bread, and the next day at school Darcy was distant and cold with Cali, even though she didn't really understand why. Now she didn't like to confide in anyone except her mother; telling anything to strangers made her especially afraid. But her mother was gone, and if she had another choice, she didn't know what it was.

"My mom disappeared yesterday," she told Ansel, "and I'm trying to find her."

He seemed not to have heard.

"Darcy, what brings people like us here in the first place?"

"What? What are you talking about?"

"Money. They have it, we don't."

"Who's 'they'?" Darcy asked. "The circus people?"

The crowd noise had thinned from a rush to a trickle and then to a series of driblets with dead space between them. A man shouted something that sounded like "Monkey!" and a woman laughed, and then silence.

"Lucky girl," Ansel said. "You are ignorant in the ways of our world."

Darcy turned away from him into the empty black.

"Fuck you," she said. "I've been working since I was fifteen. All I ever had was my mom. Now she's gone and no one will help me. I know as much about the world as I want to know."

"As you wish."

She heard a shift and sliding of the sleeping bag as he too turned away. She listened for Sunshine's return but heard only Ansel's breathing. Then from above, the drips of talk came back, as though time was switched around and running backward, replaying the circus from the beginning. The voices multiplied and swelled, and then the man with the suspenders began to respeak his lines, and then with a fumbling rustling sound the curtain went back up and teams of toes went dancing back along the stage.

"How many times a day do they do this?" Darcy asked.

"Today, probably five."

"And how many have they already done?"

"I think this is the third."

"Jesus."

Darcy pulled the sleeping bag over her head. Through it she could still hear the man with the suspenders announcing something about "great mainland apes." She heard new footfalls above her, lighter and more numerous, jumping and scuttling and stopping: more monkeys. Darcy remembered the one in the dressing room, its small intelligent malign face, the flowered dress bunched over its tail. Probably it too had been about some private business when someone grabbed it by its shoulders, muzzled its biting jaw, and bent it with drugs or beating or sheer captive time into a life of performing and obeying. Darcy felt a red hate pooling behind her eyeballs. Her ankle was sending shots of pain all the way up to her hip. She needed to find her mother and she didn't know where to look and she was trapped in the dark and she had become the kind of person that people could just do things to.

"Are you crying?" Ansel asked.

"No."

She didn't mean to shout it, but she heard the word bounce loud and ragged all around the dark. They both froze. Swirling music was playing overhead. A wheel was rolling on the stage. A door opened and a little light stained the space where they lay. Darcy saw a slice of Ansel's face—it was brown-skinned, hawkish, and hungry. Her body clenched into its smallest self. A man and a woman exchanged some indecipherable words. She saw Ansel looking at her. The crowd clapped overhead. The light went away.

"Sorry," Darcy whispered.

She heard Ansel shake his head.

"You're the reason this island never gets any better."

"What," Darcy whispered, "because I'm loud?"

"You lack what I like to call a larger awareness."

"Try having a larger awareness when your mom disappears, asshole."

"My mom died when I was a kid. She had parrot fever."

The monkeys were gone and in their place was someone speaking loudly in the stop-start cadence of a joke. The audience was booing.

"I'm sorry," Darcy said.

"How long has your mom been gone again?"

"She didn't come home last night. She's been gone all day."

"And you went to the guards?"

"And I went to the guards."

Cymbals crashed. A few gasps floated down through the stage floor. A pair of boots and a pair of high-heeled shoes *tick-tock*ed above their heads. Someone onstage was speaking. He said something that sounded like "chamber."

"And they didn't do anything?"

"And they didn't do anything," she said.

A scrawny-voiced macaw began to call—more gasps, some cheers. Then something was wheeled out onto the stage. A door opened and closed.

"Tell me, my fellow Eskimo, don't you think the guards would have been a little more helpful if you were a little higher on the totem pole?"

"I guess, probably," Darcy said.

"Are you aware that the families of Board members are actually exempt from arrest by the guards? They literally can do no wrong."

"How do you know that?" Darcy asked.

"I have my sources," he said. "But I can't reveal them to just anyone."

Darcy was getting frustrated. She was worried that he was messing with her, that he didn't really know anything she could use.

"Fine," she said. "Who can you reveal them to?"

"All my knowledge is freely available," Ansel said, "to members of my organization."

"Can your 'organization' help me find my mom?"

"Absolutely," said Ansel, "if you're willing to do something for us."

A sudden downward rush of air. A thud and a scramble. Then light pouring down from the stage, a clearer, closer sound of cheering. A woman in a spangled dress, dusting herself off, looking right at them.

"What the fuck are you doing here?" And then, in angry recognition, "Are you that girl that pissed off Nanook?"

The light went out above them but the woman was running through the dark calling, "Tug, you better take a look at this!"

Then more light, the heavy sound of running, and Ansel standing, pulling at her, saying, "Come on, we've gotta go."

"I can't," she said. "I can't stand."

So he lifted her, threw her across his shoulder with his good arm, pinned her to his chest and ran zigzagging through the dark, with feet bashing all around them, until they burst out into the flashing night and Darcy's eyes went white with the brightness of the Strip. They wove through a circle of cowboys singing for change, past three prostitutes teetering in their shoes, and around two monkeys fighting over a tangle of cotton candy, shrieking and hopping and scattering the pink shreds in the rain. Ansel was panting and Darcy could feel his body sagging under her weight. She smelled blood on his shoulder. He half ran, half fell through an open doorway and into a wide, round room with a vaulted ceiling.

Right away Darcy realized they were somewhere they weren't supposed to be. The carpet Ansel set her down on was clean and patterned with roses. The ceiling was painted light blue, with fluffy clouds unlike any that ever hung over the island. All around them were tables where women in short shiny real-fiber dresses played cards with men in old-style suits. The air smelled like the kind of fancy cigarettes you could buy only in Manhattanville. And unlike any of the places where Darcy was usually allowed to be, the room was air-conditioned. Cool air blew down the back of Darcy's neck and dried the sweat underneath her arms. She felt weightless and almost reckless, the way she imagined rich people felt before they spent a bunch of money.

Darcy followed Ansel over to a green felt card table where four elegantly dressed people were waiting for their hands. A woman with a saggy wattle and a diamond necklace pursed her lips at them. The dealer, a small severe young man in a burgundy vest, shuffled the cards without looking up. A middle-aged man with a red silk tie was holding forth about the defense budget.

"We simply have to raise taxes," he was saying. "The Hawaiians could attack again any day. We got lucky that the Seaguards shot them down this time, but next time who knows how many ships they'll bring? Who knows what kinds of weapons they'll have?"

When Ansel pulled a chair out for Darcy, the man turned his bluster on them.

"Hey lasties, this is the thousand-dollar table."

Ansel made his voice change completely. He flattened the vowels and clipped the consonants so he sounded like a Manhattanville executive.

"Our costumes must be pretty good, eh December?" he said to Darcy. "We better watch out—they might not let us back in our building."

The man in the tie changed his expression from disgust to skepticism. He might not believe they were Manhattanville execs, but he was at least entertaining the idea. Darcy felt a kind of power flowing from Ansel into her. She didn't know how to do a Man-hattanville accent, so she threw back her head and tried to laugh like someone who had fired a lot of people and liked it.

"We've just come from a last-boat party," Ansel told him. "Ever been?"

"What's a last-boat party?" the woman in diamonds asked, eye-ing the limp sleeve of his coat, "and what happened to your arm?"

Ansel looked serious for a moment.

"I had cancer as a child," he said. "I almost died."

"I'm so sorry," said the woman. "How insensitive of me to ask."

Ansel patted her shoulder.

"Not to worry," he said. "Anyway, last-boat parties are a big deal now. I'm surprised you've never been to one. You don't shower for a few days, you put on some ratty Seafiber clothes from an Our Lady store, then everybody crams into a really small room to drink palm wine and eat cheese food."

"That doesn't sound like very much fun," the woman said.

"Well," said Ansel, leaning in close to her, "it depends on how much you like rubbing up against people."

The woman giggled, her neck flesh reddening.

"Honestly, though," Ansel went on, "I think it's good to do that kind of thing once in a while. The last-boaters, they experi-ence everything more viscerally. They're capable of appreciating some of the simple things in life in a way that's harder for people like us."

"I think that's absolutely true," the woman said. "I met a last-boat girl once, *such* a nice young lady. I was on the scholarship committee for the University then, and I recommended her very highly. She wanted to be a doctor, very driven. Not like these lazy Manhattanville kids you see these days. Of course, she didn't get the scholarship—so few of them do."

Ansel looked pointedly at Darcy. Then he made his face calm and solicitous and turned it toward the woman.

"Why didn't she?" he asked. "I mean, if she was as good as you say?"

"Oh, I didn't look at her file very closely. I assume it was something with the values test—it usually is."

Darcy remembered the kids trudging grimly back from the scholarship exams at her high school—she wondered which of their values had been tested. Ansel anticipated the question.

"What's on those tests these days?" he asked. "I haven't looked at one in years."

"Questions about politics, support for the Founder. It's important to make sure people are really loyal, you know, and not just pretending so they can get a free ride."

Ansel gave Darcy another meaningful look. She hadn't thought of this before, that Tyson might be testing people's loyalty. She guessed it made sense—he wouldn't want the Board paying for people's education if they were going to turn around and use it against him. Still, the flyers always made the scholarship winners sound like the smartest kids on the island, not the most obedient.

The woman was looking at Darcy now.

"December, was it?" she said. "You don't say much, do you December?"

Darcy turned to Ansel. He didn't speak for her; he just looked back at her with a mild, easy confidence, like he did this all the time. Then she clenched her throat and whispered, "I lost my voice at the party."

"Last-boaters do a lot of yelling," Ansel added.

The dealer was getting impatient.

"You buying in?" he asked. "If not, you've got to leave."

Ansel patted the pockets of his coat with his good hand. He put on a look of exasperation.

"I'm an idiot," he said. "December, do you have any money?"

Darcy shook her head. The feeling of power weakened a little. She whispered to Ansel, "What are you doing?"

"Just play along," Ansel whispered back.

"Listen," he said to the woman. "I left my wallet back at the party. They make you check them at the door, for authenticity. I could go get it now, but we're having such a nice time. What if you were to stake me? If I win, I'll give you half. If I lose, I'll go get my wallet and pay you back."

The woman looked around her as though someone might give her advice, but she had obviously come by herself.

"I don't like this," said the man in the tie to no one in particular, and this seemed to make her decision.

"I do," she said. "Of course I'll stake you."

She handed a green Seafiber bill to the dealer, who nodded and said to Ansel, "Snow kings, flakes wild, no flipping."

Ansel nodded, and the dealer began laying cards on the green felt table. Their backs bore a picture of a cottage with warm light in the windows and heavy snow covering the roof.

"Do you know how to play this?" Darcy whispered. She didn't. Cards were a rich kid's game — when the kids at her school wanted to gamble, they flipped cheese-food lids or bet on back-alley games of baseball.

But Ansel whispered, "Of course. Relax."

He lifted the first three of his five cards. A king, a scepter, and the crown. Darcy looked around at the other people at the table — the man in the tie chewing his thick lip; a thirtyish woman with beautiful iridescent skin that turned out, as Darcy stared at it, to be very carefully painted and powdered; another man with a real-fiber handkerchief sticking out of his pocket. Darcy sat up straight. These people thought she was one of them. If she'd known how easy it was to fool people, she would have done it more often. She could have crashed student parties at the University. She could have gone to the boutiques on Fifth Avenue and tried on expensive real-fiber dresses. She smoothed her hair; she could be anyone.

"What kind of work are you in?" the man in the tie asked Ansel.

"GreenValley," Ansel said, not looking up from his cards.

He said it as casually as if it were the truth.

"I'm GreenValley," said the man. "What department?"

Ansel hesitated a half second before answering.

"Research and development," Ansel said.

A line of concentration or concern appeared between his eyebrows. He laid down the scepter on the felted table and asked the dealer for two more cards.

"How come I didn't see you at the last meeting with Tyson?" the man asked. He didn't take any new cards. The line between Ansel's eyebrows deepened.

"I was busy," Ansel said.

His two new cards were both serfs, bent-backed and trudging through deep snow.

"That's not much of an attitude for a young man like you. Your department isn't going to keep getting subsidies if you don't come and show support."

Ansel smiled—a little weakly, Darcy thought. She started to feel nervous.

"Thanks for the advice," he said. "I'll take it into consideration."

The woman in the diamond necklace got three new cards, which she looked at quickly and then laid facedown. She watched the man's conversation with Ansel as if it, not the game, were the main event.

"Who's the head of research and development?" the man asked. "I can't quite remember."

The cards in Ansel's hands were shaking slightly. If she were rich, she wondered, would she be able to sense a poor person's fear? Or would that sweaty, caged-up feeling be so alien to her that she would look right past it? She hoped it was the latter.

"It's funny," said Ansel, "I can't remember either."

"You can't remember the head of your own department? I hope you can at least remember the CEO's name."

The man wore a smug expression now, one Darcy had seen on her teachers when, as they expected, she didn't know the life span of the jellyfish or the number of days it had taken for the boats to cross the Pacific. Ansel looked like Darcy had looked then— panicked, foiled, caught. She was angry with him for offering something he couldn't deliver, for making her feel strong when they were both still weak. That delicious recklessness deflated on itself, sagging like an empty solvent bag. Then Darcy thought of the steak in her shirt, her fake tears. She hadn't gotten out of the pay cut with them, but she hadn't gotten fired either. And this time maybe she could do better. She put on a pained face, pressed her fingers to her temples, and croaked at Ansel in her laryngitis voice, "I think I'm going to faint. Will you come with me to the bathroom?"

"You can't leave the table during a hand," said the dealer, but Darcy said, "It's an emergency."

She stood up unsteadily and hobbled toward the gold-on-burgundy sign marked RESTROOMS.

Ansel followed her; no one else did. The women's bathroom was beautiful—sinks shiny and white as rich people's teeth, cloth towels folded in a wicker basket on the counter, a hamper underneath where you could throw them after just one use. Above the mirrors was a window with real-fiber curtains and frosted glass.

Darcy wanted to linger, to use one of the spotless toilets peeking out behind the stall doors, but she knew someone would come after them soon.

"Nice work," she said. "I thought you had this under control."

Ansel shrugged, his anxiety apparently relieved.

"Sometimes I overestimate myself," he said. "Can you blame me?"

"Yes," Darcy said. "How are we going to break that window?"

Ansel heaved himself up onto the counter with his good arm, then calmly turned the window latch and lifted the frosty pane. The sound of rain came rushing in, and then the rain itself, spattering the sinks.

"They didn't bother to lock it," Ansel said.

His smile was both triumphant and apologetic, both seeking approval and confident that he would receive it. In that moment she liked him again. He reached down to her and helped her up onto the counter.

The window was three stories off the ground. Looking down from it, Darcy saw a dumpster full of green Seafiber trash bags, rainwater pooling in their folds. A smell of rotten cheese food and something fecal came oozing up.

"Is it far down?" Ansel asked her.

"Fuck you," she said, and jumped.

The bags squeaked and squelched around her, and one of them split open and wet the back of her neck with what felt and smelled like partially fermented fruit cup. Something she hoped was refried beans squished up between the fingers of her left hand. She had fallen well, at least, on her back instead of her hurt leg. Ansel came down a second later; his arrival sent up new clouds of fetid trash scent.

"Well, we almost had them," he said, peeling a wet wad of Seafiber tissues from his coat.

"What was the point of that?" Darcy asked.

"We almost made some money," he said. "Besides, we needed a place to hide from Tug."

"Have you ever heard of laying low?"

"Laying low is for the low. And I, my friend, consider myself high."

"You *must* be high," Darcy said.

"I am not currently on any intoxicating substances. But I have been told I have an abnormal zest for life, an unusual joie de vivre."

It was raining lightly but steadily. A cockroach darted in and out amid the garbage. At the end of the alley, Darcy could see the Strip. Through the wet air, the lights of the casinos wept like wounds.

"You could've gotten our asses kicked," Darcy said. "We could've gone to jail."

"Didn't you hear them, talking about Tyson and subsidies and shit? That's money he could be spending repairing the cave-ins or giving poor people parrot-fever drugs so they don't die with pocks all over their faces. Those fuckers are taking something away from you every day of your life. Don't you want to take something away from them?"

Darcy didn't care about the people in the casino, or about Tyson or subsidies or cave-ins. She was tired, she wanted her mother, and Ansel seemed like he was going to be no help at all. She crawled across the trash and hoisted herself up onto the dumpster's edge.

"Give me a straight answer," she said. "Do you have any idea how to find my mom?"

"Not as of now," Ansel admitted, "but my organization is very adept at such things. If you'd like to consider joining—"

The rain made tracks of dirt across his skin; his thin long pleading face looked almost sweet. And it had been a long time since someone had wanted to help her. Then she remembered the woman with the diamond necklace, her blush, her naked desire to believe what Ansel said. She had money and jewels and a family and time; she could afford to be conned. Darcy could not.

"I'm going home," she said.

"Where's home?"

"Little L.A. On the Avenida."

"You really should stick with me," he said. "I can help you."

"It doesn't look like it," she said, and she lowered herself down into the alley and hopped away.

3

I'm sorry to hear about your mother," Marcelle said, "but you missed an entire day of work. And you haven't exactly been a model employee lately. Besides, if I grant you an excuse, I have to do the same for everybody."

Darcy had seen Marcelle's office only twice before—once when she was hired, and once when she made a batch of jellyfish sausages with two parts real pork instead of one. It wasn't a pleasant place— or rather, it was a place designed to be pleasant to people other than Darcy. Drawings of and by Marcelle's children simpered and twinkled across the walls—they went to a better school than Darcy had, one that could afford glitter. On her large but slightly flimsy-looking desk was a yellowing photo of Tyson with a light-skinned black man—Darcy assumed he was Marcelle's father. He looked young and happy and lucky, probably second boat, some-one important enough that his children were managers of places like World Experiences. Behind the men in the photo was the scaf-folding of a building, not yet covered in Seaboard, still full of promise. Tyson looked the way he looked in the few existing pho-tos of him: shifty, stoop-shouldered, and strange.

"Not everybody's mom disappears," Darcy said.

Marcelle had a way of talking to Darcy that made her look like she was reading from a script posted somewhere behind Darcy's head. Her teachers in junior high school had talked like this too.

"World Experiences depends on its rules, Darcy. If we break them, we all suffer."

Then she did another thing Darcy's teachers used to do—she screwed her face into a parody of conspiratorial friendship and said, "But I'll tell you what I *can* do."

Darcy waited. One in every ten times or so, that conspiratorial look meant something good. Sometimes a person who had something Darcy wanted—a teacher, a shop owner, the landlord, even Marcelle—also wanted something Darcy had. Usually it was affection. Even when people had power—maybe especially then—they wanted to be liked.

"I need someone to take vitals on the non-ambulatories. We had to let Nancy go. It won't make up for the dock, but it will be something. What do you think?"

At first Darcy was angry—more work for less pay didn't sound like a favor to her. Then she thought of the non-ambs themselves. They were the oldest of World Experiences' residents, the most likely to be first-boat—the most likely to have known her mother.

"Sounds great," she said.

Her ankle was swollen and sore inside its wrapping, and walking up stairs felt like stepping on nails. Darcy had to devise a kind of crab walk to get to where the non-ambs lived, along the Hall of Africa, a narrow low-ceilinged hallway packed full of fake animals. Paint wasn't enough for whoever had designed this hall—a stuffed Seafiber lion gave a lopsided roar by the stairs, a leopard lay splayed like roadkill beyond it, an elephant raised its trunk toward room 203, and some sort of cowlike beast Darcy couldn't identify made a loopy expression near the bathroom. More than once Darcy had crashed a lunch cart into one of these animals when she was on delivery duty; the dented haunch of the elephant in particular displayed the ill effects of its poor placement.

Some of the non-ambs lived in private rooms and some were obscured from one another by a flesh-colored Seafiber curtain. They were wheeled down to the Rainforest Dining Room once a week or whenever important people were visiting, and they were no more cranky, demanding, or capricious than the other residents. But they were more distant, further along on their slow journeys out of the world.

The first on Darcy's route were the twins, Evelyn and Elvina. Their hospital beds were pushed close together, and identical IVs pumped drugs into their identical arms. Evelyn's nose sprouted an oxygen tube; Elvina's left leg ended above the knee. They had a photo too—good quality, framed, only slightly orangey with age—of the two of them as fit, smiling fortysomethings standing in front of a tent in Founders' Village. They looked rugged in ripped T-shirts and cargo pants—one of them showed the camera a mango with a hearty bite taken out of the center. The photo was the only thing on their bedside table; it was probably their most valuable possession.

"Time to check your vitals," said Darcy, trying to affect the chipper yet domineering voice she'd heard the nurses use. In her mouth it sounded slightly crazed, like the uncomprehending voice of a parrot.

The twins looked at her placidly. Then Evelyn turned to Elvina and said, "Thew thana doe."

Some of the non-ambs—and some of the ambs too, for that matter—had retreated into gibberish worlds of their own making. Rainbow Dog Maclean spoke mostly in bird noises, and Angie Cho strung together her words not by sense but by sound, *bad-badge-badger-hatcher-hatching-matching-match,* so that a conversation with her was a long unfunny pun. A few of the nurses had the gift of treating someone like a human being even when she had stopped talking like one, but Darcy had never mastered this. She approached the twins mutely, warily, undoing the fasteners on the blood pressure cuff.

"You don't happen to know a Sarah Pern, do you?" she asked.

"Doe dinga thana," Evelyn said to Elvina, and both women let out airy halting cough-laughs. They looked at Darcy, looked at each other, and laughed some more. Darcy realized she was being mocked. She did what she had done in school when the hard girls from the Twentieth Street houses had made fun of her for bringing her lunch in a bag—she lifted her chin and looked off into the middle distance like nothing in her field of vision could possibly interest her. Evelyn and Elvina laughed harder. Elvina hacked, then went into a fit of long, low, rumbling coughs that sounded like animal moans. Darcy tried to feel her pulse—Elvina pulled her hand away and covered her spasming mouth with it. Then Evelyn reached across the space between the two beds and clutched Elvina's other hand.

"Daffin doe," she whispered. "Daffin pin ren daffin doe."

Elvina's coughs grew softer and further apart. She let Darcy feel her pulse and put the blood pressure cuff around her arm. As Darcy wrote down the results, she saw the women exchanging mirthful, private glances. When she turned to go they called out, "Ring thana," and laughed some more.

Next was Armin Abcarian. Darcy had heard that he had once been on the Board, and she wondered what had happened to bring him here. He didn't look impressive; he looked like a long vertical line down the middle of the bed. He gazed up at Darcy out of a face pared down to its foundations, like a hasty drawing of a face.

His mouth was a single stroke, his brow a stark shelf, his cheek-bones clear half circles below his eyes. A little pulse of excitement lifted his lips and eyebrows as she crab-walked into the room.

"Are you new here?" he asked.

"I usually work in the kitchen."

"I see, I see."

He held his arm out for the cuff. His wrist bones stood out smooth and round, the skin like a layer of lacquer over them. It looked like it had once been olive; now it was grayish green.

"Do you know a Sarah Pern?" Darcy asked, in a voice she hoped was casual.

"Sorry," he said, "I've never heard of her. But maybe you can tell me something. Do you know someone named Marina Ionova?"

His blood pressure was low. She wrote it down.

"Sorry, I don't."

His face sagged a little, then tightened again.

"She might go by Marie."

Darcy held a finger to his wrist to take his pulse.

"I know a Maria Jimenez."

His eyes swelled. Darcy had learned to look into a person's face and tell if his mind had gone out beyond the bounds of reason. Some of the residents had the blank-eyed look of people for whom the world holds no familiarity—old age had flooded their bodies and washed out their brains. Others turned to Darcy with expressions of concentration, as though making a physical effort to fix the room, the day, her face. Others still looked out of their furrowed faces with eyes that, though perhaps less keen than Darcy's, were no less comprehending. Armin looked like he belonged in the last category, but his expression seemed out of proportion to the situation. Nothing Darcy could possibly offer should make anyone so excited.

"Is she a little younger than me, maybe sixty-five?" he asked. "Kind of a sharp chin, green eyes?"

He stared at Darcy now with bug-eyed fixity. His eyebrows twitched; his mouth opened a little.

"No," Darcy said. "She's my age. She went to school with me."

He nodded and shut his eyes. When he opened them again they were as unfocused as eyes on a bus, eyes on an elevator, all the excitement gone out of them. Darcy wrote down his pulse.

"Why did you want to know?" she asked.

He lifted two long fingers to the bridge of his nose and pressed, like he was pushing energy back into his brain.

"She lived in Portland," he said vaguely. "She was working as a nurse."

"A friend of yours?"

His smile was as wry and lurid as any young man's.

"That's what I called her. When we knew each other, I was married." There was mischief in his voice, but there was also the damp tone of still-unhealed sorrow.

"She had this funny tic," he went on. "She used to pull her left earlobe, then her right. She said it was to keep away frostbite, but she did it all the time, even indoors. She was always thinking, always trying to survive. And she had to be. She had a rough life — her mom was a drunk, they were poor. She never got enough to eat growing up. But she knew how to get what she wanted."

He smiled and shook his head, as though remembering a part of the story he didn't want to tell.

"I told her I'd get her over here. I left word to put her on a boat. It was very competitive, you know. Many people were turned away. But I had influence back then."

He looked around his room, as though comparing. A little blue card by his bed reminded the staff that he couldn't have sugar.

"I keep looking for her," he finished, "but nobody can tell me anything."

"I'm sorry," Darcy said.

"It's all right. If she was here she'd have contacted me by now. Either she doesn't want to see me, or she didn't make it after all."

Darcy began walking out of the room, but he kept talking.

"She was the one who told me we'd all have to get away. I didn't believe it would really end—the cities, all those people. Even when the roads closed down, even when we were eating cats. Even when the vitamins ran out and all the kids were getting rickets and scurvy. I still don't. I can't make myself believe it."

There must have been hundreds of people like him on the island, separated from their lovers by ocean and ice, years of unsaid greetings and good-byes dammed up in their throats. Darcy knew other people who had been separated from their families— Dolores Beltran's husband hadn't been able to get passage, because of something he had written once in a magazine. Everything about that time was shadowy to her—who got to go on the boats and who didn't, who chose and how. Tyson never mentioned that time in the "Mainland Reminiscences" column he published in the news flyers, and Darcy had been eight years old before she understood that not everyone had made it over. In history class they learned about the first boat, and the second, and about how an influx of boats had then brought thousands to the island, but after that there was no more mention of the mainland, and they moved on to learning about Board elections and the accomplishments of the Founder. But the school's janitor was a last-boater, and he told some of the older boys something that quickly trickled down. He said the last boat, an old freighter they hacked out of the ice at the Port of Los Angeles and patched up with car doors and tin roofs and whatever they could find, could fit only five hundred people.

They all pressed together with their stashes of potatoes and cabbage and their contraband vitamin pills and their family heirlooms and their guns, and then when there was no more room and they could barely breathe, and the babies were shoved down between their mothers' breasts and the little children were crushed against their fathers' legs, people were still streaming up the gangplanks, trying to shove their way on. The janitor was only a child then— he didn't know who started shooting. But he saw the men fall backward into the icy water; he saw the women clawing at one another's eyes; he saw the body of a teenage girl slump red-stained across her family. Then someone gunned the engines and the boat pulled away from shore, and people were stripped off the sides into the sea, and more people were gathered on the dock, screaming and throwing stones. It was so cold that the ice knit up in the boat's wake, and they all knew they were the last to get out, and they clutched one another, and the mothers sang quietly to their children, and none of them could bring themselves to rejoice.

Darcy asked her mother if it was true, and after Sarah tried to distract her with a knock-knock joke about monkeys, she said, in a calm and serious voice she rarely used, that there were many more people on the mainland than on the island, and that many of them had been left behind.

"What happened to them?" Darcy asked.

"The winters were getting colder," her mother answered, "and even when we left people said it would only be a matter of time before they were just too cold."

"Too cold for what?"

"Too cold for anything."

"You mean they died?" Darcy had asked then.

Her mother got a look on her face then, an upward twisting of the mouth and eyebrows, a deep and old and impotent guilt.

Darcy had seen that look since, she had felt it in the crowd on Remembrance Day, and she saw it on Armin now. Darcy didn't want to hear any more from him. She didn't like to think you could lose someone forever.

The other non-ambs were almost all women; they slept and knit and complained and lived out their long fragility. Ginnifer was quiet, Madison was bawdy. Courtney slept until Darcy put the cuff on her, then caressed her face as one would a child's. None of them knew who Sarah was. The last room in the Hall of Africa was Yuka McKenzie's.

"You're not Nancy," Yuka said when Darcy walked in.

She had thick full white hair, cut blunt at her shoulders, and a little body coiled up under the sheet. Her face was broad and colorless and minimally lined—a stroke had twisted and pulled the left half so her mouth tailed off in a scowl and her left eye tilted up at the ceiling. Her right eye bored into Darcy like a corkscrew.

"I'm filling in," Darcy said.

Yuka must have learned to talk around her grimace—her speech was quick and clean.

"She get fired?"

Darcy paused, then answered truthfully.

"Good," Yuka said. "She was too fat. Panting all the time. I don't know how somebody so poor gets so fat."

How does someone so rich get so mean? Darcy almost asked. Instead she slid the cuff wordlessly onto Yuka's arm. She knew a way of pumping the cuff that applied sudden and painful pressure.

"What's your name, new girl?" Yuka asked, apparently oblivious to the abuse.

Darcy answered her.

"I knew a Darcy once," Yuka said. "Not a very common name anymore though."

"No."

"Nowadays everybody names their kid Sunroof or Shitstorm or whatever."

Darcy said nothing. She wrote down Yuka's blood pressure. It was high. She screwed up her last bit of hope and asked Yuka, "Do you know Sarah Pern? She's my mom."

"Did she live in Seattle," Yuka asked, "in a co-op?"

Darcy's heart rose in her chest. She looked at Yuka. Her left eye lolled freely, but her right eye met Darcy's gaze and held it. She wasn't going to let herself float off into the past like Armin. Her mind was firmly in the present, and it was watching.

"That's right," Darcy said. "Arete."

The old woman's whole face cracked open in a smile — even her bad eye rolled momentarily forward, centering Darcy in the full strength of its stare.

"Sure, I remember Sarah. She was a little sexpot, that one. I caught her with Duncan Harrison once — well, I won't tell you what she was doing."

Darcy felt like she'd been pinched. She let out a little barking laugh.

"She was ten years old when they left," Darcy said.

Yuka widened her good eye as though to transmit a remembered shock.

"I know, and he was fifteen! I reported it to the council, but they didn't do anything. They didn't give two snowflakes for those orphan kids. No wonder a lot of them turned out the way they did."

Darcy thought of the years of boyfriends, the nights her mother would spread a blanket on the floor, and then another blanket on top of that, so that Darcy could sleep between them.

"Think of a pair of hands," her mother would tell her, and then she would ball up toilet paper and put it in Darcy's ears, "so you don't hear him snoring." And then her mother and the man would get in the bed, and Darcy would make her breath sound low like that of a sleeping child, and she would hear the furtive shifting and muttering that she understood as sex before she was sure what sex was, before her sixth-grade science teacher explained that sex for girls like them would probably happen sooner rather than later, and that they should use a condom, but they probably wouldn't, because girls like them couldn't think about the future since they had too many problems in the present, and so really it was Tyson's fault that five or ten of them would be pregnant by the time they left junior high. That teacher disappeared—transferred to the refinery, someone said—but sex remained on the girls' minds and on their tongues, and pretty soon on their bodies. Autumn and Marisol and Killer Kirkorian were all pregnant in eighth grade, but Darcy wasn't curious. Sex was already in the room with her a few nights a month, less during her mother's period, more when there was someone new, and so when boys came up to her with their looks of studied carelessness she insulted them, treated them like children or idiots, and got a reputation as tough and mean and cold.

She remembered how she would wake in the morning—having finally gone to sleep after all—to see the man putting on his shirt, his pants, once pulling his underwear over a purplish penis, and kissing her mother on the mouth or on the forehead and walking out the door. And then her mother would kneel to her, and kiss each ear as she took the toilet paper out; and if it was a Sunday, she would whisper, "He's gone—now we can play."

Then when she was fourteen, one of the men—a long-armed, bowlegged refinery worker with a parrot-fever scar in the center of his forehead—knelt to her in the middle of the night and pressed his lips against her cheek. It was almost fatherly, almost like a good-night kiss for a sleeping child, but this man was not her father and his mouth stuck to her skin a little too long, long enough to awaken a new insight in Darcy, the realization that she could be desired. It disgusted her. She called out for her mother, who woke immediately—had she even been sleeping at all?— and who took the man by the arm and whispered to him fiercely in the hallway for a moment before coming back alone and shutting the door behind her. After that, no more men came to the apartment, and if Sarah missed them, she didn't show it.

Yuka had made her face politely blank, but Darcy saw a smile fighting up toward the surface. She might be lying, of course, but why would she lie? To confuse Darcy, maybe, to set her on edge, to make her lie in bed at night and wonder if her mother, who seemed so innocent when she bit her toast into a heart shape and placed it on her heart, had ever been innocent at all.

"She's missing," Darcy explained. "I'm trying to find her."

"Well," said Yuka, "I'm very sorry to hear that. Have you been to the guards?"

"They weren't any help," Darcy said. "You don't know anything about where she might be, do you?"

"Is there a man in her life?" Yuka asked. "Maybe you should ask him."

"There's no man in her life," Darcy said.

"You don't really know that, do you?" Yuka asked.

"I know my own mom."

The good half of Yuka's face took on a haughty serenity then. She crossed her hands on the bedspread—small, soft hands like a girl's.

"Obviously you don't know her as well as you thought," Yuka said, "or you'd know where she is."

Darcy tried to think of something mean to say to her, something sweet on its face with barbs underneath, something that would keep cutting Yuka in the brain as she huddled by herself in her medicine-smelling room. But Yuka's twisted face looked impervious to her, her wasted body weirdly strong.

"So there's nothing you can tell me?" was all she could think of to say.

"Oh, there's plenty of things I could tell you," Yuka said. "I could tell you why this island is so fucked up, or what a lion really looks like, or how it feels when a clot cuts off blood flow to half your brain. But I've got no idea where your mother is. And if you'll excuse me, I'm an old woman, and I'm tired."

Someone had slid a comics flyer under Darcy's door. It lay pale and alien amid the familiar mess of the apartment—the splayed bedsheets, the empty cheese-food cans, the few old makeshift toys under the window. On the front of the flyer, Max the Monkey was stealing money from the overflowing pocket of Mr. Moneybags, then using it to buy soda, which made him so dizzy and confused that when he looked at a dog, enormous hearts jumped out of his eyes. Across the top of the cartoon, above Max the Monkey's head, someone had written six names:

Cricket Thomson
Simone Krull
Orion Wu
Duncan Harrison
Esther Rosen
Sarah Pern

She stared at the list a long time. Her mother's name in writing shone out at her like the sun on water. Duncan Harrison's made her smack the wall and pinch the bridge of her nose to drive the image away. She tried to place the other four names but could not. She flipped the flyer over and saw an ad for the Big Top—a polar bear and a wide-mouthed, bug-eyed Eskimo. "Brrrrring Your Family to the Big Top," it read. Darcy left the flyer on the bed and hopped up and down each hall of each floor of the building and out onto the street, but Ansel was nowhere. Then she felt stupid—she had no way of knowing when he'd left the note, and of course he could be anywhere by now.

She searched the apartment for a pen, but all her school supplies were long lost in the cracks of bus seats and the halls of World Experiences and the big open maw of entropy, and she couldn't even find a pencil stub. Finally she took the ketchup out of the mini fridge and, making a silent, aimless apology for wasting food, squirted it onto the paper in the shape of the question, "WHAT?" She left the new note in her hallway, its message peeking out from under her door like a bloodstain.

The next day was Treat Day, and Darcy brought flat glossy brownies to each of the non-ambs. Yuka had been waiting.

"You're late," she said.

Darcy opened her mouth to apologize. Then she said, "I had things to do."

Yuka made the right half of her face faux serious.

"A meeting of the Board, perhaps?"

Darcy didn't take the bait. She set the brownie down a little out of Yuka's reach. Yuka's right eye darted toward it hungrily. Darcy strapped the cuff around Yuka's arm.

"Just some things," she said. "Did you know Cricket Thomson?"

"What an interesting question," Yuka said. "Why do you want to know?"

"Oh, no reason," Darcy said. She moved the brownie a little farther from Yuka.

Yuka's blood pressure was low. She began to laugh. Her laugh was as dry and harsh as sticks rubbed together.

"Are you having fun?" she asked.

"Fun with what?" Darcy felt herself sweat a little.

"Playing around with my brownie," Yuka said.

"I don't know what you're talking about."

Yuka reached out and patted Darcy's hand.

"You think you've got the upper hand and you're going to get something out of me. But don't worry, I'll tell you what you want to know, and you don't even have to play with my food."

Darcy stood up as if to leave.

"It's not that important," she said. "I was just curious, since you knew my mom, if you knew a Cricket Thomson. Or an Orion Wu."

Yuka smiled, the slack left corner of her mouth quirking up a bit. Darcy wondered if that side was really as immobile as it seemed.

"And I'll be glad to satisfy your curiosity, Miss Darcy Pern, if you just do me a little favor. I want Marcelle's notes on me."

Darcy had never seen Marcelle with a notebook. She had never even seen her write. For all Darcy knew, she kept World Experiences running entirely by memory.

"Her notes?" she asked.

"You're not very high up on the totem pole, are you? Marcelle keeps notes on every one of us: whether we're eating, whether we're moving our bowels regularly, whether we're getting depressed and need a little Solzac in the old IV—and other things too. I want her notes on me."

"I can't do that," Darcy said. "I'll lose my job."

Yuka turned away from Darcy slightly.

"Well, I certainly wouldn't risk losing your job over some idle curiosity. You seem like a clever girl; I'm sure you'll find some way of learning what you need to know."

Darcy came home to find the note lying crumpled at the bottom of the stairs. The ketchup was smudged—it looked like something or someone had licked it. Darcy threw it against the wall, where it made an unsatisfying soundless impact. Then she kicked the wall with her bad leg, made a loud crack and a dent the size of her big toe, heard Jorge open his door by the stairs, and had to hop up five flights and collapse onto her bed in a cloud of pain.

She thought of going back to the Big Top and asking about Ansel, but if she showed her face there again, she'd probably get her other leg broken. And how could she even get into Marcelle's office by herself, let alone find and steal her notes? Darcy imagined beating Yuka across her misshapen face. She imagined her mother coming in and sitting cross-legged on the floor, bright-eyed, saying, "You won't believe where I've been." She held her throbbing ankle, and she remembered how her mother used to stand on top of her feet and tell her, "I don't want you to get away." And how, on the rare days when the wind turned cool and people went out in their long sleeves, she would sit by the window in the fading light and answer Darcy's questions in monosyllables, or not at all.

"I really need this," Darcy said as she poured oil on a strainer full of slimy noodles. "I wouldn't ask you if I had any other ideas left."

"You're crazy," Trish said. "We shouldn't even be talking about this."

Trish scraped the inside of a tomato-food can and shook the results into a pot.

"I just need twenty minutes. Just tell her you need her to look at something in the kitchen. I don't care what you tell her. Come on, Trish, this is someone's life."

Trish shook her head as she scooped beef powder into the pot.

"It won't work. Odds are we both get fired, your mom stays gone. I'm sorry, Darce, I really am, but I can't afford to lose my job. You have to figure this out on your own."

Armin had visitors: a woman in an expensive real-fiber shirt and low-heeled leather pumps, a man in an old-style suit. The woman had the composed, studied look Darcy had seen before on the faces of rich women, a look that implied she had been taking great care in her appearance and behavior for so long that this care had become indistinguishable from pleasure. The man was big and loud and profligate of gesture—when he saw Darcy, he made a great sweeping arc with his right arm.

"Aha!" he shouted. "One of our Florence Nightingales!"

Darcy didn't know what he was talking about. His face was wide and red and open, but his little mobile eyes said he wasn't as stupid as he looked. Darcy gave him her company smile.

"Darcy's come to give me my sedative," Armin said. "I have to get my rest."

The woman looked confused—a tiny ripple traveled across her composure.

"During visiting hours?" she asked.

Armin turned to Darcy, his face both pleading and conspiratorial. Darcy reached down into her lungs and pulled up her most authoritative voice.

"In his condition," she said, "properly scheduled sleep is very important. It helps with fluid balance."

The woman looked at her, and she felt the prickly heat of her appraisal. Her eyes, unlike the man's, were large and still. They were used to sizing people up. Darcy wondered what it would be like if your approval were worth so much you had to be careful where you bestowed it.

The woman nodded.

"Well if you need your rest, you need your rest. Come on, Jacob, we'll come back next week."

She allowed the man to walk ahead of her, so he wouldn't seem to be following. On her way out she looked at Darcy again, this time as though she were memorizing.

"Thanks for backing me up," Armin said when they were gone. "I just can't stand my sister for more than twenty minutes."

Darcy strapped the cuff around his arm.

"Why not?" she asked.

His face took on the same abstracted look it wore when he talked about Marina, but now he sounded lost, frightened, like a child alone on the sidewalk.

"I was eleven years old when she was born. My mother didn't want to have another baby. Already we were having trouble getting by — my parents had an online store, and it was getting harder to ship things; the power was out all the time. But my dad, he joined the church around that time. One of the new ones, the Revelationists. He wouldn't let her get an abortion. He said Christ was coming to make a paradise for all of us, where we would all eat manna and the dead would come back to life. He actually said that."

His voice was high and boyish, freshly outraged.

"And so they had my sister, and things just got worse. Even

when she was a little baby, she'd give me this look, like, *I'm hungry, but I'm not going to complain about it*—every day when we were kids, every time I got an orange or a cake for my birthday or a good coat for going outside. When she followed me here she didn't lose it. But now it's changed. Now I'm not a big Board member anymore, I'm just an old man wasting away in a bed. Now her look says, *I'm so hungry, but I'm about to eat.*"

Darcy looked into his face and saw a coddled child, someone for whom the hardened, the uncoddled, had a mysterious power. She imagined Marina—thin, short, malnourished, a raw pointed look to her chin and cheekbones, a little furtive economy of gesture. A quick awareness of all the exits in the room, like a thief or a mouse.

"I need something," she said.

At first he looked at her with confusion—was it distrust?—and Marina faded from her mind and she became for a moment her uncertain self. But then all the reason went out of his eyes, even as he tried to make them look shrewd and withholding, and he said, "I'm not sure I can do much for you," but she knew he meant, *What do you need?*

"Marcelle keeps a record on all the residents," Darcy said. "There's one I need to see."

Armin's face turned pinched and annoyed.

"I don't know anything about any records," he said. "You'd know more about that than me."

Whatever he had wanted to do for her, this wasn't it. Darcy tried to conjure the image of Marina again, but all she saw was Armin's face in front of her, turning away into the pillows.

She sat down on the bed.

"Listen," she said. "My mom disappeared last week. She's the only family I have, she's all I have, and I have to find her. I think Marcelle's records might help."

He was looking at her again, but skeptically, his eyes cool. She imagined him as a boy, his unsunned skin soft and white as bread. She thought of begging him, telling him he was her only hope. Then, instead, she rose as though to leave.

"It's all right," she said. "Forget it. I'll ask someone else."

She put her hand on the door. She heard him shift beneath his covers.

"Wait," he said. "Which ones do you need?"

Another sheet of paper peeked out from under Darcy's door. She scrambled down to snatch it, as though someone might get to it before her. It was a pornoflyer—a cartoon woman was pressing her round breasts together, the nipples peeking out through her fingers. She wore a bikini bottom in a strange pattern—not checks or stripes, but tiny crosshatches and squiggles. A speech bubble said, "I'm waiting for YOU."

Darcy flipped the sheet over—an ad for a strip club. She flipped it again. The woman's breasts stared at her. She threw it on the floor and yelled at it for making her think it was a message. She started to feel light-headed. Her ankle was doing something more complex than throbbing. It was speaking to her, bubbling words up through her leg. It was saying random dirty words like a crazy person. *Shitfuckevilfucktit,* it was saying.

She unwrapped the cloth that Sunshine had tied for her. It looked like it had been a T-shirt—now it was printed with dirt and sweat. She looked off into the murk of the apartment for a minute before she could make herself look at her leg. She counted down from three.

It looked like someone else's leg. Darcy looked at her left leg and felt a little purr of familiarity, the soft, semiconscious "yes" that the brain gives itself when it sees a place where its own blood flows. She looked at her right leg and saw the limb of some other person, some person who was lying alongside her and seemed to share with her a knee and part of a calf, but whose ankle and foot had turned a color that no one should ever allow skin to turn, a blackish gray not so much bruised as stony, as though the leg were slowly becoming a statue.

Darcy retched but forced herself not to vomit. She took the T-shirt to the bathroom and rinsed the dirt away. She carried it still damp back to the apartment and put it in the mini fridge. When it was cold, she wrapped her ankle up again. The voice didn't stop, but it grew soft, like children through a window. She imagined her mind as a hand reaching out, closing the window. She lay down on the bed. The flyer lay upside down next to her head—the bikini bottom was level with her eyes. The pattern looked different now. It looked like letters.

She sat up. She held the flyer close to her face. She read the letters on the woman's crotch. They said, "LIST OF THE MISSING."

Armin was sleeping. His knees were drawn up near his chest and his hands were pillowed under his head. It was only when he lay crumpled like this that Darcy understood how tall he must've been when he could still stand. Stretched out, his attenuated limbs got lost in the blankets. Folded, they took on weight and became visible. His bony calves were as long as a four-year-old child. His hands were big as palm fronds. He was murmuring in his sleep, secret tiny prelinguistic sounds. Darcy knew she shouldn't wake him. It was policy to come back later if a resident was sleeping, and his murmuring face held a kind of calm intention, so different from the shifting, questing look he showed her when he was awake that it seemed like a small act of violence to shatter it. She hesitated. Then she walked forward and shook his pinioned arm.

He woke like an animal, inarticulate and snarling. His lips pulled back over graying teeth. She had seen that face before on a dog in the alley behind her high school, when a monkey tried to grab its can of cheese food. She almost expected him to snap at her, but then his lips closed, his eyes widened, his human brain awoke and sealed itself around the animal one.

"I was dreaming," he said.

"What about?"

He gave her a kind of bent-mouthed leer.

"How old are you?" he asked her.

She tried to imagine how Marina would've responded, cold but somehow not discouraging. She lifted her chin, turned her face a few degrees away.

"Old enough."

But his eyes darkened, his mouth fell into a rueful frown.

"You're not old enough."

Darcy didn't know what to say. She felt his pulse. It was slow, but his skin was sweaty.

"Did you get the reports?" she asked.

He nodded.

"Can I see them?"

"Would you do something for me first?"

She tried to take stock of what she would be willing to do. She would unbutton her jumpsuit to the waist, but would she take it off? Would she put his penis in her mouth?

"What is it?" she said.

"Marina used to wear her hair in a braid, kind of wound up into a coil at the back of her head."

"All right."

"She never took it down while we were together, except when she thought I was sleeping, and it was really cold, and she would undo it, and pull it down around her ears, and wind her fingers up in it to keep them warm."

Darcy reached back to divide her hair for braiding. He shook his head.

"No," he said, "if you could—" He looked down at his hands, embarrassed. "It's not the same if I see you braid it."

"Can you shut your eyes?"

He scratched his index finger with his thumbnail.

"Can you go outside?" he asked.

She stuck her head out the door—no one was in the hallway.

"Okay," she said, and she shut the door behind her.

The hallway was thinly coated with human sounds, with the yelp and mutter and breath and rustle of men and women in their beds. Darcy tried to twist the noises on their way from her ear to her brain, to hear lovemaking instead of coughing, night terrors instead of the ravings of old age. She imagined a hotel from the time before, how the chill would seep in through wooden walls, how her feet would sink into the bearskin rugs. The hotel in her mind was a place both luxuriant and frigid, where bony hips knocked together on feather beds, and women's heavy jewels bruised their famished skins, and hungry mouths chewed orange rinds and dried flower petals. How would someone act in a place like that if she had never known any luxury, if she had gone to bed hungry three nights out of every week for as long as she could remember, and worn old bedspreads to school throughout the ever-lengthening winters, and opened her legs at thirteen and a half to a boy with ragged fingernails and a sore on his upper lip? Wouldn't she smile a little, as she did up her hair in the morning, to see these people brought low as her mother always said they would be? And wouldn't she braid her hair tightly, and coil it up neat, so that even in these threadbare times, no one could see the squalor that she came from?

As she found a way to tuck the end of the braid so the coil stayed tight, she imagined the man waiting in the room for her. She imagined him young, anxious, clutching the pallid hothouse flowers that had cost him two weeks' salary. He would try to compose the face he liked to show to her, the face of someone familiar with affairs in hotel rooms, someone who might even meet another woman in another hotel later that day. He would say to himself, "I don't care if she comes today," and he would try to make himself believe it, and not think of her lying curled in the snow somewhere, or putting her mouth on the mouth of someone with more money and better connections than him. He would pretend to read, or turn on the television and watch part of a western. Then he would hear the door handle, and he would forget how to make the face he'd practiced, so that when she entered—cheeks still flushed from the cold, hair done up neatly—she would see how life had shrunk for him, dwindled down until it was the shape of the air around her body as she moved toward him.

She opened the door. She could see his young face on his old face. She could feel the other woman's skin lying over her skin. She reached up to take her braids out. Her hair fell across her shoulders; she had never been so conscious of it before, the way it felt, the way it must look. She felt beautiful. She saw that Armin was crying.

"What's wrong?" she asked him.

"She's dead," he sobbed. "I left—I left her and she's dead."

"She's not dead," Darcy said, breaking character. "She's probably on the island somewhere. I bet she has a really nice apartment in Sonoma."

He pressed his long bony hands to his face.

"No," he said. "I left her there and she died. They all died. We abandoned them."

"It's not your fault," Darcy whispered.

"There's always one more person we could've taken," he said to her. "If not Marina, then someone else. We didn't do all we could."

She knew it was true, but then again, for every extra person they brought over, there would be one less patch of earth here on the island, one less jellyfish bar or can of cheese food in the convenience store every day, one less job. She had things she needed now, and Armin's guilt seemed far away, frozen, and antique.

"It's not your fault," she said again, and then, "By any chance, did you get a look at Yuka's files?"

He was still crying. He put his face in the pillow and made a noise like a hurt cat.

"I've failed everyone," he said.

Anger rose up in her.

"You didn't see them?"

He shook his head.

"Marcelle wouldn't let me," he said. "She says they're confidential. I'm sorry, I just—I wanted something of Marina so badly. I wanted to see her again."

Yuka's hands lay on her bedspread, tense and compact as cats' paws. When she saw Darcy the good half of her face went taut and sly. Her bad eye stared out past the walls of the room.

"So, did you bring me something?"

Her voice was teasing, like a girl's. Darcy imagined her as a teenager, the two halves of her face matched up in a haughty smirk.

"I couldn't," Darcy said. "Marcelle says they're confidential. I'm sorry."

Yuka reached for a glass of juice on her bedside table and took a sip from the straw. Her expression was obscure now, impossible to read.

"That's no good for either of us, is it?" she said.

Darcy put her blood-pressure cuff and notepad down on the table.

"Look," she said. "Why don't you just tell me what you know? What's the point of holding out?"

Yuka took another sip of her drink. A little clear liquid dribbled out the slack side of her mouth and she wiped it away with her good hand.

"I have something you want," Yuka said. "Why should I give it away for free?"

Darcy sucked her anger and confusion down into a ball in her gut.

"Why do you want to see your chart anyway? What's so interesting about it?"

Yuka was silent for a moment. She seemed to be studying Darcy's face. When she spoke her voice was quieter than usual.

"I had friends, people on the Board. People I worked with, people I trusted. I want to know why none of them ever visit me."

"Maybe they're busy," Darcy said.

"Maybe. But I think Marcelle might be keeping them away from me."

Darcy understood Yuka's face now. It was bereft.

"Why would she do that?" Darcy asked.

"I don't know," Yuka said. "I can't tell."

Darcy felt sorry for her then, and for Armin. She knew what it was like to be alone, to feel your world shrink down to the diameter of your skull. She knew what it was to crave someone powerlessly, to wake up every morning and have to remind yourself that this was life and not a nightmare. And at the same time, she saw an opening.

"I could be your friend," she said to Yuka. "It's not like I have any of my own."

Yuka looked at her for a moment. Then she shook her head.

"You wouldn't understand," she said.

"I might," Darcy said. "Try me."

"You know how long I've been living here?"

Darcy shook her head.

"Five years. When I came to World Experiences, I was eighty-one. I'd had parrot fever twice already, plus a stroke, and I couldn't speak or eat or shit on my own. I had to relearn everything, like a baby. And still I can't walk, and the medication they have me on makes me see things. Sometimes I see the face of a dead woman hovering over the end of my bed."

"That's terrible," Darcy said.

"I'm not stupid. I know not everybody has a nice hospital bed and rehab treatments and medicine. But not everybody did what I did, either."

She was speaking loudly now, and Darcy could hear a younger voice wrapped in the old vocal cords, straining and failing to reassert itself.

"What did you do?" Darcy asked.

"I was here from the beginning. I was one of the first people to set foot on the eastern beach. And even before that—you could say I'm the reason we're here in the first place."

Darcy looked at Yuka's eyes, saw pride in the good one, need in the bad.

"What do you mean?" she asked.

"Well, it's all ancient history now. Everyone else has forgotten about it anyway. Maybe it's time for me to forget too."

But Darcy could see that Yuka wanted to tell her—she just wanted to be cajoled a little. She sat down on the bed next to Yuka's tiny hip.

"I'm interested," she said.

"Don't you have other patients to visit?"

Darcy bet that Yuka would want to feel superior. She made a dismissive wave of her hand.

"They won't notice if I'm late," she said.

Yuka took a little preparatory breath, like she was diving into water. Then she began to speak, and she spoke quickly and without pausing, as though she were worried about being stopped.

"When I first got into the Pacifica thing I was married. Daniel. He was an idealist. We both were. We were twenty-five and we'd been living in Arete for two years, ever since our college got shut down. At first it was fun, living in that great big house out in the pines. Lots of the neighbors left, trying to get to the compounds by the Gulf or maybe to South America, and we made fun of how soft they were. Every time we saw a car leave we'd go take what we wanted from their houses. They never locked them—they weren't coming back. We got a nice big couch for the living room that way, a whole cabinetful of spices, a dog. Once I found a big box of family photos—an outdoor wedding, kids in bathing suits at the beach. All the way back to this young woman sitting in one of those old cars—a Model T—grinning. Of course, we didn't know how valuable photos would be later—we used them as playing cards until they fell apart.

"Then we started hearing about the hurricanes in the Gulf, and people getting shot down at the Mexican border, and we started getting all these refugees from the north, from British Columbia where the ice was knocking out whole towns. We had seventy people living in Arete finally, in a house built for twenty. There were ten, fifteen people in every bedroom—even the two big communal sleeping rooms that the hard-core hippies liked were packed to the gills with people. And then the road closed, and we were all alone out there. The electricity went out, the gas went out, we were heating the house with wood and lighting it with candles. We had to feed all those people on just our five chickens and the vegetable greenhouse, and the cans in the pantry. That winter six kids got scurvy, and we had a full-on food riot—ten guys beat up the kitchen manager over two cans of corn.

"That's when Tyson showed up. He came from downtown, he said, and everyone there was talking about this volcanic island. It was uninhabited, and it was small, but you could build it out with landfill. Best of all, it was really, really warm. We could live there the way we used to—grilling hamburgers for lunch, going for a Sunday drive with the windows down. He even knew about this procedure for making fuel out of ocean bacteria—he wasn't calling it solvent yet—and we could have electricity again. America Pacifica, he called it, and a lot of people were skeptical, but I knew right away that this was something big.

"Tyson started showing us how it would all work, how we'd travel to the port and fit out the ship, how more people could follow after. He had contacts as far east as Denver, as far south as L.A. Our world had shrunk to the size of our crowded, dirty house, but he made it big again. But then Daniel started to pull back. He thought Tyson was moving too fast, he thought we needed more information. More than that, he thought the whole premise was wrong. He thought we could never go back to the way things were before. He said that living the way we used to—trying to shape the world rather than letting it shape us—he thought that was what got us into the Ice Age in the first place. He thought we needed to learn to live with the ice and snow, adapt to it. And he thought we could learn to do it; we just needed a little time.

"I guess I should mention how much I was in love with him. I don't know if you'll know what I'm talking about, but sometimes you feel like no matter how close you get to someone it will never be enough. We'd been married three years and I was still hungry like that, every single day.

"Anyway. Daniel started telling people the whole plan was flawed. He was saying we'd end up just as bad as we were now, if not worse. He said it looked like an easy way out, but really it wasn't at all. People had always listened to Daniel; he was very inspiring. It started going around that there was going to be a vote—if Daniel won we'd stay, if Tyson did we'd go. Daniel wasn't sleeping anymore—he spent every night making maps and plans. He had this theory that some places along the coast would be warmer than others, because of ocean currents or something. And he thought we could grow food more efficiently if we were willing to use our own shit for fertilizer. It was all he could talk about—all the changes we'd have to make, the new ways of doing things.

"That's when Tyson came to me. He had a different way about him from Daniel. He wasn't handsome; he had this way of walking like he had some kind of injury he hadn't quite recovered from—his arms all hanging funny from his shoulders. And when he talked to you he didn't seem convincing. He had this weak voice, like there wasn't enough air behind it. He said what Daniel was doing was going to be disastrous for all of us. He said almost certainly we would die—I already knew the temperature projections, but he told me anyway. He told me to imagine it, the food getting scarcer, the fights getting worse, people killing each other over the last leaf of cabbage. He told me that in situations like this, people often turn to cannibalism. And even if we didn't die, even if we could make a life for ourselves in the snow and ice, did I really want that kind of life? Did I want to stay inside forever and raise kids who never got to see the sun? I asked him why he would come to me, of all people, and he said I was the only one who could stop Daniel.

"At first I was angry. I almost hit Tyson. I was so offended that he'd try to turn me against my husband. But that night I didn't tell Daniel what he said. I lay in our sleeping bag while Daniel wrote, and Tyson's words just stuck like burrs in my brain. I lay there listening to the young people drinking and shouting, and the mothers singing to their children, and the children crying or talking in their sleep, and Daniel writing and writing, and I thought about what would happen if Daniel got his way. Tyson was right—most likely we would die. But death—death I couldn't really imagine. What I could imagine was what would happen if we lived, how we'd start making accommodation after accommodation. We'd start thinking rickety bent-up legs were normal, we'd paint trees on the walls and pretend we were outside. We'd forget what apples looked like, how beef tasted. And I didn't want that. I wanted my old life back, when I was a child and the days were warm, and I didn't have to scrabble for every little thing. There was something else too. I didn't want Daniel to become a leader. Ever since we met, we'd been so close; weeks went by sometimes when the only people we talked to were each other. I wanted him to be great, I'd always seen greatness in him, but then when all the people were listening to him, hanging on his words, I got jealous. I wanted to be his only audience—I didn't want anyone else taking part of what used to be mine. So the next day I went to Tyson and I said, 'What do I need to do?'

"He knew just how to talk to me—no glee in his voice, no gloating. He put his hands on my shoulders and said, 'You won't regret this.' And then he told me what to say.

"The next three days I got myself on vitamin duty. I went around to all the little circles—there were couples bedded down in the bathtubs by this point, babies in the old washing machine—I went around handing out the last of our multis, one pill for grown-ups, half for the kids. I told everyone, 'This is it, enjoy it. Pills like this, they're going for a hundred dollars a pop now, and it's only going up.' Then I'd remind them about the vote. Daniel was planning for it day and night, I'd say, and then I'd tell them how methodical he was, how thorough. I'd say—and this part was a lie—that Daniel had made population calculations, that before his plan had a chance to work, one in three of us would probably starve. And I saw the mothers look at their children, the husbands look at their wives, the young people look down at their own shivery bodies, all of them thinking, *One in three*. Then I'd toss off something about Tyson, how his plan was too reckless and untested, and how no matter what, Daniel's was better. By the end of the third day I saw how they all looked at Daniel differently—skeptical, peering. When he talked to our friends they started to look embarrassed, turn away. Daniel just worked harder, and I heard him whispering to himself at night, trying to find a way to get people back on board. During that time I felt incredibly tender toward him. I gave him my blankets and slept in just my parka; before the meeting I made him breakfast with the last of our ham. I told myself it would be easier for him when Tyson was in charge—he wouldn't have to worry so much; he could sleep curled around me like he used to.

"We had the meeting in the morning. I'd lost track of the time of day because it snowed so much, the light was always the same, but that day I knew it was early because we got a little sun, just for ten minutes or so, a little red dawn across the snow. I remember thinking, *I'll never see sunrise on icicles again, I'll never see pine trees sparkling with ice.* We hadn't voted yet, but I already knew we were leaving.

"At the meeting Tyson just stood up for a minute, but Daniel talked and talked. After we voted he wanted to have a revote—he said people hadn't been listening. Tyson let him do it, but everyone voted the same. Then Daniel got up and walked out of the house.

"It was way below zero that day, and we didn't find him for a long time. He was huddled up against the menu at a broken-down fast-food place almost a mile away. His tears were frozen to his cheeks. We took him back and I stripped him down and crawled naked into our sleeping bag with him. While I was holding him and feeling him shiver back to life, I realized that I was as close to him as I wanted to be, and then I knew I didn't love him anymore.

"After that we started getting ready for the move, getting together provisions for the boat, stocking up on trash so we could start the landfilling. Daniel didn't help with any of that. He started spending a lot of time with the orphan kids. We had a bunch of them, six or seven, kids whose parents couldn't be bothered with them anymore and just dumped them on us. Schooling wasn't too organized at that point, but he got them all together, from little Simone all the way up to Cricket, who was sixteen—"

"Cricket Thomson?" Darcy finally interrupted.

"That's right. All those names on your list were protégés of his. Your mom too."

Yuka's story changed shape in Darcy's mind. Where before it

had been populated by dim-faced strangers, now her mother's face shone out of the crowded co-op rooms, the assembled masses lifting their hands to vote. Her face looked just like it had the day she disappeared, except smaller, and more hopeful, and bright as the clean ocean at the horizon. Her mother had never said anything to her about Daniel—all this was news to her.

"Do you know why that would get them in trouble?"

"No idea," Yuka said. "Daniel and I weren't talking much by that point. For all I know he was just teaching them their ABCs."

Darcy's brain sputtered. What good was it to know about Yuka's life, about Daniel? The story about Tyson was strange—it disturbed her a little that the Founder had built the whole island on a lie. But that had been so long ago, before Darcy was born, and it didn't seem to have much to do with her.

"Of course," Yuka said, "it might help if I knew what you were looking for."

To tell her anything felt like giving something up, but Yuka's face still wore its lonely look. If anything it seemed that telling the story had made her sadder, as though it hadn't relieved her as much as she had hoped it would. Darcy relented.

"After my mom disappeared," she said, "someone gave me a list of names. All those people were on the list. He says they're missing too."

Yuka pursed her lips like she was sucking something sweet.

"Now," she said, "that's interesting."

"Interesting why?"

"Well," she said, "somebody wants those kids gone. Or at least quiet. Now that somebody could be a lot of people—could be one of the gangs, could be some kind of serial killer, could be the guards. But if I had to guess, I'd say it's Tyson, or somebody close to Tyson."

The idea that Tyson would even know about her mother, let alone wish her ill, was bizarre to Darcy.

"Why do you say that?" she asked.

Yuka smiled her half smile. "Call it a hunch," she said.

"So how do I find them?"

Yuka spread out her good hand in the air in what Darcy realized was her version of a shrug.

"That's your problem. But I'll tell you one thing that's funny. Esther Rosen had a twin, Ruth. She wasn't on your list. Now maybe your source just didn't get her name. But if she's not missing, you should talk to her. I bet she knows more than anybody."

"How do I find her?"

Yuka shrugged again.

"How should I know? I'm stuck here, remember."

Her voice was wry, but Darcy heard real sorrow in it.

"I'm sorry," she said, "I interrupted you. You can go on if you want to — I have a little time."

Yuka looked bleakly at the wall.

"It's all right, I know you have things to do. Everybody does. I know you just listened to me so you could get your information."

"No, I—"

"Don't pretend," Yuka said. "But do this for me. If you find out anything, I want you to tell me what you know."

"All right," Darcy said, but as she was agreeing she saw a new expression flash across Yuka's face. Yuka corrected quickly, and looked bereaved and put-upon again, but that new expression was so prying and calculating and sly that Darcy wondered if she had ever really been lonely at all.

4

It had been five days since she wrote the note, and still Darcy had heard nothing from Ansel. Every morning before she went to work, she checked its positioning—"COME MEET ME," written in real pen this time, in large letters all around the head of the topless woman, the whole thing affixed to the baseboard by her door with a wad of hardening cheese food. But every night she returned to find it untouched and Ansel nowhere in sight. Armin didn't look Darcy in the eye when she came in now; Yuka was bored and laconic; the twins chattered happily in their gibberish language. Trish never asked about her mother—they made pancakes and burgers and imitation-crab salad and joked and complained as they always had. There was a big cave-in near Sixth Street, and Trish heard they were going to have to condemn everything east of Salinas Avenue. Win heard there was going to be a tax hike to pay for more retrofitting, and they all wondered for the fiftieth time how come all the rich people got to live inland.

"They'll be safe if the Hawaiians come back, too," Trish complained. "It's the people on the coast who are going to get torpedoed or whatever."

"What about the safe houses?" Darcy asked—a sign reading SEA-ATTACK SAFE HOUSE had popped up on a community center near World Experiences, and Darcy passed it on her way to work.

"Yeah right," said Trish. "I heard there's only, like, four of those. If they come back, we're toast."

"But how much you wanna bet we start paying higher Seaguard taxes too?" Win asked.

Darcy didn't answer. Discussion of the attack couldn't hold her attention. She was living as though it were possible to be normal, but every morning she still felt for her mother beside her, and then pummeled the empty bed as though it might yield her up.

On the sixth day Jorge came for the rent. She had just walked into the apartment, bus sweat clinging to the small of her back. He stood in the hallway, eyeing the room like he was measuring it.

"I'll have it by Tuesday," Darcy said, "I promise. It's just been hard, with my mom and everything."

"Maybe you should get a roommate," Jorge said. "I have a friend who's looking for a place."

Darcy stared at him until he looked away.

"She's coming back," she said.

"Of course. But even if she does, it might be easier for you. You could split the rent three ways then."

He looked at her again, this time with sly eyes.

"My friend's a nice guy," he said. "I think you two would get along."

"Tuesday," she said. "I promise."

His voice went a shade darker.

"No later," he said.

She waited for him to leave, and then she reached into her coin cup—bus fare, if she didn't shower tomorrow. There was no way she was going to make rent without her mother's salary. She would have to live with Jorge's friend. And if she didn't want that, she'd have to move, but where could she afford to live on just her paycheck, minus refinery tax, minus the special Seaguard tax, minus the electric bill and bus fare and showers and a month's worth of cheese food and seaweed crackers and jellyfish powder, all of that not even counting anything that could possibly bring her any respite or pleasure? She was going to find Sarah before she had to worry about that.

She smelled her hair. It smelled like jellyfish and crab flavoring and smog. She pulled it back, folded it into a quick braid. She wondered what Marina's hair had smelled like. Were there any bad smells in a world of snow? She found a ripped T-shirt under the bed and wrapped it around her head in what she hoped looked like a scarf. Then she went out to wait for the bus.

The number 17 was unreliable. It had a strange route, scything through Little Los Angeles on its way from Manhattanville to the Strip. Usually Manhattanville types were rich enough for taxis, or even had their own cars, so the number 17 was often packed with fourteen-year-olds skipping school to talk their way into the casinos, or University kids with dreadlocks slumming it for the day, or escorts coming back worn-looking from all-night gigs with Pacifica Bank execs. Unlike on the number 32, where fights were relatively predictable, there was no telling what would happen among the heterogeneous assortment who packed themselves together on the number 17. It could be a half hour late because some college student who fancied himself an anarchist refused to either pay or leave, or it could be early because a bunch of rich, stupid teenagers were trying to treat it like a cab, paying the driver to skip stops and take shortcuts down alleyways so they could lose the rest of their allowances at a craps table. Tonight Darcy waited with a pair of joyless, baggy-faced gambling addicts and a woman in a purple corset heading to her night job. As the busless minutes ticked by, they tapped their feet in a spastic rhythm, and the gamblers began to scratch and look about themselves fearfully, like solvent-heads. Darcy thought about walking—it was only a half hour or so, but you had to cross the canal at Barstow Road, whose banks this time of night swarmed with junkies and crazies and people who would drag you down from the bridge and never let you back up again. The gamblers coughed and scraped at the skin of their upper arms. The woman adjusted the dimpled flesh that squeezed up out of the top of her corset.

When the bus finally came, a nun from Our Lady of the Talking Birds was walking up and down the aisle, collecting donations. The parrot on her shoulder fixed Darcy with its lizard eye and said, "Blessed are they who speak for the voiceless."

"I don't have any money," she said to the nun, whose face remained absolutely still as though she were deaf and mute. Darcy didn't like the Talking Birds nuns, their creepy parrots, their vow of silence—she wished they would just do their own begging instead of making the birds do it.

"Bless you," said the bird, its voice like gravel in a cheese-food can. "Bless you, bless you, bless you."

The nun looked at Darcy with the same weird fixed stare they all had, like they were counting up a column of numbers written inside your face—a look that would earn anyone else a beating. Then she reached into her pocket and handed Darcy a flyer. On the front was a picture of a church and an Avenida address. On the back were the words "DRUG COUNSELING, YOUTH GROUPS, FREE MEDICAL CARE."

"Services Sundays," the bird was saying now. "Eleven and four-thirty. Blessed are those who hear the Word."

Darcy put the flyer in her pocket, and the nun passed Darcy by, her flat, thin-soled shoes softly brushing against the floor of the bus.

On the Strip Darcy kept her head down. She hoped the T-shirt would obscure her face from any circus people, but every time she saw a man who looked like Tug she tried to duck behind someone else, until a woman in a Seaboard headdress shaped like a boat turned and growled into her face. When she got within sight of the Big Top she pretended to stand in line for the midnight show at the Desert Palace, peering around the nervous businessmen and drunk University kids to search the street for a sign of Ansel.

A block ahead, a street show was beginning. Two players held up a Seaboard cutout of a house and made it bob in orange Sea-fiber waves.

"Help me!" called a man in a flowered dress. "My house is in the ocean and my babies are drowning."

The actor playing Tyson pranced and preened.

"I have an idea," he said. "Let's all watch a baseball game to take our minds off our troubles."

"That's a great idea," said the man in the dress. "I love baseball."

"Wonderful," said the player Tyson. "That'll be three thousand dollars."

"But I don't have three thousand dollars!"

"Well then, you can read about it in the flyers the next day. It's just as much fun!"

It wasn't raining yet, but the air was thick and wet and hot and it bent the shapes of people on their way to Darcy's eye, making pushers sashay like dancers and dancers slither like snakes and one tall drag queen seem to melt from the knees down into a flume of liquid metal. Darcy squinted and blinked, but the colors ran and bled, until the street was dappled and reticulated in maroon and lemonade and green.

"Ticket?" someone said to her, and she jumped back as though shaken from sleep.

"Sorry."

She moved out of the line, rubbing her eyes.

The ticket taker muttered "cunt," matter-of-factly, like it was a number.

She crossed the street so she was opposite the Big Top, tugged the T-shirt down low over her eyes, and half hopped, half hobbled her way past. She could manage walking if she let only the outside edge of her right foot touch the ground. The polar bear poster was gone, replaced by "Pecos BILL and the Giant RATTLER." The line out front looked shorter than before. Tug was working the door, smoking a fat seaweed cigarillo—he looked Darcy's way and her muscles clutched around her guts. Then she saw him turn and argue with a couple in wedding clothes. She passed the Big Top, passed the chapels, stopped by the side of the Ring Road to catch her breath. She didn't know what she'd been expecting—Ansel standing on the street, waiting for her? He couldn't be very welcome at the Big Top either.

Five hookers by the side of the Ring Road waved at passing cars and fattened their red mouths in kissing shapes. One of them was dressed like a cowgirl—ten-gallon hat, fake leather boots, Seafiber minidress with sheriff stars painted on it. She held a flaccid lasso in her sharp-nailed hand. It was a long shot, but a whore might have cause to know someone in a shady information-gathering organization—if Ansel's organization was even real.

"Excuse me," Darcy said, "do you know someone named Ansel?"

The cowgirl gave her a look of sleepy half attention. She was tall on top of her cowgirl boots. She looked like she didn't have time for anyone.

"I don't ask for names," she said.

She sounded like she said this a lot. Two of the others turned to look. They were in costumes too—a rich girl, with too-bright blond hair and a pink skirt suit, and a last-boater, with smeared eyeliner, a torn tank top, and an empty solvent plug hanging from one earlobe by what looked like Seafiber thread.

"No," Darcy went on, "I mean—he used to work around here. At the Big Top?"

The cowgirl shrugged. A minicar drove up, black and waxy with only a few salt scars on its hood, and she switched her lasso and called out, "Giddyup!" in a high-pitched baby voice.

The car slowed to a stop, and the cowgirl leaned into the passenger-side window, resting raw elbows on the frame.

Someone tapped Darcy on the shoulder. It was the girl in the pink suit. Up close, Darcy saw her nipples poking through the thin material of the jacket. The skirt was slit all the way up to her faded red panties. She wore thick pink lipstick and false eyelashes. Darcy thought of the girls from Manhattanville and Upper Chicagoland who sometimes came down to the Avenida in nervous groups of three and four, talking about "authentic Mexican food." They wore stranger, better clothes than this, and they always looked clean, even when they began to sweat in the nighttime heat.

"I know Ansel," she said. She wasn't smiling. "Hey Christmas, you remember Ansel Adams Rivera?"

The last-boat girl disengaged herself from her hip-first stance and came over, graceful in her high-heeled shoes. Her arms were covered in colorful tattoos.

"Mr. Big Idea? Of course I do."

They laughed together in a private way that made Darcy jealous. They reminded her of the hard girls she knew in school, girls who acted like they were the only ones who knew about solvent, or sex, or how to get what you wanted. The girl in pink recovered first. She adjusted her blond hair; a spider leg of brown escaped from beneath it.

"What do you want with Ansel?" she asked. "He owe you money?"

"No, he's helping me with something. Do you know where he is?"

The girl in pink turned to Christmas.

"Ansel ever help you with anything?" she asked.

"He helped my mom get rid of all that extra food she had. That was a big favor."

"He's bad news," the girl in pink said. "He used to hang out with my brother, and he'd get this look in his eye. He's going to do something dangerous someday."

Christmas rolled her eyes.

"Nah," she said, "he's just a freeloader. He's not going to do anything except what he's always done—hang around and mooch."

"Whatever," said the girl in pink. "Free advice: if you're looking for help, don't look for Ansel."

"Oh, and don't look for help either," Christmas said. "Unless you're willing to—" She mimed a penis going in and out of her cheek. The girls cackled.

"Thanks," Darcy said. "I don't need any advice."

"Oh yeah," Christmas said. "You look like you're doing real well for yourself. What happened to your leg? Slip in the shower?"

"Are you kidding?" the girl in pink said. "Look at her hair. This girl's too good for showering."

She wanted to say something cutting, to show she was better than them even if she didn't look like it. But everything about her was as it seemed—she had dirty hair, her leg was busted, she was not doing well for herself. When she was little and other kids made fun of her, her mother had told her to imagine living inside an egg, a cool yellow-white place no one could see inside. But now no place she could make for herself seemed pleasant, nothing of hers was worth keeping safe. She let them jeer and yell at her as she limped away, and she said nothing in return.

The night was hardening around its core. The air was cooler—sweat dried on her skin and stuck there, spit-thick and itchy. The wind shifted and blew the smoke in from Detroitville. Below that was the ominous smell of the coming rain.

Darcy hobbled a block north of the Strip and headed back toward the bus stop. Her whole lower leg was starting to seize up with a cold pain like ice against a sensitive tooth. Against the door of a dark pawn shop, a woman lay crumpled in a solvent sleep. Darcy envied her for a moment—whatever was the most awful thing in her life, she wasn't thinking of it now. The street was badly lit—a man emerged from a stain of dark and whispered at her, "Solve your problems?"

Darcy still had seven dollars in her pocket. She could buy a hit of solvent, sink into its springy surface, and not climb out until morning. She'd had the powder kind once, at a party with some older kids from the high school, and it had melted time, condensing her birth and her childhood and her adolescence and the six frenetic hours of the party itself into a single homogeneous substance, translucent and crystalline like amber. If she took a hit now, maybe her mother would come back to her, smiling across the eternal present like a painting on the inside of her eyelids. She stuck her hand in her pocket and pressed the money against her palm. Then she remembered running down the street inside the yellow room of her fear, and she imagined that feeling cooked down into a liquid and mixed with every second of her life before and since, and she retched and tasted bile in her throat. She shook her head at the man and walked on.

She expected her leg to stop hurting when she got on the bus, but when it finally came and she lowered herself onto the duct-tape-mended seat, the pain only spread out around her like a skirt. When she moved her leg, she thought she could feel edges of bone grinding against one another. She remembered the flyer the nun had given her, the words "free medical care." She pulled it out of her pocket and looked at the address: 1219 Avenida, near Sixteenth Street.

It took her three passes to find the church, wedged in between a convenience store and a place that sold solvent pipes. Its Seaboard sign was small and rain-faded. Even this late at night, a narrow door stood open, and through it she could see a row of folding chairs. She walked inside. The room wasn't air-conditioned, but it was cooler than the street, and pleasantly dim, and it smelled like clean laundry. She listened for birds, but heard nothing; she looked around for a doctor's office, but saw only a line of light from underneath the door of an inner room. She walked toward it and was forming her hand into a fist for knocking, when a woman opened the door.

"Can I help you with something?" the woman asked. She was shorter than Darcy, small and indeterminately old, and her hair was put away underneath a green cloth. A blue and red macaw sat quiet on her shoulder.

"I thought you guys weren't allowed to talk," Darcy blurted.

"I can," said the nun. "I'm the extern. Ann."

She extended her hand, gnarled but with beautiful nails. Darcy shook it.

"What's an extern?" she asked.

"Somebody has to order the Communion wafers, deal with the landlord. The birds aren't real good at that."

The macaw turned its vibrant head and regarded Darcy balefully. It opened its beak; its tongue was black as asphalt.

Darcy held up the flyer. "I hurt my leg," she said. "It says 'free medical care.'"

Ann motioned to one of the folding chairs. "Sit," she said. "I can take a look at it."

She unwrapped the filthy shirt from around Darcy's ankle. Even the air on her skin seemed to hurt a little. Darcy looked away as Ann moved her fingers down the inflated flesh. Then her thumb hit a spot of perfect pain. Darcy cried out.

"Yup, that's a break all right," Ann said. "I can give you some medicine and wrap it up for you, but you need to get it set properly or it's not going to heal right."

"Yeah, okay," said Darcy, mentally calculating the cost of a hospital visit. Especially without Sarah's salary, medicine and wrapping were going to have to be enough.

Ann went into the inner room, and Darcy heard her rummaging in drawers. Through the door, she could see a drawing of a man in brown robes surrounded by strange animals, and another of a man in some sort of jail, with white birds flying around him. Ann came back with a tube, a Seaboard splint, and a roll of clean white gauze.

"This is a topical preparation," she explained, squeezing cream from the tube into her palm. The cream was the color of an old tooth and smelled like basil. When she put it on Darcy's ankle, the skin went hot like it was blushing, and then numb.

"We'll want to let it sink in a minute before we wrap it," Ann said, and then she sat down in one of the folding chairs and looked at the wall with such fixity and serenity that Darcy was immediately uncomfortable. The bird, on the other hand, craned its neck to look directly at Darcy.

"What's the deal with the birds anyway?" Darcy asked, trying to direct the question to Ann and not the macaw. "Are they in the Bible?"

Ann laughed. Darcy looked at her blankly.

"Sorry. No, they aren't in the Bible. It's a thing our founder came up with. We take a vow of silence to symbolize the plight of the voiceless, and then we talk only to the birds, who have voice but no understanding."

"But who are the voiceless?" Darcy asked. "I mean, besides you."

Ann's smile was like her laugh, full of mirth and bitterness.

"I used to wonder that," she said. "Then I lived on the island for a while."

She knelt again, and without asking slid off Darcy's clammy shoe and sock and wound the gauze under her instep.

"You want to keep it wrapped pretty tight," she said. "Tighter than you had that shirt."

She held the splint against Darcy's leg and lashed the two together firmly.

"This should hold you for a while. But like I said, you should see a professional. How'd you do that, anyway?"

Darcy looked at Ann's calm face, the bird's sly eyes. Ann seemed trustworthy enough, but she didn't know what went on in that inner room.

"Long story," was all she said.

Ann nodded, as though satisfied.

"Well good luck, and God bless you."

She put the tube and the remaining gauze in Darcy's open

hands. As Darcy stood to leave, the macaw lifted its feathers so she could see the pink skin underneath, almost like a human's.

"Blessed are they who inherit the earth," it said, "for they will speak for the voiceless."

Ann shook her head.

"Sometimes they get mixed up," she said. "They write their own scripture."

It was after 2 a.m. when Darcy walked home, and the Avenida wore its dismal late-night dress. Empanada wrappers twitched in the breeze. A monkey under a streetlight fiddled with a woman's shoe. She opened the door to her building; the inside smelled like its inhabitants, their restless nights and sweaty days. She heard a baby begin to fuss and imagined a cool hand reaching down to cup its face. She turned onto her hallway and saw Ansel standing at her door.

He was wearing his trench coat, and she noticed now how tall he was, how there was something regal in his slender head, his beaky nose, the way his shoulders leaned back away from his chest. She saw how he could pass for a Manhattanville executive, someone who assumed good things were due to him in life. Both his coat sleeves were full, and she wondered if he'd been conning her earlier, if he'd somehow faked his amputation just to see what she would do. Then he held his right hand out.

"Shake?"

The hand was the size of a baby's, chocolate brown, and furry.

"What's that?" Darcy asked.

"I got it from a stuffed monkey. Look, I got his arm too."

He rolled up his sleeves and showed her a skinny monkey arm lashed to a piece of plastic tubing.

"Where's the rest of the monkey?"

He pulled a doll out of his coat pocket. It was Monkey Max

from the comics flyers, with white plastic eyes and a laughing, pink-tongued mouth. She imagined a real monkey making short work of it.

"In case I need any more parts," he explained.

She turned the doll over in her hands. It was exactly the kind of toy she'd never had as a child, the kind of toy she'd seen in the hands of children in Sonoma Hill or Upper Chicagoland and yearned after with a brainless and unfocused craving. She opened the door to let Ansel in; the only toys she'd ever had were the ones lined up under the window, the crown and the dolls made of rocks.

"I was looking for you," she said. "I went back to the Big Top."

He sat on the floor. He picked up the cheese-food crown, balanced it on his head.

"You risked the Tug treatment? You must've really wanted to see me."

He slid the crown over his monkey arm, wore it like a bracelet.

"I wanted to know where you got the names," she said.

"You know, it was the funniest thing. A bird came to my window—a big, ugly macaw with its feathers falling out—and it just squawked out all these names and then died right there on my floor. I think it'd been poisoned."

"Ansel, come on. My mom is missing."

He put the crown back on his head, clasped the monkey hand with his real hand and brought both up to his chin.

"I see. You wish me to be serious."

Darcy hated how beholden she was to him, this man with a monkey hand sticking out of his coat. The hookers could be right—he could be a worthless freeloader. But in his presence she could feel her joints loosening, the sour panic leaving her blood.

"Please," she begged.

He pressed his lips together and lowered his brows in a parody of grim resolve.

"You have to understand, Ms. Darcy Pern," he said, "that my seriousness comes at a price."

"Right," said Darcy, "your organization. Explain to me for real what you guys do."

"We are a multifaceted subversive organization pursuing many avenues of endeavor—"

"Ansel," said Darcy, "just tell me what you *do.*"

His face lost its humor then, and she saw what was behind it— something roiling, like rage or desire. A little of the recklessness she'd felt at the casino came back to her now, but darker, not like a rich person's but like an animal's.

"There are fifty thousand people on this island," he said. "About five hundred are first-boaters. Another five thousand or so are second-boat, or they came in the influx, but they've managed through crime or connections or, very occasionally, intelligence to acquire wealth. The rest are people like us. We don't have money, so we don't have power. My organization is going to change that."

"How?"

"Rich people have friends everywhere. The guards, the big companies, the Board. Tyson most of all. We're making friends of our own."

He spoke like he didn't have to think, like he had a grand plan in his head and he was just breaking off chips of it to show her. She liked his certainty, and she liked the anger crackling in his voice. She hoped he was dangerous—she needed some danger on her side.

"What do you want me to do?" she asked.

"It depends on where your skills lie," said Ansel. "But in general—talk to people. I have a lot of contacts, but I'm not always able to get the best out of them. In some situations, you might be better."

She had talked to so many people in the past few days, it didn't seem like much to promise. But she thought of the guard and his minty tongue, and she was wary.

"If you want me to talk to someone, and I don't want to, what happens?"

"What are you suggesting?" Ansel asked.

"I mean, I don't know how many guys you have. I don't know whether you have guns or what."

"I'm not going to divulge any information about our weaponry—yet. But I'm not trying to indenture you. We want enthusiastic allies or none at all. You won't have to do anything you don't want to do."

Darcy hoped the girl in pink was right. And she hoped Ansel did have weapons. She was so small now, and she wanted to step into the middle of something big.

"Okay," she said, "I'm in."

"Very well," he said. "Kneel, and I will knight you."

"I'm not going to kneel. Tell me how you got the names."

He spoke into the monkey hand.

"Let the record show that the subject refused knighthood." He dropped the monkey hand to his side. "I know someone who knows someone in the guards. Thus, I obtained a list of all the missing persons from the week your mother disappeared. Usually only one or two people are reported missing per year. We live on an island, if you haven't noticed. But ten people were reported in that week alone. I thought that was interesting. Don't you?"

"I know someone who lived with my mom, back on the mainland. She said everyone on the list was a child on the first boat."

"Who was that? Did she say anything else?"

"Yuka McKenzie. She lives at the nursing home where I work. She didn't know why, but she said there was another kid, someone who wasn't on the list. Ruth Rosen. Does that sound familiar at all?"

He shook his head.

"Did she say anything else about her?" he asked.

"She's Esther Rosen's twin sister. And Yuka seemed to think that she'd know what happened to the others. You think your friend in the guards could find her?"

"My friend's friend. Perhaps. But he'll need some convincing."

"Can you convince him?"

"Oh, he doesn't like me. He prefers women. Maybe you could convince him."

She thought again of the young guard at the Avenida station.

"I'm not going to sleep with this guy," she said.

"I don't think it will come to that."

"You don't *think?*"

"It never has, with my friend."

"So why doesn't your friend talk to him then?"

"They've had a bit of a falling-out. And anyway, you'd be good at it. You seem like someone who gets what she wants."

Darcy thought of listing all the things she'd wanted and never gotten, from the chicken sandwich in some rich kid's hand at a bus stop when she was eight to the freedom to look forward to the next day without a dollar-by-dollar plan for getting through it, but she was too exhausted to begin. The black sky was turning yellow at its corners like an old comics flyer. She had the slightly unreal feeling that comes at the end of a sleepless night, the feeling of burrowing under time. The days and nights could pass, and she could crawl beneath them, like a mole or an insect in the earth, hidden from whatever parsimonious eye kept track of the minutes and hours. She shook herself. She had to be at work soon.

"Where do I find this guy?" she asked.

"He's at the Boat in Hell City every night. He'll be by the bar. Do you have any clothes besides that?"

She looked down at her jumpsuit, then at the small stack in the corner.

"Just some T-shirts and shorts. And my old school uniform, but it doesn't really fit anymore."

"That's perfect," he said. "Wear that."

"It's going to look pretty stupid with this splint sticking out."

He looked her up and down, again paying her more attention than she was accustomed to receiving.

"No," he said, "you'll look great. I promise. Just go to the Boat tomorrow night, around eleven o'clock. He'll be there. You can't miss him—he wears this dumb visor all the time. And make sure you compliment him. My friend says he likes to be flattered."

Then he stood, took the crown off and returned it to its place on the floor.

"If you need to find me," he added, "I live in Hell City, near the market. There's a green bucket outside the door."

He used his monkey hand to wave good-bye.

5

At 10 p.m., Darcy turned off the Avenida and walked up Eighteenth until she got to the gray blocks where the Seafiber factory dribbled out its workers. Then she joined the jumpsuited crowd—grimly rowdy, smelling of salt and ash—as they all waited for the Hell City bus. Three women in front of Darcy shared a low, shapeless laugh. Darcy saw them pass a stained Seafiber bag from hand to grubby hand, saw each in turn lower her face into its mouth and breathe slowly in. When the last one had huffed her fill she lifted her face to the sky and let the rain pound her in the cheeks. A fat teenage boy to Darcy's left began to lead his buddies in a song.

"I wish all the ladies," he called.

"I wish all the ladies," they answered.

"Were just like Aunt Jemima."

"Were just like Aunt Jemima."

"'Cause then they'd taste like syrup."

"'Cause then they'd taste like syrup."

"When I ate out their vaginas."

A dark square opened out of the silver rain and the bus thundered forth into it. The fat boy peeled away from Darcy into the crowd crushing against the curb. The bus wheels sent up wings of black water and the people jumped and slapped at their plastered pant legs. Then the bus made a terrible metal ripping sound and stopped in a cloud of oil-stinking exhaust. Darcy wiped the rain from her face and struggled forward across the melting sidewalk to the scrum of men and women crowding the bus doors.

She had never ridden the Hell City bus before. It looked like a junkyard. Its headlights were bashed in and covered over with clear tape. A long stripe of tape also bisected the windshield. The side of the bus was patched in two places with Seaboard and in one place with what looked like a blue jumpsuit. Scrawled across these patches was an epic swath of graffiti: the image of a naked girl with head-sized breasts and a fat-lipped, gaping mouth, above a firing gun and the words "First Street Girls = RAT BITCH SLUTS." A ladder made of old metal pipes hung down over the girl's legs; the three women with the solvent bag handed a coin each through the driver's window and hoisted themselves up the rickety rungs. The roof of the bus was already covered with a thick layer of wet and fractious humans who squatted hip to hip with one another and clutched the rusty, gum-spattered guard-rails. When Darcy's turn came she dragged herself up with both hands, pulling her bad leg up the wet rungs behind her.

Two hollow-eyed teenagers made room for her in the back left-hand corner of the roof. She lowered herself onto the little damp square of metal they uncovered, slung her bad leg to the side, grabbed the handrail as the bus shuddered and screamed and began to move. The roof pitched and yawed so fast and hard that Darcy felt her gut rise to meet her throat. All around her the young and old were laughing or sleeping or smoking hand-rolled seaweed cigarettes; a group of girls were tossing around a ball made of what looked like old underwear.

They passed through Lower Chicagoland, down Wabash

Avenue, where the GreenValley Vegetarium squatted, gray-green and humming. Darcy had heard it had twenty different climate-controlled rooms for growing luxury produce, like strawberries and apples. The air above the building was bruised with solvent exhaust; the air-conditioning drums groaned like old men. Darcy realized she hadn't seen one safe-house sign on the whole ride—she wondered if Trish was right that there weren't nearly enough to protect all the islanders.

The bus hung a harrowing right—the roof pitched into the turn, and everyone slid sideways in a crush against the railing. A general yell faded into grumbling as they righted themselves. They were on Chickadee Court now. Darcy could see the remnants of the old Founders' Village—the stucco single-family homes with their circle driveways, now encrusted with lean-tos and rusted-out metal sheds. The few floss silk and frangipani trees that still rose out of the wet black earth held tree houses slapped together out of car doors and cheese-food crates and old Seafiber shower curtains. As they rumbled eastward, the world seemed to get smaller. Precarious extra floors were piled on top of the houses; tall teetering shanties squeezed between. Seaboard and scrap metal crowded out the air. Then the street began to narrow—shacks and sheds were built on the shoulder, jutting out into the path of the bus. Children ran out from sagging doorways as the bus approached, jumping and trying to grab on to its sides. A little girl wearing only a pair of pink polka-dot shorts leapt and caught the ladder. She held her open palm out for money. Someone gave her a high-five. Someone else handed her a green beer bottle with a finger's worth left in it. The bus slowed on its way up to the intersection—there were no stoplights in Hell City, only clots of honking, rusty cars. The little girl jumped off and ran whooping between the drivers, waving her green bottle in the rain.

The bus slowed as the road got worse. They were on landfill now for sure. Darcy could almost feel the heaped-up trash and sand and sea muck giving under the wheels. This was where Tyson and the Board had first tried to expand the island, before they knew that landfill had to be reinforced, and there were so many cave-ins here that the flyers didn't even bother to report them. Of course the last-boaters lived here—nowhere else would take them.

Darcy smelled something gamy cooking, and then the unmistakable sweet stink of solvent boiling down. Supposedly the hardest junkies ended up in Hell City because there were no guards to bust them. Some of the shacks had iron-red troughs in the doorways where solvent-heads had poured pot after pot of cook water. Darcy passed by one Seaboard shed now roofless and whorled with char marks from a cook gone bad; someone had spray painted the front wall with the words "FOR ReNT, TeN DolLARs A Yr."

The other shacks and tree houses were dun and rust and gunmetal, occasionally plastered with wet ads cut from magazines. One low-lying thin-walled hut was plastered with naked women from pornoflyers—inside, Darcy could hear techno music beeping and hammering. Another shack was spread with doll parts: legs on the roof, blind breasts over the windows, heads above the door. All the objects in Hell City seemed broken off or torn out of something: a movie poster was a baby's swaddling, a hubcap was a frying pan, a shower curtain was a roof.

A hundred feet ahead the road ended. A long low building made of rusted metal squatted in the bus's path. As they drew closer, Darcy could see portholes in the sides and peeling silver paint. A keel pointed outward toward the bus, dinged and salt-scarred, its sharp edge dulled by its long-ago push through the waves. Beyond the boat was a great soupy no-man's-land, a

sucking swamp of orange mud and rusted cans and pools of standing water. The remnants of old shacks, built in the days when the
land looked sturdy, sank into the mire, their walls warped and
swollen, their roofs caving in. A few were still inhabited by people
so desperate or marginal that even Hell City proper had no place
for them — Darcy saw a skinny naked form, its long stringy hair
obscuring its face, dart from a doorway and crawl, with a terrible,
broken-hipped gait, across the sand. Fifty yards east of the last
busted shack was the seawall, its barbed wire now a mockery.
Once it had kept people off the restricted beach — now there was
nothing beyond or before it worth restricting.

All the other boats — the first two cruise ships, and the numerous large and small craft of the influx — had been broken down
and made into cars or pipes or factory parts or expensive jewelry
for ironic rich people, but this one had hobbled in two years before
Darcy was born, with passengers so scabbed and sored and rickety
that no one wanted anything they lived in. The Boat itself was
patched and rotting too, no square foot of metal without some
scratch or flaw, so that looters had given up on it and scrap men let
it be. All around it the pitted road was so full of men, women, and
children hustling, dancing, tripping, and yelling that the bus
driver didn't even come to a full stop outside, just slowed down
long enough for Darcy to jump off. With the new splint and the
cream, she could walk as long as she kept most of her weight on
her left leg. She kneed and elbowed her way through the sweat-
and-solvent-scented crowd to where a bouncer stood with a light-
ning-bolt tattoo bisecting his forehead. He looked her up and
down — she saw that his lightning bolt had been clumsily inscribed
and was furred and faded at the edges like a bruise. His eyes lin-
gered on her eyes for a count of five before he jerked his head over
his shoulder to let her know she could go in.

The door of the Boat was a jagged hole cut in the metal. Darcy passed through it and into a darkness the color of tobacco juice. The high metal ceiling scrambled the music into a tinny tattoo, and in several places the rain was falling freely through it. The walls had their own smell, rust and brine and rot and something older, some foreign mainland chemical that had since fallen out of the world. Darcy ran her hand along one and felt the rivets holding it in place. Someone had screwed these in twenty years ago or more, with the last of the mainland metal, so that a last few, lucky or unlucky, could creep across the ocean and collapse in a heap in Hell City, where they were now writhing together like snakes.

Darcy pushed through the crowd. The inside of the Boat was one enormous room, bigger than the Manhattanville High School gym her class had been allowed to visit on alternate Wednesdays, bigger than the dining room at World Experiences. In the middle, a solve-core band was playing—a man plucked out a loud, slow, aimless riff on his cheese-box guitar while a singer wailed in a voice like air blown across a bottle neck.

"My home is a worn-out shoe," she sang. "My home is a pizza box. My home is a solvent vial. My home is the open sea."

A short woman grabbed the air in front of her and turned it like a knob. A man was licking space in a conical shape. As Darcy looked for Ansel's contact, she felt hands climb up her. A finger made its way into her pocket, and when she wheeled around, its owner disappeared into the crowd.

The bar was at the back of the Boat, next to a rusted-out boiler. Girls with solvent-glazed eyes and skirts made of cut-off jumpsuits crowded around it, singing along to the music in sludgy voices. A bartender with fever-ravaged skin handed out jars of yellow-green palm beer. Around the bar were a handful of tables. At one sat a crew of young men in the red bandannas of the Kings, their toughness belied by the anxiety at the corners of their eyes and the still-soft down on their upper lips. At another were three refinery workers, one of them badly burned across the forehead, all of them grimly filling themselves with beer before the bus ride back to their dark Lower Chicagoland efficiencies. And at a third were a skinny, pointy-faced woman smoking a cigarette and a man in a Seaboard sun visor. He looked about thirty-five and was light-skinned, black-haired, and strong-jawed, like an advertisement for the guards.

He turned, and she felt his eyes on her. She tried to compose her face to meet him. She wanted to look invulnerable, like she belonged in this place and was never intimidated or afraid. But she also wanted to look like someone worthy of help. The skinny girl put out her cigarette on the Seaboard table and looked at her with a skeptical eye. She had a tattoo of a mouth next to her mouth. Darcy drew her shoulders back, made her face hard, resisted the urge to tug on her shorts.

"I'm Darcy Pern," she said. "I'm a friend of Ansel's."

She wondered if she should have given them a false name. She wished she had asked Ansel more about the guard. He was looking at her the way job interviewers once looked at her—smug and bored and lazily confident that they had something she wanted.

"And?" he said.

And what? She searched the air around the table for something complimentary to say. She thought he was handsome, but she didn't want to tell him that. She looked at the cigarette-burned tabletop, the smeary portholes, the jar of cloudy beer in his hand.

"I like your hat," she said.

The skinny girl laughed. Her front teeth were gray and jumbled together. Her tattoo was an amateur job, like the bouncer's; the mouth opened much wider on one side than the other. It looked like it was burping.

"Is that so funny, Pine? Just because you don't find my hat attractive doesn't mean nobody does. What do you like about it, Darcy?"

She remembered the GreenValley interviewer asking about her experience, remembered the sucking feeling inside her chest as she realized there was no right answer she could give. She pushed the feeling away. The guard leaned back. He was wearing a fifty-cent Seaboard visor, the kind boys on the Avenida made themselves, and he was drinking palm beer in the Boat with a girl even more last-boat than a last-boat hooker. Darcy took a breath.

"It's not pretentious," she said. "Someone like you, I'd think you'd shop at those Manhattanville boutiques. But it looks like you don't waste your money on that stuff."

Pine rolled her eyes and looked at the guard. For a moment his expression didn't change. The band stopped playing, and dancers shoved past Darcy toward the bar, fumes and laughter on their breath.

"See, Darcy, some people—"

Pine snorted. The guard gave her a look, she went quiet, and he began again.

"Some people think your circumstances define you. They think if you happen to grow up in, say, Manhattanville, if you happen to be a professional person, you're fundamentally unlike, say, someone who comes from Hell City. What do you think about that, Darcy? Do you agree?"

A keenness came through his smug face. It reminded her of Armin.

"I think your character defines you," she said.

He turned to Pine.

"See! Character. That's what I've been talking about. Darcy, sit down. My name is November, but you can call me Glock. Have a drink with us."

He motioned to a waitress with a tray of sloshing beer jars. She set one down on the table, and Darcy watched the easy passage of coins from his hand to hers.

"Where do you come from, Darcy?" the guard asked. "What's your story?"

"I'm from Little L.A.," she said. "I work at World Experiences."

She saw his interest flagging already, his eyes sliding from her face.

"Before that I went to school, I went to Seventeenth Street School, near the Seafiber factory."

He was looking at Pine now. She whispered something to him, and he laughed the way people laugh when they're not supposed to. She took a sip of the beer. It tasted like spit.

"I had to drop out when my mom's hours got cut at the docks," she went on.

He focused on her again.

"How old were you?"

"Fifteen."

"So you dropped out, and you got a job at World Experiences. Did you do anything in between?"

"I interviewed for a lot of places—GreenValley, the printing presses—"

He looked away again. She didn't understand what he wanted from her. She was spending all her time these days figuring out what people wanted.

"I did some odd jobs for a while," she went on.

"What kind of jobs?"

"I collected bottles, I cleaned some apartments."

"Did you do anything more unorthodox?"

Pine drained her jar.

"I want another beer," she said.

"Hang on," said the guard. "I want to hear what Darcy has to say."

Darcy tugged on her shorts. She had worked lookout for one of her classmate's brothers, a solvent dealer with a lazy eye, but the money wasn't very good, and it became clear that she'd have to sleep with someone or beat someone up if she wanted to advance. She'd stopped after a couple of weeks. But even that could get her jail time if he chose to turn her in. A lie formed in the back of her throat. But she saw how he was looking at her, the thinly veiled nervous expectation tightening his mouth and eyes. The lie in her throat changed shape.

"That doesn't seem like a very smart subject to be discussing with a guard," she said.

A vein was beating in his temple.

"Pine," he said, "am I a typical guard?"

Pine shrugged.

"Don't ask me," she said.

"Well," he said to Darcy, "do I look like a typical guard to you?"

Darcy wasn't in the habit of examining guards critically. On the street, she always avoided looking directly at them, for fear of drawing attention to herself. She remembered the one she had talked to about her mother, his false helpfulness, his hand on her back in a parody of comfort. This one was different—his hands always moving slightly on the table, his eyes drifting and locking, drifting and locking. The first one had probably pulled the same trick with five women a day. But this one was restless, on the lookout for something new. She wasn't sure which one was typical, but she knew which was more dangerous.

"Typical or not," Darcy said, "you could get me in a lot of trouble."

Glock turned to Pine.

"Could you give us a minute?" he said.

Pine's eyes turned from scornful to frightened and she leaned in close, whispering to him again. He whispered back, and her face softened a little. She nodded. Then she turned to Darcy, scrunched her face up in fake sweetness, and trilled, "Byee!"

When she was gone he moved his chair closer to Darcy's. She wondered if Ansel had been right that he wouldn't want to sleep with her. He smelled expensive, the way she imagined the cool inside of a fancy store would smell.

"Let me ask you something," he said. "The guards, who do you think they work for?"

"Tyson?"

"Sometimes. Sometimes not. Some of them work for the gangs or the drug kingpins."

She had heard this before, but mostly dismissed it as paranoia. She thought of feigning surprise, then settled on worldliness.

"I've heard something about that."

He ignored her.

"But me," he continued, "I work for myself. Not Tyson, not some wannabe with a few solvent vials. I work for me."

He might have been all talk; for all Darcy knew, he was the most loyal guard on the force. But the way his eyes and hands stopped moving, as though everything in his body were waiting for a response from her, made her think that part of the thrill for him was telling the truth. He liked to keep a secret, to hold on to it, and then when the mood took him, he liked to tell it in a bar to a girl he barely knew. He liked to feel that he was putting himself in danger. But of course, the danger wasn't real. He hadn't told her anything of importance, anything she could use. Darcy wondered if he'd ever felt really at risk.

The band started to play again, and the people at the next table stood up to dance. The whole crowd of swaying, addled humans turned their backs on Darcy. No one was watching her.

"Are you carrying a gun?" she asked.

He looked confused.

"I always do."

"Can I see it?"

"Why would you want to do that?"

Darcy gambled. "It's just been so long since I held one."

Actually she had never held a gun. She had seen one only a handful of times—in the belt of a solvent dealer, sticking out the window of a car one rainy morning in her childhood. But he looked like he believed her. He looked like he wanted to.

"You won't do anything stupid?" he asked. But his hand was already inside his jacket.

"I've never done anything stupid in my life," she said. Some unfamiliar part of her was choosing her words, making her lips move.

He passed her the gun under the table. It was heavy, and it felt old, covered with scratches and some thin, alien grease. She could imagine a cowboy pressing it to an outlaw's temple, a gangsta pointing it at a cop on a crisp Old Los Angeles night. She could imagine it traveling over the ocean in a dark hold, coming ashore in an unmarked crate.

She moved close to him so that their legs were touching. She had seen people shoot guns in gangsta flyers: she knew where the safety was. She clicked it off. She pressed the barrel against Glock's gut. His eyes went wide and she could see all the way down them. She saw fear and excitement and, at the bottom of his retina, she saw a dangerous, unpredictable woman who might be about to murder him. Darcy smiled and the woman smiled.

"You scared?" they asked.

"Should I be?"

His voice was hot and thick. Darcy was happy and the woman was happy. They fused.

"I want something," she said.

"What is it?"

"I want to find someone named Ruth Rosen. I want to know where she lives."

"I don't know if I can get that for you."

His brain was wriggling. He was testing her. She pushed the gun up under his rib.

"Yes you can," she said.

"I'll need a few days."

"One day," she said.

His eyes glazed over for a second, and she couldn't tell if she still had him. She imagined pulling the trigger. Blood would spurt out and pool on his chair, and she would stick the gun inside her uniform and run. She could do it. She stared at him and he stared back and he saw that she could. But then where would she go? She hardened her face, tried to hide this thought from him.

"Where do you live?" he said.

"Let's just meet back here tomorrow," Darcy offered.

He could see that she wasn't so unpredictable, that she needed something from him and that she had only a few ways to get it.

"I'd rather come to your place," he said, his voice easy.

She was still holding the gun, but he knew it was a game now.

Darcy lost her hold on the dangerous woman and was herself again, questing and striving, putting on a disguise.

"I have to go now," she said. "I'll see you here tomorrow."

She let the gun fall into his lap.

"We'll see," he said, and he clicked the safety back on and stuck the gun in his pants.

6

The next night Darcy sat in her apartment, staring at the wall in a paralysis of anger and doubt. Would Glock even be at the Boat if she went back? She hadn't given him any compelling reason to help her. If she went back there, would she find herself alone among the whirling bodies, in her ill-fitting school uniform, looking around like an idiot for someone who wasn't there?

It was almost ten—she'd been back from work for two hours—but still she couldn't bring herself to leave the apartment. Instead she knelt under the windowsill, with her old toys. The rock dolls lay on their sides, their eyes pointing at the floor, like flounders. The crown sat empty, with no head to honor. She opened *An Animal Atlas of the West Coast* and flipped its brittle pages. She'd learned the names of all the animals before she could read, and they felt somehow normal to her, even though she had never seen them and never would. The salmon leaping over Oregon, the grizzly bear in Yosemite, the mountain lion stalking across Southern California—they were like Santa Claus to her, both fictional and familiar, unseen but known. But the maps were so alien they might as well have been random markings—tracings of water stains, or accidental pen tracks across the page. The frilled lip of

Southern California, the little northern notch, the deeper dent plunging down through Washington, at the base of which her mother once had lived. She couldn't imagine anyone living on these greenish shapes. Least of all her mother, the most familiar person in the world, whose absence made the angles of the walls seem off, the shape of the air feel wrong. How could she once have fit into another space, a space Darcy knew nothing about, could not even picture? Why hadn't Darcy absorbed some understanding of this space, learned how to see it in her mind the way she had learned to predict when her mother was about to sneeze or sing or cry?

Why hadn't Sarah ever talked about the mainland? When Darcy asked, she usually got an abstracted look on her face, like longing poorly hidden, and answered Darcy's questions as briskly as possible before steering the conversation toward something inconsequential. Darcy assumed it hurt her to remember her first home, the place she could never return to, but her reticence always churned up a sour jealousy in Darcy. Did Sarah wish she had never left the mainland, that she had never started the life that made Darcy possible? Did she consider the co-op her real home, instead of the apartment she shared with Darcy? And if not, if she didn't feel for the mainland some secret and competing love, why did she hold all knowledge of it away from Darcy, a privileged part of her Darcy wasn't allowed to share? If she hadn't, if she had told Darcy what went on with Daniel at Arete, Darcy might have a better idea of how to find her now.

Darcy put the book down. She shucked off her jumpsuit, and was halfway into her school uniform when the apartment door opened. She felt such a flood of excitement and relief that her vision went gray for a moment, and a ringing filled her ears. All the things she had wanted to say to her mother in the days she'd been missing, the important ones and the inconsequential, tiny ones she had not even realized she was storing up—all came rushing up into her throat. She imagined how her mother's face would look—tired, exhausted even, but glowing, glad to be home.

Then she turned around and saw Glock in the doorway, wearing his visor and grinning. As she rushed to button her uniform shirt, she remembered what the Seaguard at the docks had said— they had everyone's address. From the moment she told him her name, he had known how to find her.

He was wearing what looked like a University kid's version of gangsta wear—a sports jersey with "Los Angeles Dodgers" printed instead of painted, a pair of dark jeans, their real-fiber still crisp and rustly around his legs. Darcy saw now how young he was, not more than twenty-five, though he tried to move like an older man. He put his hands on his hips and looked around at the room like he was surveying a great landscape.

"I like this," he said. "No paintings, no coffee table, no antiques. No bullshit, just the basics."

"I wasn't expecting you," she said lamely.

Her armpits were sweating. She glanced at the window and imagined jumping out of it, but it was three stories up, not two, and there were no dumpsters waiting on the Avenida.

"A pleasant surprise, then," he said, and his face was open and without irony.

He sat on her bed. He was close enough that she could smell him—a thick cologne, womanish in its sweetness, and below it a hint of sweat. She looked at his waist for the square bulge of a gun, but she saw only the blue folds of his jersey. He might have it strapped to his leg under the jeans—wherever it was, he wouldn't let her get at it as easily as before. Its hidden presence made her vision vibrate with apprehension; his body on the bed made the whole room strange. She wanted both of them gone.

"So," she said, "did you find Ruth Rosen?"

He moved away from her. The grayish blanket bunched beneath his thighs. He looked annoyed and bored by her question, like she was a nun on a bus trying to push a flyer on him.

"I thought we could talk a little first. I brought something."

He reached into his jeans pocket. Darcy's muscles tensed all along her body, like a zipper closing. But all he held was a flask. It was metal, another expensive version of something you could get for a few dollars on the Avenida, with a detailed and overly realistic Snoop Dogg face stamped into the side. He unscrewed the cap and handed it to her. She considered the possibility that it was drugged, but she didn't think Glock was interested in a passed-out girl. She drank.

It was good whiskey, with a smoky roughness in place of the weird sweet tang of palm fruit. She wondered if it was made from real rye. She'd never had rye whiskey before, but this tasted so old and rich and foreign she thought it must be the real thing. It reminded her of steak and pinewood and paper, and all the other mainland things that were almost gone from the world, so that luxury had a museum quality to it, a musty, decadent obsoleteness. He took the flask from her and drank with his head thrown back. His neck was pale and smooth, like he'd never had a pimple in his life. He came back up from his drink as from a dive, his eyes wide and staring.

"You wouldn't have shot me," he said.

Darcy tried to find the dangerous woman from the night before, but all she could do was imitate her, like an actress in a bad street show.

"What makes you so sure?" she asked.

He didn't seem to notice the change in her. He was looking at her face, but his eyes were unfocused, like he was watching an image projected on her skin.

"Because you're like me," he said. "And I know you know it."

He took another gulp of whiskey and handed the flask to her. As she drank her second sip, she felt the first one steaming up her brain.

"Ever since I was a kid," he went on, "I've been different. I lived in Manhattanville; my parents were second-boaters, GreenValley executives. They were really popular in the neighborhood—we had lots of parties. But I never wanted to play with the other kids, I never felt at home with them. And one day I realized—they were too soft. They were going to play with their toys and their cars and their girlfriends, and then they were going to become GreenValley execs too, and eat nice food and wear real-fiber clothes and never worry or think about anything. But that wasn't me. I was destined for bigger things. And I can tell you're the same."

"You don't know anything about me," Darcy said, still acting.

"But I do," he said, "I know that you're special. You're strong. People like you and me, we're the next generation."

"What do you mean?" Darcy asked.

"Stick with me," he said. "You'll see. A change is coming, and you and I are going to be a part of that."

Darcy couldn't help but be intrigued by him, the weird fever in his eyes, the sweat on his upper lip. In his crisp jeans and his nicely printed jersey, he looked like someone who wanted to be something he wasn't. But she thought he was right about himself—he wasn't complacent. He might have the power to become whatever he wanted.

"What kind of change?" she asked.

Then he put his hand on her leg. She knew she should have expected it, but still she jerked her leg away, as if he had burned her. He reached to touch her again, and she stood up from the bed.

His face flushed baby pink like the corner of an eye.

"What," he said, "you're going to try to deny it? I know you feel the same."

He stood. She backed up against the door. He moved onto her and sealed his mouth against her neck and she felt it foreign there, like a scab.

"I don't do this with everyone," he told her. "You're different. Because you're like me."

She thought of the other guard with his soapy smell. She thought of the men who had been here with her mother, their breath pounding through the toilet paper into her ears, their grunts and farts and the shapes of their asses in the air filling the quiet space of their apartment and staying there for days, long after they themselves were gone, crowding the simple sealed universe that had been hers and her mother's alone. Her hand was on the doorknob. She was going to spring herself out into the hallway and run until she was far enough away that he wouldn't look for her, that he would go home to Manhattanville and push his way into the body and brain of some other girl instead. She turned the knob.

Then she imagined what would happen next. She would pant in an alley off Figueroa for a little while, congratulating herself on her escape. And then she would look around at the dumpsters, and the solvent vials, and the monkey chewing on a piece of moldy pizza, and know that she was packed into a dead end with no way of prying herself out.

"Wait," she said.

He laid his hand on her breast. It felt like a lid.

"You don't really want me to wait," he said.

"Will you give me the address first? Otherwise I'll just keep thinking about it—"

His mouth was on her ear. The sound of his breathing covered up all other sounds, like a hot wet wind whistling in her skull.

"After," he said. "I promise. I want to help you."

He put his hands on her hips and tried to steer her to the bed. She made a decision. She took a proud part of herself and she locked it away.

"Not there," she said.

She moved and he held on to her, so that when she sat down on the floor he sat on top of her, his legs around her legs, his hands still on her hips, his eyes on her eyes. He looked at her like he knew her, like she was a simple machine he'd taken apart and figured out.

"Of course," he said. "I should've known you'd like it this way."

And then she let him unbutton her uniform, and slide it down to her ankles, and take off her shoes so she could pull it off over her feet, and when she was lying on the lukewarm floor in her old gray undershirt and her stained underwear, with the gauze wrapped around her bad leg, she let him kiss and lick her body like a lover, like the men in the romance flyers who made women moan and cry because they knew exactly what the women wanted without having to ask.

When he removed her underwear—again, not roughly, not businesslike, but sweetly, like she would enjoy it, like if he touched her in the right way he was sure she would enjoy it—and kissed the light brown part of her hip where the bone came up against the skin, she thought of the day her mother taught her how to swim. She was seven, and the solvent contamination wasn't so bad yet—in many places, the water was still blue. They went to the unrestricted beach near Venice Boulevard, and usually the ocean would've been clotted with people, so thick it was more flesh than water, but her mother took her on a weekday, she skipped work to take her, and it was cloudy and raining a little, and the only other people were an old lady with a big belly in a black bathing suit, and three teenage girls trying to share a cigarette, and two pale naked children dancing in the shallows like ghosts. Sarah swam out into the neck-high water with one arm around Darcy, and then she told her just to hold her head under the water, because that was half the battle. But Darcy was afraid of water. Even in the shower her mother had to get in with her or she'd waste their two dollars shivering outside the stall while the hot water poured down over no one. She didn't want to put her head down and be alone under the ocean, where long-tendriled creatures could wrap themselves around her ankles and drag her down and make her one of them. She shook her head. She was seven years old and she had a life to live on land. Her mother was wearing her diving mask, but she took it off and fastened it over Darcy's face and pulled the straps tight, and then she told Darcy about all the things she could see under the water if she looked for them, the sea urchins, and the flatfish with both eyes on one side of their bodies, and the sand dollars, and even action figures dropped by children coming in on the boats, their plastic limbs covered in lichen, capes of algae streaming out behind them. But Darcy didn't care, wouldn't stick her head under the water unless her mother's head came with it, temple to temple, like they were Siamese twins, and even when they did that she opened her eyes and saw nothing but grayish muck with splotches of black in it, and came up sniveling and asking to go home.

"Try looking up," her mother said, and then they tried again, heads pressed, eyes pointed at the sky this time, and Darcy saw the skin of the ocean above her. The skin was thick, and where the rain fell it turned a color that was no color, an unsilver silver from some alien spectrum, and the clouds through the skin were bent and rippled and doubled, and a bird through the skin was like a crazy person's drawing of a bird. Then her mother's face appeared above the skin, and Darcy did not register that her mother's head was no longer beside her, only that it was also now above, and that the skin of the water was rippling across her mother's skin, and turning her from a person into something else, an image, like a print of a hand on a steamed-up window or a set of clothes laid out on a bed. And it was this image, this thing related to but not her mother, that Darcy thought of as Glock parted her legs with his left hand, and put the head of his penis against the outside part of her labia, and pushed until she felt it crush the lips apart, and kept pushing as a dull internal hurt spread all the way up to her belly button, like the whole inside of her was a bruise and he was carefully but insistently poking at it. And she thought of this image as his head moved back and forth above her head, and as his sweat dropped on her, and as she in spite of herself began to sweat, and as he fit his mouth over her nipple like it belonged there, and flicked it with his tongue, and began to breathe like a sick person, and then like a dying person, and then clutched her upper arms with his fingernails and shuddered and bucked with his lower body in a way she didn't know was possible, and choked, and grimaced like a dog, and then lay along her with his skin against her skin as though they loved each other, as though touching made them both happy.

An amount of time passed that Darcy couldn't measure. Then he touched her hair.

"That was great," he said.

The image of Darcy smiled at him. He rolled off her and lay on the floor looking at the ceiling. She could feel contentment steaming off him. She could see him looking at her leaky ceiling and liking it. A piece of pain was lodged inside her, underneath her belly button, vibrating. Her labia felt swollen. She had scratch marks on her arms. She waited for his relaxation to become unbearable, and then she asked him for the address again.

He laughed.

"You've got a one-track mind."

She didn't answer. He crossed his arms behind his head. His penis was going flaccid at the center of the body. It was a color she had never seen before, an obscene kind of blush.

"I couldn't find any Ruth Rosen," he said. "There's a Naomi, a Snow, a Bruce, and a Nathaniel."

Darcy felt the hard floor through her hair. She felt the fear pressing down on her that this had all been for nothing.

"Could you write them down?" she asked.

Again he laughed, like he had all the time in the world, like answering her questions was a luxury to him, and he tickled her stomach and, almost without thinking, it was disturbing how nearly without thinking, she made the image of her giggle and flinch. She put her uniform back on and found him a pen and the back of a tomato-paste label. While he was writing, some of his semen ran out of her and pooled in her underwear. When he was finished he kissed her on the ear. Then he gathered his clothes up off the floor and pulled on his real-fiber underwear with an easy motion.

"You'll be here tomorrow, right?" he asked her.

"I don't know," Darcy said, "I might have to work late."

"I can wait."

He pulled his jeans up, and Darcy saw the gun distending the front pocket.

"Sometimes I have to work the night shift," she lied.

"I'm sure you can get away," he said.

He took hold of her chin and kissed her on the mouth. He wasn't rough, but she felt a new insistence in the muscles of his lips, the press of his fingers. When he pulled away she saw again his youth, the pale smoothness of his skin—she saw a child with the power to take what he wanted.

"I'll see you tomorrow night," he told her.

He hooked his thumb in his jeans pocket and his fingers pointed down at the gun. She wasn't sure he was doing it on purpose, but she knew what it meant.

"I'll be here," she said.

Darcy sat on an overturned cheese-food crate pushed up against a grease-stained Seaboard wall. Ansel sat on a yellowish couch cushion against the opposite wall. Sunshine was facing away from them, lighting a coal grill. The only window was made of plastic wrap; through it Darcy could see a solvent-barrel fire and a pack of ragged children roasting chunks of unidentifiable food over it. They were maybe a quarter mile past the Boat—Darcy could hear the thrumming music if she listened for it—but it had taken her an aching hour to find the shack in the gridless tangle of dwellings that huddled door-to-door and window-to-window against one another after the road ended. The market Ansel had mentioned was a handful of old women pressed together where the alley met another, selling dented cans of cheese food and expired jellyfish powder and a few desiccated macaws. The green bucket sat outside collecting rainwater that sluiced off the roof, which was half Seaboard and half garbage bags. A little orange light came from a solvent lamp in the middle of the floor. There was no bed.

"I told you she was just going to make things more complicated," Sunshine said. "Now he's going to come after us."

"He'll go to the old place," Ansel said. "Nobody there knows we're here. It'll take him a long time to track us down. Anyway, none of this would have happened if you hadn't quit."

Sunshine turned around. She was dressed in street clothes now, a man's white undershirt and a jumpsuit bottom cut at the waist and belted with string. Her hair radiated from her head in red-brown kinks. Without her makeup she looked older—her breasts under the thin shirt were low on her chest, but full and round with dark, pointed nipples. Her eyes were full of rage.

"I didn't quit," she said. "It just wasn't going anywhere. And then you went and pimped her out to him."

Ansel sat up straight. His monkey arm was lying on the floor next to him; his half arm stuck out of his T-shirt, its tip pink and hot-looking.

"You told me he never had sex with you. You said it wasn't like that."

Darcy saw that he was angry for her. His forehead creased; a flush came up beneath his skin. Under her thick pain, something in Darcy kindled.

"It wasn't like that because I wouldn't do it," said Sunshine. "I didn't want the information bad enough, and he knew it."

She turned away and got the coals to light. That coal-smoke smell came up from them, like seaweed mixed with chalk.

"You should've told me," Ansel said. "I wouldn't have—"

"Wouldn't have what? Wouldn't have sent her? I know you, you'll do whatever you have to do."

"Auntie—" Ansel said. He crossed to the grill and began to whisper to Sunshine. She turned her face toward him—she had naked sorrow in her eyes. Then he put his hand on her shoulders and his face in her hair and whispered something more, and she broke into a rueful, private laugh.

"You always say that," she said, "and I always listen."

Sunshine shook her head, but Darcy saw how her face was calmed, how whatever he had said had relaxed her in spite of herself. There was a warm charge in Ansel's eyes as he looked at Sunshine, a strong private attention and understanding. But what did they understand?

"Okay," Darcy said, "are you going to explain any of this to me?"

Ansel looked at Darcy, then back at Sunshine. The charge dissipated. Sunshine untied a plastic bag and took out three milky sacs—jellyfish. The sight made the nausea that had been riding low in Darcy's gut rise all the way up to her throat.

"If we're going to let her stay with us," Sunshine said, "you might as well trust her."

Darcy didn't like the way Sunshine talked about her, like she wasn't even in the room.

Ansel sat back down on his cushion. He scratched a little at the stub of his arm, then pulled the T-shirt down as though to cover it. Sunshine smirked and shook her head.

"We're going to get rid of Tyson," Ansel said.

Darcy wasn't entirely surprised. She remembered what the hookers had said about Ansel's ambitions. Still, out loud it seemed ridiculous. Tyson was a drawing to her, a hand waving at an annual parade, a name to call everything ineluctable and unchanging about the island. She couldn't imagine trying to get rid of him.

"Why?" she asked.

"He's the reason the last-boaters stay poor and all the assholes in Manhattanville stay rich. Tyson just picks the people he knows will never challenge him, and then he keeps them happy with kickbacks and subsidies and cushy jobs for their kids. You heard it yourself—those values tests the woman at the casino was talking about. The only way to get rich is to kiss his ass. What does he care if Hell City or Little L.A. falls into the ocean? Those people have no power, he thinks; they can't do anything to him. We're going to prove him wrong."

What Ansel said made sense—she too thought of the woman at the casino, and of Yuka's story about Tyson's original lie—but it didn't excite her the way it obviously did him. His words sat heavily in her brain.

"Great," she said, "sounds easy. What's your plan?"

Ansel paused. Sunshine raised her eyebrows at him. The jelly-fish sizzled on the grill, turning transparent, smelling like glue.

"You're our plan," Ansel said.

Darcy remembered the first time she'd seen the back of the Sears Tower and realized it was only Seaboard supported by struts. All she could do was stare at him.

"Sunshine's right," he went on. "We weren't getting anywhere before. Then we met you, and now we have all these names. It's a smoking gun."

Darcy found her voice.

"How is it a smoking gun?" she asked.

"Say all those people were kidnapped. If we can prove that Tyson's behind it, it will turn people against him. Right now everyone's just trying to get by, nobody wants to rock the boat. But if we convince them that Tyson could steal their mothers, kidnap their children, we could get them to rise up. We could get them to revolt."

"We don't know Tyson's behind it," Darcy said. "We don't even know for sure they were kidnapped." She felt bereft. What little safety she'd felt before had come from being part of some machine, however rusty. But if she was the center of Ansel's machine, it was no machine at all.

"Come on, do you think they all happened to disappear at the same time, for no reason? We live on an island, Darcy—there aren't that many places to go. I'm betting your mom knows something Tyson doesn't want anybody to find out. We're on the right track, and with the names Glock gave you—"

Darcy put her head in her hands.

"Those names are shit," she said. "For all we know, Ruth Rosen could be dead. She could be a popsicle on the mainland. Glock didn't tell me anything."

"But Yuka said she came here," Ansel said. "We'll go, we'll ask them all. One of them must know something."

"I don't care about Tyson," Darcy said. "I don't care about any of this. I just want to find my mom."

Ansel came and sat beside her.

"And you will," he said. "I promise."

His voice calmed her a little, as it had calmed Sunshine. There was something in the way he talked that felt convincing, as though he believed what he was saying so much it had to be true. Darcy thought of him growing up—not far from here probably—with the two little girls who would grow into Ring Road whores, and their brothers and all their scrawny, pocked and pitted neighbors. Why had the rest of them slotted into their last-boat places, cooking solvent or turning tricks or slamming into one another outside the Boat, while Ansel was here with Sunshine, one-armed, trying to change something Darcy had always thought as unchangeable as weather? Something within him would not let him rest, and it would not, she thought, let him fail forever.

"We'll help each other," he said. "We'll both get what we want."

Darcy looked down again. She had been used, she would be used again, but she hadn't gotten anywhere on her own, and he might be the best person she could find to use her.

Sunshine slid a grilled jellyfish onto a coffee lid and handed it to Darcy. Its glistening shapeless body filled her with despair. She dropped the lid on the floor and crouched down on her cheese crate, hiding her face like a child. She heard Ansel apologize, and Sunshine shush him, and then she heard the door open and shut. She tried to blank her mind of all thoughts. She sang a song to herself:

> *"Have you heard the tale of Sweet Betsy from Pike*
> *Who crossed the wide desert with her lover Ike*
> *With two yoke of oxen and one spotted hog*
> *A tall Shanghai rooster and an old yellow dog*
>
> *The alkali desert was burning and bare*
> *And Ike cried in fear, 'We are lost, I declare!*
> *My dear old Pike County, I'll go back to you.'*
> *Said Betsy, 'You'll go by yourself if you do.' "*

It was the only part of the song she knew, and she sang it to herself over and over, until the words meant nothing, until time meant nothing, until she was nothing but a mouth that murmured the words. When she had almost erased the existence of even the mouth, the door opened again. She heard footsteps, and then a sound of cloth moving against Seaboard, and then the lamp went out, and someone was kneeling beside her. She smelled a woman's sweat.

"Are you all right?" Sunshine asked.

"Fine."

"You were shaking."

Darcy turned away.

"I made you a bed. It's just some shirts on the floor, but—"

Darcy ignored her.

"Listen, I know how you feel."

Darcy sat up and looked at her. She was balanced on her knees with her long calm hands on her thighs. Her face was weary and haughty and knowing. Darcy abruptly hated her again.

"You don't," she spat.

Sunshine gave her a look of pity.

"You think you're the first person to do something you didn't want to do? How do you think everybody else around here gets along?"

"Don't tell me how people get along," Darcy said. "I've been getting along all by my fucking self for a while now."

Sunshine's face barely moved, but the tiny tightening at the corners of her eyes was enough to show her anger.

"Without Ansel," she said, "you'd still be fucking around Las Vegas asking stupid questions."

Darcy stood. The wall of the shack shook a little from her movement.

"And now I'm what?" she yelled. "Squatting in a box with two circus freaks whose idea of a plan is getting an arm bitten off by a retarded bear?"

The slap came fast, hard enough to shock but not to bruise. Darcy held the side of her face and felt her blood rising to meet her skin. No one had ever slapped her before. She was used to punches, scratches, school-yard fighting, but this was a new language.

"I can talk shit about Ansel," Sunshine said, "and you can talk shit about me. But if you talk shit about Ansel, you leave here and you don't come back."

Darcy sat back down. Sunshine's face was unreadable now.

"Is there any reason why I shouldn't?" Darcy asked. "Just go, I mean."

"It's up to you. But I wasn't all that different from you when I met him. I pissed off this guy from Death Row. He put a hit out on me. Ansel got it fixed, he never told me how. He gets things done. He seems like he won't but then he does. That's why I stay, in spite of everything."

Darcy wondered now what Sunshine's stake was. Why had she gotten Ansel the job at the Big Top in the first place? Were they lovers? Did she want Tyson gone too, or was there something else she wanted Ansel to do?

"What do you mean, 'everything'?" Darcy asked.

Sunshine looked out the window.

"Shh," she said, "he's coming back."

She lay down on the floor with her head on the yellow cushion and her long, bunioned feet pointing up. Darcy hesitated for a moment and then lay down next to her.

"Are you really his aunt?" Darcy asked.

Sunshine didn't answer; she just barked a single laugh out into the dark.

7

Naomi Rosen lived in Lower Chicagoland, in an Orthodox neighborhood. She came to her door smiling, in a Seafiber wig with hairs thick as noodles. She had a little boy, two or three years old, with enormous fearful eyes, and when he clutched Naomi around her knees Darcy was murderously jealous of him. Naomi was about twenty-five. She didn't know a Ruth, or an Esther, and in fact, she told Darcy, her husband's family had changed their name when they came to the island.

"Too many bad memories," she said, still smiling, like her cheerful, pockless face was part of the erasure of those memories.

Snow Rosen, of Fifty-third Street in Manhattanville, didn't open her door. Darcy heard laughter and conversation in her apartment and no matter how much she banged, she couldn't produce a pause in it. So she waited in the hallway for an hour, and then two, and then for a period of time that had no definite duration, shaped only by the comings and goings of other people in the building, all of them dressed in real-fiber and wool and leather, some smoking tobacco cigarettes, one cuddling a tiny tame dog, three carrying briefcases, one holding a cloth bag brimming with leafy green vegetables Darcy didn't recognize.

The hallway was decorated in understated Mainland Nostalgia—deep red carpet, wallpaper with pictures of bridges, apartment numbers engraved on gold plates on the doors. Darcy had cleaned a building like this once, in her short stint with a bucket and mop before she landed the World Experiences job. That building had been in Upper Chicagoland, not as nice as this one but even more nostalgic, with Cubs cards on the doors and signs advertising deep-dish pizza. Darcy didn't completely understand Mainland Nostalgia. She was curious about her mother's home, that world of ice and snow and malnutrition, but the Old Mainland of bridges and pizza seemed not just far away but pointless. Most of the people on the island were from the West Coast anyway—something about the highways shutting down—so what did they care about Old Manhattan or Old Chicago? Darcy wondered if they even noticed what was on their walls. Maybe they were so comfortable all the time that they didn't need to look around them. The red carpet was very deep and soft. Darcy sat down, leaned up against the wall, and let her waiting slide imperceptibly into sleep, a sleep in which she dreamt of waiting, so that the only difference was the flock of brightly colored birds flapping up and down the hallway, squawking at Darcy in a strange but distinctly human language. Then the apartment door opened and the birds faded back into the walls and a woman's face filled up Darcy's field of vision. The woman was young, maybe a few years older than Darcy, her hair was bleached yellow-white and gelled back into a ducktail, her lips were frosty pink, and her eyelashes were long and silver and spiky, like the legs of a metal bug. She was wearing a white fur coat that she held closed with her hand.

"Hi," she said, wide-eyed and slow-voiced, the single syllable as long as a deep breath in and out. "Wanna party?"

Darcy followed her into an enormous room painted entirely

white, and at first Darcy thought she was still dreaming, only her dream had taken her inside an ice cave or a snowdrift or a shining, pristine bone. Then she saw the three white sofas arranged in a box, the white coffee table in the center, the white refrigerator and white countertop, a man and a woman in white bomber jackets and tight white jeans, and the only nonwhite thing in the room—a standing rib roast, untouched, oozing red-brown juice onto a white platter. Darcy's stomach leapt with longing.

"Are you Snow Rosen?" she asked.

"Sure," said the woman, "and what are you about?"

"I'm looking for a Ruth Rosen. Do you know her?"

Snow knit her brows like she was working on a math problem. She opened her mouth to speak and shut it, opened and shut it again.

"Oh man," she said finally, "you need to give me a minute."

She sat down on the sofa—her head rocked back, and her arms fell limp at her sides. Her coat slid open to reveal a silvery-white minidress, a triangle of white chest set with narrow bones, and one bluish thigh.

"Hope you're not in a hurry," said the man. "She might be gone for a while."

"Do you know Ruth Rosen?" Darcy asked him.

The man shook his head. He was wearing a white knit cap pulled down to his ears. His eyes were blue.

"Northstar, that ring a bell with you?"

The woman's voice was low and rich and sleepy.

"Snow's the only Rosen I know," she said.

"That sounds like a poem," the man said. "Snow's the only Rosen I know. Snow's the only Rosen I'm nosin'."

He pressed his nose into Snow's neck. She stirred but didn't open her eyes.

The apartments Darcy had cleaned in Chicagoland had looked like she expected a rich person's home to look—ornate, with antique-style furniture, real photographs on the walls, mainland flowers from the Floridatown cold-houses slowly wilting in their crystal vases. Scented candles that pumped out apple or rose smells when she lit them. Here the blinding walls, the cold, the unsweet smell that was no smell, all made the room seem like the world's cleanest morgue. Probably this was what came after comfort, she thought, when you were too rich even to want things to look pretty. She wondered if these people were also too rich to be mean, to fend off her encroachment the way the lesser rich learned to do.

Darcy looked at the roast. It was so dark against the white counter that it looked like the fabric of the room had ripped open, exposing glistening flesh.

"Can I have some of that meat?" she asked.

Northstar looked momentarily confused.

"Oh, I totally forgot that was there," she said. "Sure, let me get you some."

Northstar put her hands on the roast and tried to break off a piece. Bits of shiny meat came off under her fingernails. She looked apologetically at Darcy.

"It's really hard," she said.

"Do you have a knife?" Darcy asked.

Northstar smacked herself in the forehead. "I can't believe I didn't think of that."

"I can," said the man, but she ignored him. She opened a white drawer and scrabbled around in it, her hands clumsy as paws. Finally she got her fingers around the handle of a big kitchen knife and began haphazardly wounding the roast.

"Here," Darcy said, "let me."

Roasts like that were too expensive for World Experiences, but she'd seen them in the training manual. She slid the knife in between two ribs and sliced downward, then made another cut so that a fat slice of meat five ribs wide came off in her hand.

"Do you want some?" she asked Northstar.

"Um." She considered for a moment. Her eyes were smaller than Snow's, and so far apart that the whole middle of her face was white, featureless wasteland. Her eyebrows were severely plucked.

"Yeah," she finally decided.

Darcy cut another, smaller piece for Northstar, then one for the man, and then she sat on a couch and sucked the bloody meat off the bone. It tasted gamy, foreign, old-fashioned—she thought of Glock's rye whiskey and smacked the thought away. Northstar and the man ate with guileless concentration, like children.

"You know what would be good with this, Mistral?" Northstar said to the man, her mouth full of meat. "Strawberries. Strawberries and, like, cream."

"Want to get some?" he asked.

"I'm too tired," she said. "Let's do it tomorrow."

"But then our guest won't be there to enjoy them," said Mistral.

"You should just stay," Northstar said. "Stay here tonight, and tomorrow we'll all go get strawberries and cream."

Darcy imagined a world in which this was possible. She thought about just leaning back against the white couch cushions, sinking down into these people's lives. They were so relaxed, they might let her stay for a week, a month, forever. They probably didn't even have jobs—they probably sat around the apartment all day, eating real meat and snorting the classy powdered solvent, which cost twice as much as smoking it and three times as much as huffing. They probably had big all-night parties with beautiful lazy people in expensive clothes, and went to other people's fascinating pristine apartments, and drove cars, and walked at all times on solid, well-paved, high-rent ground that was never in any danger of falling into the ocean. Northstar was giggling now, even though no one had said anything, and Darcy imagined a life so carefree that laughter could become a stock response.

"Wait," Mistral said, "don't we have that meeting tomorrow?"

"What?" Northstar looked at Mistral like he had just pointed out a monster.

"You remember. With the Board. They're going to talk about the Hawaiian attack—defense spending or something."

"You guys are on the Board?" Darcy asked.

"We're junior members. We have to go sometimes so that when we replace our parents, we'll know what to do."

"I thought you had to get elected," Darcy said.

Mistral waved his hand. "I think that's, like, a formality. I *wish* somebody else would get elected. It's so boring. All we do is sit around and they tell us how to vote."

Darcy felt her breath quicken. She had believed, in an abstract way, Ansel's claim that Tyson kept rich people rich and poor people poor. But she'd always assumed that the Board was legitimate, that if she bothered to vote she would have some say in governing the island. It shocked her how easily Mistral admitted that this wasn't the case, how easily she could have found out years before if she'd bothered to try.

"Who tells you?" she asked.

"Some woman," said Mistral. "I think she works for Tyson. My dad said Tyson used to come himself, but he's too old now or something."

Mistral stared down at his thumbnail, which was perfectly

square and had a slight, unnatural sheen. He seemed bored with the conversation, but Darcy wasn't ready to let it drop.

"So she just tells you how to vote and then you do it?" she asked.

He sighed. "Well, I mean technically we can vote however we want. But if Tyson doesn't like how I vote, then bye-bye subsidies for Dad's GreenValley division. Which means bye-bye to this." He ran his hand vaguely through the icy air of the room. "I don't really care about voting though," he finished. "What's gonna happen is gonna happen."

He put his white shoes on the white coffee table, laced his fingers behind his head. Darcy hated his easy languor—here was someone who sat on the Board, who had the power to fix the cave-ins, feed everyone in Hell City, and pave the sidewalks of the Avenida with real concrete, and he didn't even care enough to use it. But why would he, when he had enough money to let a rib roast go to waste on the counter? Why would he want to change anything?

Mistral shut his eyes for a moment, and Snow shifted in her drugged-out sleep. Northstar was picking at her rib with tiny, even teeth. Part of Darcy still wished she could stay with them and eat strawberries and think about nothing all day. She couldn't exactly blame them. She hadn't cared about Tyson or the Board or voting or what was fair or unfair until her mother disappeared. She was surprised to find that now she did.

Darcy put her rib bone down on the coffee table.

"I need to find Ruth Rosen," she said.

Mistral didn't seem to register her change in tone.

"How come?" he asked.

"Someone important to me is missing," Darcy said, "and I'm trying to find her."

Northstar looked up from her rib as though waking from a dream.

"Oh my God," she said, "who's missing?"

Darcy looked at her little empty face and decided there was no harm in telling her.

"My mom," she said.

"Oh my God," Northstar said again, "that's terrible."

"Did you go to the guards?" the man asked.

"I did," she said, "but they didn't help me."

"That's terrible," Northstar said. "You should tell me their names. I can get them fired."

"I don't know their names," Darcy said. "All I know is Ruth Rosen."

Northstar hoisted herself up off the sofa and began shaking Snow.

"Come on," she said, "wake up. We need to help this girl."

Snow's head rolled loosely on the axis of her neck.

"I'm tired," she moaned. Her mouth went slack.

Mistral filled a glass of water in the white sink. He brought it close to Snow and then splashed it across her face. She didn't rouse right away; instead she curled inward like a wounded cat, brought her hands up to her face and began wiping ineffectually. She went still, and Northstar moved to shake her again. Then she spoke, her voice thick as a child's after crying.

"Okay," she said, "okay, what?"

"We need to do something for this girl," Northstar said. "We need to—"

She stopped. She looked up at the ceiling like she was trying to read something written there.

"Tell me if you know Ruth Rosen," Darcy finished for her.

"Yeah," Snow said, "yeah. Here, wait—" She made grasping

motions in the air with her silver-nailed hands. "Here, I'll write it down."

Northstar crawled under the coffee table and found a white leather purse. She took out a white leather-bound journal and a shiny white pen. Snow took both of them and began to write with minute concentration. Darcy felt her heart pounding in the cold room. She wondered if Snow would be able to write clearly. She was taking a long time, and Darcy wondered what she was writing. Was it an address, or some crazy incoherent story Darcy would have to decode? After several minutes Snow made a decisive final stroke, handed the paper to Northstar, folded her hands in her lap, and looked up at Darcy with an alert and expectant expression. Northstar folded the paper in half and handed it to Darcy. Darcy opened it and saw this:

"There's nothing here," she said.

"It's the new white ink," Mistral said. "You have to look at it the right way."

Darcy squinted, and held the paper close to her face, and rotated it, but it stayed blank.

"I can't see anything," she said.

Mistral took the paper and squinted at it himself. Snow pulled her legs up on the couch and shut her eyes again.

"Oh," he said. "Looks like Snow doesn't really know anything after all."

"There's no address?" Darcy asked.

"It's a drawing of some kind of fruit. I think it might be a strawberry. Hey, Snow"—he shook her—"can't you do any better than this?"

Snow made a little throaty noise and covered her eyes with her hands.

"She gets like that sometimes," Mistral explained. "I don't think she really knows any Ruth Rosen. But you should still stay and have strawberries and cream with us."

Five minutes later, Darcy was out on the street again, filled with an ineffectual, angry energy. She had even less control over her life than she'd ever thought, and it made her want to break something. She saw a coffee cup sitting on the sidewalk, the only piece of trash on Fifty-third Street. Kicking it made her bad leg hurt and produced an unsatisfying papery sound. In front of an apartment building, red flowers were growing in a raised bed, the pipes of their special cooling system poking out of the soil. Darcy snapped four fat blooms free of their stems and left them lying in the dirt, then walked off feeling like a child.

Darcy tried to visit Bruce Rosen the next morning, but he wasn't at his apartment, in the bad part of Floridatown. She had given up on World Experiences entirely—she wasn't going back to her apartment, so she didn't have to pay rent anymore, and when she found her mother they'd have to figure out some other way to make a living. She waited for Bruce all day in his dank and narrow hallway, listening to rats skitter in the walls. He came home at 9 p.m. wearing a smelly Seafiber clown suit and carrying three badly dented juggling pins. He said he didn't know a Ruth Rosen, never had, never would, he had come over with his mother, Caroline, on the fourth boat, and she had told him they were going to a place full of fruit and sunshine, and within a year she was dead of parrot fever and he was forced to support himself, first by taking bottles and cans to the recycling plant and then, when he was old enough, by working as a clown in the down-market nursing homes, and he had been doing that for sixteen years now and he'd never have enough money to get an apart-ment with a bathroom or even to take a girl out for a nice meal, and he wasn't interested in meeting anyone, let alone someone with the same last name as his mother. So Darcy said she was sorry, and he made a noise that was half laugh and half sneer, and Darcy went outside and got back on the bus again.

Nathaniel Rosen lived in Sonoma Hill. His building was not as nice as Snow's, but its hallways were clean and high-ceilinged and smelled like frangipani. His apartment was on the third floor. As she rang the doorbell she heard cooking sounds inside the apart-ment—the clack of a knife against a cutting board.

When he opened the door there was a crackling of mutual appraisal. Darcy tried to look serious but undesiring: not like a sales-woman or a criminal. Nathaniel had a small head and narrow, cau-tious eyes. He was bald; his eyebrows were thin; concern wrote two vertical lines above his nose. Darcy could see a slice of his kitchen through the door—a counter with a large mixing bowl and two fresh tomatoes, a pot on the stove, a table with a single glass of wine.

"I'm sorry to bother you," Darcy said, "but do you happen to know a Ruth Rosen?"

Nathaniel looked afraid for a second. Then his face went stony.

"I'm sorry," he said. "Now is not a good time."

He paused for a moment and Darcy saw an opening to argue. She opened her mouth. He shut the door.

Darcy tried to look through the peephole. His blue shirt receded out of view. She banged on the door.

"Please," she called, "my mother's disappeared, and I'm just trying to find her."

She heard footsteps grow louder, pause, then grow softer. She banged again. She heard the knife again, now insistent, almost showy.

"I'm staying in Hell City," she yelled through the door. "It's a shack with a garbage-bag roof, sort of near the Boat. There's a green bucket outside. Please come see me, if you change your mind."

She knocked a third time, quieter now, hope ebbing. The knife only got louder.

Ansel was alone in the shack when Darcy got there. A big Sea-fiber map of the island lay across his knees, covered in notes and symbols. Darcy sat on the floor and put her head in her hands.

"Worthless," she said.

"You didn't find Ruth, I take it?"

"No, I didn't find Ruth. Two of the people didn't know any-thing, one was drugged out, and one wouldn't talk to me. That list was a total waste. Everything I did was a waste."

Ansel folded the map and sat down on the floor with her.

"No, it wasn't. I'm sorry, I'm so sorry you had to do it, and if I'd known, I never would have put you in that position. But it wasn't a waste. Everything you do brings us closer."

"You mean closer to your crazy plan? I don't care about that. I don't give a shit about Tyson, I just want to find my mom."

"I know," Ansel said. His face went somber. "But what about if—when you do find her? Are you just going to keep working at World Experiences?"

"I probably can't," she said. "I'll have to get another job."

"But you're just going to go back to your ordinary life, knowing what you know now?"

Darcy raised her head. She felt like an empty refrigerator. She felt like the wind blowing through trash.

"What do I know?" she asked.

"You know that our founder and president probably kidnaps people. You know he's a criminal, and that he's trying to hide something. And you know that you have the power to do something about it."

All the bleakness turned to rage inside Darcy's chest.

"Power?" she yelled. "Look at me. I'm sitting on a floor in Hell City, I just fucked some asshole guard, and I didn't even get anything useful for it. At least whores get paid."

Ansel was quiet for a moment. Then he said, "When the guards wouldn't help you, you didn't stop. When Yuka wouldn't help you, you didn't stop. And when you had to do the one thing you swore you wouldn't do, you still didn't stop. Tyson should be afraid of you."

He was looking at her in a way only her mother had looked at her before. He was looking at her with respect. She had a strange feeling then. She wanted to be close to him, to touch his skin. It wasn't desire, exactly—not the kind of feeling she'd gotten the handful of times she'd made out with boys at solvent parties. It was both deeper and shallower than that—shallower because it didn't reach down through her gut and between her legs (the guard had frozen out that route), and deeper because she felt, for the first time since her mother had disappeared, a flicker of kinship with someone. She wondered if other people—people whose lives were less isolated, who never formed a tiny, sealed-off world with one other person—felt this kinship with lots of different people. She wondered how they managed it.

And she wondered, too, if she would keep fighting when she found her mother. Maybe Ansel was right, maybe Glock was right—maybe she had some sort of extraordinary quality, secret even to her. Maybe she did have the power to alter the things she'd always assumed she'd have to endure. She thought about Mistral, lazing back on the white couch. What would he do if Tyson kidnapped his mother? Would he beat down the doors of the other Board members, his fish-pale skin all flushed and slick with rage? Or would he saunter up to Tyson at some party in the Northern Zone, stick a gun in his back over the strawberries and cream? Of course, Tyson would probably never kidnap the mother of a junior Board member. He must've assumed he could get away with taking Sarah because she was poor and her family powerless. Darcy wasn't sure he was wrong.

"What do I do now?" she asked Ansel.

"Well, the last guy sounds weird. Why do you think he wouldn't talk to you?"

"I wouldn't necessarily talk to me if I came to my house," said Darcy. "But he looked scared. He looked like I hit a nerve."

"Maybe you should try him again."

"I don't know how I'll get to him. I knocked and knocked."

"Did you mention your mom? That might get his sympathy."

"I did," Darcy said, "and it didn't."

They sat in silence for a moment. A naked boy ran by the window and down the alley—he was ten or eleven, too old to be outside with no clothes on. His bare feet sent up little splashes where they fell. Darcy hated Hell City.

"Maybe you should ask Yuka," Ansel said. "If this Nathaniel guy does know Ruth, she might know him."

It wasn't a good idea, but it was an idea, and it made Darcy feel slightly less alone.

"Okay," she said, "thanks."

"Thank me when you find your mom," Ansel said.

"You're not supposed to be here," Trish hissed. "You don't work here anymore. You didn't even give notice."

"Just let me in for ten minutes," Darcy said. "I promise I won't let anyone see me. I just need to talk to someone."

Darcy was standing in the rain outside the service entrance to World Experiences. The gauze around her ankle had soaked up dirty water, and she had nothing else she could use to rewrap it. Trish stood in the dry hallway, her hairnet on, her expression skeptical.

"Who?" Trish asked.

"Yuka."

"What do you need to talk to Yuka for?"

"I need to ask her about my mom," Darcy said.

"Your mom's still missing?" Trish asked.

Darcy thought about how she must look—her hair dirty, her jumpsuit soaked, a tail of wet gauze coming out of her pant leg. Her voice desperate. She must seem like a derelict, like someone who had fallen off the edge of life. Trish's face showed that special pity people feel for those who were once their equals — pity mixed with disgust, mixed with fear.

"She's still missing," Darcy said.

Trish looked behind her, into the kitchen.

"Fine," she said. "But if Marcelle sees you, you broke in. I didn't have anything to do with it."

She let Darcy into the hall.

"And try not to drip all over everything, okay?" she added.

Win was washing pots in the kitchen. He looked up at Darcy and opened his mouth to ask her a question, but she walked by without waving. She crossed through the dining room, empty and silent, with its between-meals smell of cleaning fluid and aging jellyfish. The empty chairs and the lonely painted prairie girl made her nostalgic for a time when getting caught swiping steak was her biggest fear. Then she came out into the Antarctica Hall, with its Seaboard icebergs and oddly proportioned painted penguins. She was halfway down the hall when Marcelle came out of room 104, talking to one of the nurses.

"You can't be spending half an hour with each of the residents," Marcelle was saying. "We need to take all the vitals and get them entered in the charts within a reasonable time frame, and you can't do that if you're socializing."

Darcy crouched behind an iceberg. She held her breath.

"I wasn't socializing," the nurse said. "Ramona had a problem with her bed. It doesn't adjust right anymore. She needs a new one."

They stopped just in front of the iceberg. If Marcelle bothered to look behind it, she would see her. Darcy could smell Marcelle's perfume — crisp and antiseptic, neither fruity nor flowery. She could feel the magnetic pull of Marcelle's authority.

"I told you," said Marcelle, "we can't buy anything until our subsidy meeting with the Board. If you really want new beds, you'll suck up to the Abcarians and the Stones next time they visit. They have Trustees in their family. Talk about what a great job Tyson's doing with the cave-ins, something like that."

If Marcelle saw her, she'd throw her out, and then she wouldn't be able to talk to Yuka. But would Marcelle also have her arrested for trespassing? Would she fine her for leaving without giving notice? Darcy was reduced to borrowing bus fare from Sunshine's stash—there was no way she could pay a fine. And what if she went to jail?

"I don't think—" the nurse began.

"It doesn't matter what you think," Marcelle said. "It matters that we show our support. That's how we get subsidies. Which is how we get beds, and how we pay your salary."

Darcy heard Marcelle take a step toward her. Then Marcelle said, "You know what? I'm going to oversee you on the next one. Then I can make sure you know exactly what the appropriate amount of time is."

They turned, and they both walked into a room on the far side of the hallway. As soon as the door was closed, Darcy ran as quietly and as fast as she could up the stairs to the Africa Hall.

The door to Yuka's room was shut. Darcy knocked softly and then, when she heard no answer, loudly.

"I said come in," a weak voice told her through the door.

It wasn't Yuka. When she entered, Darcy saw that the bed was full of a big, soft woman. She lay sipping tea and holding a magazine, mounding up the covers where Yuka had shriveled beneath them.

"Where's Yuka?" Darcy demanded.

"Yuka? I'm sorry, I don't know very many people here. I just came yesterday."

The woman's face was round and mild and uncomprehending.

"The woman who was here before you," Darcy persisted. "Where did they move her?"

"Oh, there was no one here when I came. It was very clean. There's quite a long waiting list to get in here, you know. Not as long as for Renaissance Hall, but still."

Darcy punched herself in the thigh.

"So you didn't see anyone else in here?"

"Are you all right? Do you live here? Do you need help finding your room?"

Darcy had not shut the door, and now she heard the sneakered feet of one of the night nurses behind her.

"What are you doing here?"

She had never heard a night nurse speak before. This one sounded just like her earliest teachers—pained, officious, somewhere obscurely caring. Her face was small and boneless-looking, like the steamed buns you could buy on Chinatown Avenue.

"I was just checking on her," Darcy said, sweating. "I thought I heard her call. Didn't this used to be Mrs. McKenzie's room?"

The nurse looked at her with red-rimmed eyes. For a moment, suspicion seemed to give her face shape and organization, and Darcy heard her own heartbeat in her ears. Then the nurse's cheeks went slack again, whether with weariness or trust Darcy couldn't tell.

"If one of the residents calls, you call one of us," the nurse said. She turned to the old woman. "Are we all right, Mrs. Armitage?"

"Well, I would like some more tea."

The nurse turned to Darcy. "Could you get that? We only have so many hands up here."

Darcy stood her ground. "Where's Mrs. McKenzie?" she asked.

"Her son came to get her on Monday. They're going to take care of her at home, he said." She changed her voice to a stage whisper. "Which is great, in my opinion. She really upset some of the other residents." She ratcheted her voice back up to normal. "Now, tea?"

When Darcy got back to Hell City, filthy water stood two fingers deep in the alleyway. Whatever drainage the mucky beach provided was not enough, and people were beginning to dam up their shacks with wadded-up trash. The door to Ansel and Sunshine's shack was undammed, and Darcy could see the bottom of it becoming swollen and waterlogged. Then she opened the door, and someone came running at her through the small room, pink-faced and yelling.

"What the fuck do you want from me?" he shouted, and it took her a moment to realize he was Nathaniel Rosen.

"You came," Darcy said. "Thank God."

He was wet to the skin, and shivering with rage, and he smelled like nervous sweat. Sunshine was completely calm, sitting on the yellow cushion, stuffing a dark paste into old Seafiber french fry bags. The paste smelled like fertilizer.

"He's a little worked up," Sunshine said. "He's been waiting for you."

Nathaniel put his hands on his head and began pacing around the shack. There was no sign of Ansel.

"I knew you were trouble when I saw you," Nathaniel said. "You move like her, you talk like her. You could've worn a gorilla suit and I would've known."

"Like who?" Darcy asked.

"Like Sarah. I told her I wasn't interested, because I knew something like this would happen. Then you show up, and now they're following me."

Darcy looked at Sunshine, who shrugged and went on stuffing bags.

"Wasn't interested in what?" Darcy asked. "Who are 'they'?"

He searched her face; even in his panic his eyes were steady and keen.

"She didn't tell you, did she?"

He sat down on the floor now, kneaded the bridge of his nose.

"My mom?" Darcy said. "Like I told you, she's gone. I don't know where she is."

"Did she tell you anything? About Daniel, the boats, Esther?"

"Nothing," Darcy said. "I know a little about Daniel, but not from her."

Sunshine was sitting forward now, listening, her fingers working without her brain.

"Jesus Christ, I barely even know about this, I can't believe I'm telling you. Ten years ago, your mom comes to me. To my apartment. She makes my wife—I was married then—she makes my wife leave, and she tells me Daniel's trying to contact us. She says he sent a ship."

Sunshine put her bag down.

"How did she know?" she asked.

"She said she saw it. She said she saw a ship on the horizon, and she saw the guard boats shoot it down."

"The first Hawaiian attack," Darcy said. "Why did she think it was Daniel?"

"That's what I asked. She said he had some symbol he taught us. I don't know, I think she's crazy. I don't remember any symbol."

Darcy looked at his bald head then. She looked at his hands now spread out on his thighs. The knuckles were furred with dark brown hair, but the fingers were thin and short, their tips shaped like almonds.

"I'm sorry," she said, "but are you Ruth?"

His look was wry and weary.

"Good catch," he said. "I was, until about, oh, twenty years ago."

"You must have had it done illegally," Sunshine said, "or it'd be on Tyson's records."

Nathaniel turned to her, quick and feline, his anger still warm.

"And who are you exactly?"

Sunshine just smiled her haughty smile.

"I'm nobody," she said.

It seemed to disarm him.

"I am too," he said, "or I was."

"Have you seen my mom since then?" Darcy asked him.

"Three weeks ago," he said. "After the second attack. She said that was Daniel too. She said that proved they were trying to contact us. She said she'd already sent a message to my sister, to Esther. I said so what and she said don't you understand, we have to send someone. If we show them we're listening, maybe they'll come help us. I said help us what, I have a good job, I have a fine life. Then she started crying and saying how can you not know what it's like, don't you look around you, don't you look around. And I said I don't know what you're talking about, and she said my daughter has to work six days a week, she can't go to school, just so we can live in an apartment instead of a shed."

Sunshine smirked at that, but still she bent her head in close attention and didn't pick up her paste or her bags. Darcy thought of her mother crying. The thought made her want to break something. She almost never cried. Or she did, but not over anything real. She cried immoderately whenever she stubbed her toe on the hot plate or the corner of the mattress, or when she had cramps on the first day of her period, or when the Seacafé was too hot and burned her tongue. But she didn't cry when her hours were cut, or when Darcy's pay got docked, or when they didn't have enough money to eat the last few days of the month, or any of the times when, it seemed to Darcy now, it would have made sense to break down. Instead those were the times when she was most childlike, when they stayed up all night and drew on each other's skin and acted like they were both little girls hiding from some oppressive and rule-bound mother. Had that been put on, Darcy wondered, that part of her that seemed oldest and truest and most their own? Were there other people who watched her cry out sorrows she hid from Darcy? The other divers? The people on the bus in the mornings? Darcy wanted to find all of them, to somehow extort from them the scenes she should have witnessed.

"Anyway she was just bawling, she was making a scene, and of course with the crackdown I didn't want any trouble. So I told her she had to go."

Darcy felt a pang of anger that anyone, offered an extra moment with her mother, would refuse it.

"You threw her out?"

His eyes went narrow, his nostrils pinched. This was a new, cool kind of anger.

"Listen," he said. "I'm not the kind of person who asks for pity. But I haven't had a particularly easy life, I've worked hard, and I want to hold on to what I have. Not that that looks like much of a possibility now."

"Because the guards came for you?" Sunshine asked.

"Not the regular guards. Tyson's personal force—a man and a woman in those gray uniforms. The first time was a week after I saw Sarah. They were looking for Ruth then. I keep that part of my life pretty secret, so I didn't tell them anything. But they poked around a lot, asked about my ex-wife, looked in my bedroom.

They kept saying they were 'special detectives.' Anyway, for a couple days I was spooked. But they didn't come back—until you came to see me. Today I came home from work and they were at my apartment. Luckily I happened to run into my neighbor in the lobby. She wanted to know what the guards were doing there. I didn't answer. I just ran."

"If they showed up at his place right after you did," Sunshine said to Darcy, "they're probably following you."

"That's what I assumed," said Nathaniel, "but I also assumed you'd be in on whatever your mom was doing, and you aren't. So I really don't know what you're planning, but I had a job and an apartment and now I'm on the run, and you'd better fix it."

"I'm just looking for my mom," Darcy said, "who disappeared, along with your sister, or don't you care about that?"

"You don't know anything about my sister," he said.

Footfalls sloshed outside the shack, and Ansel walked in the door.

"Who are you?" Nathaniel asked.

"I am the King of the One-Armed Men," Ansel said, "and the Duke of Hell City. Who are you?"

"I used to be the assistant vice president of marketing at Green-Valley," said Nathaniel, "and now I'm a pathetic fugitive."

Ansel was smiling, and his body was full of energy. His eyes were slightly wild.

"Hey," he said. "Do you know this guy who likes to wear a red tie? Hangs out in casinos?"

"No," said Nathaniel, his voice snide. "Do you know someone who can get the guards off my trail and get me my job back?"

"Possibly," Ansel said. "Give me some time."

Darcy had no patience for Ansel's bluffs now. She had no patience for Nathaniel either. He might have lost the job that kept him in fresh tomatoes and an air-conditioned apartment, but she had lost the only person in the world who really cared about her. She thought of the guards in the gray uniforms. They were after Nathaniel, and they might well have taken Yuka too—she had never mentioned a son to Darcy. If the guards were following her, they'd eventually find her here. And when they found her, they would either kill her or they would take her to the same place they'd taken her mother.

She stood up.

"Okay," she said again. "Fuck this. Somebody's following me, and whoever's following me has my mom. So I'm gonna go outside and stand around until they get me. You guys do what you want."

"Fine," said Nathaniel.

"You can't," said Ansel.

Sunshine was silent for a moment. Then she put a final scoop of paste into one of her bags and tied it off.

"That's a good idea," she said. "But you should wait until we have a plan."

The room seemed to organize itself along new and sharper lines. Some of the rage went out of Nathaniel's face. Ansel whispered to Sunshine and Sunshine shook her head.

"No, look," she said, "it's smart. She's the one they want, let her get inside. She can find out what we want to know, and then we'll get her out again."

Ansel looked at Sunshine. Sunshine's face was like Marcelle's in its stillness and authority. Darcy was jealous of her calm, and she wondered again what was in her mind.

"Okay," Darcy said. "I'll wait. But it can't be long."

"Don't worry," said Sunshine, "it won't be."

8

Darcy hadn't left the shack in two days. Sunshine had given her a bucket to piss in so she wouldn't have to go to the pay toilet down by the Boat; when Darcy protested, Sunshine just laughed.

"We do this all the time," she said, "and we haven't died of embarrassment yet."

Darcy rolled her eyes.

"I know you think you're better," Sunshine said, "because you're not last-boat, and because your building had running water or whatever the fuck. But let me tell you, nobody with any real money could tell the difference between you and me."

She turned to Nathaniel, her face calm but her eyes shining.

"Isn't that right?" she asked him.

"It's not like that," he said, but Darcy knew it was.

The first night Ansel had gone out to recruit help. But he had come home alone, spread the map out on the floor, and then pounded his fist down on it so hard that the grill fell over on its side and even Sunshine looked alarmed. She had knelt to him then, and whispered something Darcy couldn't hear, and Ansel had pounded his fist again and shouted, "No! I'm going to do this. I have to."

She didn't like the way he sounded, both petulant and driven.

He reminded her of Glock for a moment, of a child grabbing for what he wanted, and she wondered what would happen if he ever got it. She let him calm down for a few minutes, and then she asked him, "What happens if you actually get rid of Tyson?"

He didn't look up from his map, on which he was now scribbling with a blinkered intensity.

"There's no if," he said.

"Fine, when."

"Then we'll have elections for new leaders."

"Real elections?" Darcy asked. "Because the Board elections are fake, you know."

"Of course I know. We'll have free elections, and instead of a Board we'll have a council, with representatives from all the different workers' groups—the divers, the refineries, the factories, the service sector."

He was looking at her now, and gesturing, as though she had jolted him back into oratory mode.

"And instead of the council making all the decisions, like the Board does, there'll be a referendum system, and everyone on the island will get to vote. And we'll institute a progressive income tax, and get rid of the subsidies, and we'll redeploy all the guards to rebuild the cave-ins, at reduced pay."

Darcy was about to ask about the Seaguards, about defense against the Hawaiians, but if her mother was right the Hawaiians had never attacked at all. All those sirens and flyers, all those taxes, for nothing. She wondered if it was possible.

"You sound like you've thought about this a lot," she said.

Ansel made a flourish with his good hand, and seemed cheerful again.

"I think about nothing else," he said.

She was reassured, but the next night he was gone again, and so was Sunshine, and Darcy sat in the shack with Nathaniel and felt as hopeless as ever. She had unwrapped the filthy gauze from her bad leg, and now she rolled her jumpsuit up to stare at the skin. It was the right color again, but still as tender to the touch as a new bruise, and when she stood on it wrong it sent a cold shock all the way up her back. She walked with a limp. Of course, now she had nowhere to walk to.

Outside, it was raining so hard that the street had become a rushing brown river, carrying flotillas of candy wrappers, cheese-food cans, cigarette butts, and shit, along with the occasional dead rat or living, thrashing dog. Nathaniel crouched on the yellow cushion, his discomfort palpable. He had refused to eat anything Sunshine cooked, saying he had allergies, until the previous night when he had wolfed down a grilled jellyfish and then pretended to be asleep so that no one could talk to him. Now something particularly noxious washed by outside, filling the shack with a fetid smell.

"Somebody should teach these people about hygiene," he said.

Before she'd wanted to stand apart from Hell City and its inhabitants, but now Darcy felt insulted on their behalf. She had known hardship, and she could complain if she wanted to. He could not.

"If this is the worst thing you've ever smelled," she told him, "you're in for a treat."

Nathaniel shook his head.

"You all think I've had an easy life, don't you?" he said.

"Look," Darcy said, "you were cooking with fresh tomatoes when I met you. I'd have to work for a month to buy a fresh tomato."

Nathaniel looked out the plastic-bag window.

"My ex-wife was a schoolteacher," he said. "Not in our neighborhood—in Lower Chicagoland. A real bleeding heart. I went down there to talk to the kids once. They were all fighting and throwing things; one of them had a solvent bag right there at his desk. And I told them they too could be an assistant vice president at GreenValley Foods someday, if they just worked really hard and wanted it bad enough."

Darcy raised an eyebrow.

"Yeah, and?"

"And it wasn't true. Maybe for some people, but not for me. Hard work alone wouldn't have got me where I was."

"So what did you do?" Darcy asked.

"It doesn't matter," he said. "It's not that interesting."

But he looked at her, and she saw the same desire she'd seen in Armin and Yuka, the hunger for someone safe to tell a secret to. She remembered what the nun had said about voiceless people, and she wondered how many more the island held, how many kept quiet out of fear or isolation or the sheer apathy that came from grinding every day against so many strangers' lives. Darcy gestured around her at the yellow cushion, the grill, the warped Seaboard walls.

"Neither is this," she said.

"I don't know if you know this," he said, "but it was really hard for the orphans. We didn't understand what was happening to us. They gave us a choice, you know. The grown-ups sat us all down on the rug in the co-op and they said we were our own people, we could choose to stay or go. But we were just kids; we didn't know anything. When they said who wants to go we all raised our little hands.

"And then we were here, and it was all different—the heat, the ocean. At the beginning they hadn't figured out anything—we were eating mussels in poison month and Cricket Thomson almost died. No one was watching us. They were busy building the new world for us, they said. And they kept telling us we'd be in charge someday. The leaders of tomorrow, they kept saying.

"And then we got older, and somehow none of that ever happened. The older kids, eighteen, nineteen, were trying to get jobs, but not a single one could get a good company job, and, I mean, GreenValley only had about thirty employees at this point. It didn't make sense, unless they were *trying* not to hire us.

"I started hearing about it from the other orphans, that we were blackballed. That it came from the top, from Tyson. He couldn't trust our loyalty, because of something about Daniel. The others got angry, but I didn't really remember Daniel—I was just confused.

"One thing I did know was I wasn't a girl—once a plastic surgeon came in with the influx, that decision was easy. Of course, there were a few complications."

"Like what?" Darcy asked.

"Well, I heard about the doctor from a friend of mine," said Nathaniel, "someone I used to know when I was still hanging out with Sarah. Back then I used to go to the gay bars, these tiny little places hidden in the new office buildings and whatever. It was kind of a beautiful time, in a way—there was an excitement in that stolen space, and we all knew it would be gone soon because the offices would fill up, so we had to get in all our fun before that happened. And we had that feeling of having survived something terrible, like when you cry for a long time and then you feel euphoric after. Anyway, during the influx I heard about this guy. He was a plastic surgeon, and on the mainland he had mostly been cutting off frostbitten toes and straightening out kids with rickets, but now he was claiming he could do a sex change.

"There were so many people like that then—it's almost funny now. The construction workers who said they were architects, the students who set themselves up as lawyers. One guy was the head of the bank for a little while, and then they found that he couldn't read. And of course you could ask someone for their qualifications, but there was no way of checking anything. Still, I wanted this so bad, I would've gone to almost anybody. I had this image in my head, this muscleman. You remember Arnold Schwarzenegger? That's who I wanted to look like.

"Anyway, the surgeon was in a part of Chicagoland that was still tents—a tent for the dentist and a tent for the pawnshop and a tent for this guy. It was really hot in there, and instead of having all his instruments laid out in a tray, he just had this box, like a tool chest only less organized. There was a tarp down instead of a floor and at the corner of the tent the grass was peeking through. I had to borrow a bunch of money because he only took cash, and after I gave it to him he said back on the mainland he used to do this with stem cells, but we were going to do it the old-fashioned way. I asked what that was and he said he was going to take a piece of my thigh and attach it to my vulva with a hole in the middle so I could pee. He said it would look weird at first, but the testosterone would make it look better. He said that and the breast removal together would take six hours, and then he gave me a shot of solvent and I was gone.

"After he was done I felt good. It hurt, but he gave me some painkillers, and I bought testosterone from this other guy, who had a pharmacy that was half fresh stuff and half stuff he'd hoarded on the mainland, and every time I gave myself a shot I felt like I was becoming a man. I was only twenty years old. When it was time to take off the bandages, I was freaked out at first—it didn't look like a penis; it looked more like a slug, but after a day or so I kind of liked it, I started to feel like it was me.

"The next day the pain started. It was like someone stuck a drill into my leg and turned it on. And my whole right thigh started to swell and get red and hard, like there was a bowling ball in there. I dragged myself down to Chicagoland—I remember there was just this one bus that went there then, and I was waiting for it in the hot sun and I felt like I was rotting from the inside — and when I got there he was gone. His instruments and the operating table were still there but he was nowhere. So I got back on the bus, but this time I passed out from the pain and some old ladies took me to the charity hospital. I was there three days, and one of the days they ran out of painkillers. I was just screaming all day long — everybody was screaming, it was a horrible place — and then finally on the fourth day I was sort of coming back to my senses and they told me that I'd had blood poisoning, probably because of poorly cleaned instruments, and that they had to remove six inches of flesh from my thigh and some of my abdominal muscle, and I was lucky I got there when I did or I might have lost the whole leg or died. They didn't have to take the penis though. I was happy about that."

Darcy thought about her leg. She reached down and pressed the ankle and felt the pain come up like an answer. She wondered if it would ever stop hurting. By the time she could get to a hospital, would they have to cut it off?

"Does it still hurt?" she asked cautiously.

"Not really. I can't run very well, and I have a huge scar from my crotch all the way to my knee, and this funny-looking dent in my stomach that never went away. And I never became a muscleman. But the penis did get a little better — it still looks weird but I can have sex, or at least I could before I was divorced.

"And of course I became a different person. Nathaniel. I'd always liked the name. And once I had it I realized what I could do. I could just start cutting ties with people. Cricket was working construction, building those factories they said we'd be running, and your mom was living in a squat — none of them was going anywhere in life."

"My mom lived in a squat?" Darcy asked.

He smiled a little.

"Oh yeah, she was like a hippie queen. She lived with twenty other people in this unfinished building, this place in Founders' Village that they tried to build before they really got Seaboard right. They were always stepping through the floor. They used to all sit in a circle and she'd teach them songs."

Darcy tried to imagine her mother surrounded by friends and worshippers. Her mother who always seemed so alone when she came in wearing her wet diving suit, like she'd just come back from an expedition to the moon.

"What were her friends like?" she asked.

"I didn't know them very well," he said. "None of them had jobs. They got all their food from dumpsters — your mom weighed about ninety pounds. They were always getting parrot fever, and they never had medicine. At least two of them died."

"Did you know my dad?" she asked him. "He died of parrot fever. His name was Alejandro."

Nathaniel shook his head.

"Like I said, I didn't spend much time with them. Pretty quick, I realized I had a shot, I had this new identity. For at least a little while, Tyson wouldn't know who I was. And I could get off his blacklist — but not if I kept hanging out with the kids I grew up with."

He stopped talking, and Darcy watched him. He had a new look on his face now, some tension in the eyebrow muscles, like hope, like caution.

"The worst was my sister," he went on. "When we were kids, she used to put her hands around my head" — he pressed his small palms into his scalp — "and no matter how scared or angry or sad I was, I'd calm down, because I knew she would always be there.

But then we grew up, and she was working these really marginal jobs, trash collecting, day labor—I suspected worse but she'd never say—anyway, I knew I couldn't see her anymore."

Darcy understood now what she saw in his face. She had seen it in Yuka, and sometimes, when she happened to pass by a mirror, she now saw it in herself. It was loneliness.

"I didn't have the courage to tell her outright," he went on, "so I just stopped answering the door when she came around. I had roommates then, a couple of young second-boat guys, real clean-cut; they didn't know about my operation, they didn't know I even had a sister. The last time she came she sobbed outside my door for an hour, and I told my roommates she was a crazy person who was stalking me."

Darcy wasn't sure what to say. Here was someone who had one person who had loved him all her life and would love him until she died, and he had abandoned her. The very thing that had been taken from Darcy, he had simply thrown away.

"I'm sorry," she said flatly.

He sighed.

"No you're not, I didn't expect you to be. Or maybe I did—I don't know. You were right, I did have an easy life. It's hard to believe, but the island was doing really well for a while. New factories springing up, new jobs. GreenValley was growing. I got really settled there, rose up through the ranks. I was Nathaniel Cobb to start out with, but when I got divorced I started going by Rosen again, just because I missed it. I felt that safe. I was so stupid; I should've known they'd figure it out eventually, and that someday I'd be shit out of luck and I'd have given up my sister for nothing. But I didn't think about that."

His self-pity made her angry; she wanted to yell at him, treat him like a sniveling child. But she thought, too, of the guard, of how she'd been willing to give up part of herself to get what she wanted. It was not right that their lives had required this of them, that the island required this of them, and her anger began to take a different course—she thought of Tyson, not as he must be now, but as he was when Yuka knew him, young and power hungry and conniving. Darcy wished she had been alive then, that she had been on the mainland. She would have known not to listen to Tyson; she could've told the others. Of course, she had the advantage of Yuka and Nathaniel to tell her what had happened. Still, there must be people in the world who are not fooled, who can catch evil before it spreads. She wondered how she would know if she was such a person.

"All right," she said. "I'm not sorry. But I get why you did it."

"Thanks," he said. "I haven't told anyone that story. Not even my wife. I don't exactly have a lot of friends."

"Neither do I," she said, and she felt something like sympathy between them. For a moment she liked it, and then it became uncomfortable.

"Look," Nathaniel said, pointing at the bucket. "I'm not going to use that thing. I'm going outside."

"Are you sure? It might not be safe."

"I'll take my chances," he said. "I don't really like to go in front of people."

Darcy wondered if he was embarrassed about his penis. She imagined him cupping his hand over it in public restrooms, shielding it from view. She imagined him explaining it to his future wife, sitting on his couch with her, not touching, his eyes cast off to the side. She understood why he had wanted a job so badly—money bought privacy.

Water rushed in the door as he shut it behind him. She saw him pass the smeary plastic window, heading for the narrow space between the shacks. She thought of Nathaniel as a child, a little girl wishing for a boy's body, her sister's hands around her compact, splitting head. Sarah must have played with them, she might have shared a room with them at night, one of ten kids packed into the kitchen or bathroom or supply closet. They might have heard her cry out in her dreams. Why had Sarah never mentioned them? Why hadn't they come to the apartment when Darcy was growing up, to reminisce about old times? Why had no one ever come to the apartment? The humid closeness of their life together had always seemed natural, but now it began to seem strange.

Then Darcy heard a sound. The sound was loud—it rang out above the rain—but short, too short to have an obvious source. It could have been the truncated bark of an angry dog suddenly placated with food, or the abrupt slamming of a door—or Nathaniel's voice, trying to cry out before someone stopped his mouth. For a second she thought of hiding, but if Tyson's guards were really here then surely they would find her, and even if they didn't, she didn't want her only link to her mother to disappear. She felt a new kind of fear heating up in her belly, a fear that was almost excitement, and she let it rise up all the way to the top of her head, and then she stepped outside. She looked around her. A tiny girl with a bloody nose half ran, half swam into a nearby shack. A seagull flapped above, cackling like a witch. Darcy called to Nathaniel; her hands began to shake. And as she stood on the rushing street, she smelled the heavy fetor of all Hell City's stirred-up trash, and beneath it something different, something sharp and insistent and almost sweet, like the rain was trying and failing to clean the world it washed over, and then she heard something behind her, and then she felt hands on her arms and something sharp in her neck and she had the sensation, not unpleasant, of the sky and the shacks and even the water itself melting before her eyes.

9

When you wake up for the first time in a strange bed, you wonder not only where you are but who you are. Are you, perhaps, the person who has always slept in this cool room, between these smooth blue sheets? Are you the one who played with this stuffed owl, these smiling china ponies, who gave them names and whispered their stories to your soft pillow when you couldn't sleep? Are you the girl whose father read to you in that wooden rocking chair, whose mother gave you those roller skates for your birthday?

And by the time you realize that you are not that girl, that this room has never been your own, that you have never been the kind of person who sleeps in a room like this — by that time you are not as you were before, and all the certainties and convictions that held your brain in place are loosened slightly, like the laces of a shoe.

"Don't be alarmed," a woman said.

Darcy snapped upright, felt the pain fork up from her ankle all the way to her face, looked down to see her foot encased in some kind of blue metallic sleeve, and shouted at the woman with all the rage her muddled mouth could produce, "Who the fuck are you?"

The woman laughed.

"I should learn not to say that. 'Don't be alarmed,' right after someone's just come out of the operating room. Of course you're going to be alarmed. I'm Marie. I prepped you for surgery, remember?"

The woman was small, with a pointed chin and green, wary eyes. She had the look of someone who had been undernourished as a child. At first Darcy thought she was young, but as she came closer and set a plate with an aluminum cover down on the night-stand, Darcy saw the loose skin beneath her eyes and along her jaw, the wrinkles in her forehead—she might be fifty, or older. Her dark brown hair was cropped close to her head.

"You did surgery on me?" Darcy asked.

"Your ankle was a mess. It looked like it had never been set properly and you'd been walking on it for a while. It was a nasty break—I don't know what you did to it."

Darcy remembered the Big Top, and the polar bear, and the memory had the effect of cleaning out her mind all the way up to the moment when she'd stood outside the shack looking for Nathaniel, and no further.

"Where's Tyson?" she demanded. "I want to see him."

Marie smiled, a little ruefully.

"You'll see him," she said, "as soon as you've rested a bit. You haven't eaten in several days, and we had to give you some heavy-duty painkillers. You're going to be a little woozy for a while, and when the pain comes back, you'll probably want something a bit lighter."

Marie held out a hand with two brown pills nestled in her palm. Her fingers were short, blunt, savage-looking.

little, and if they had wanted to kill her, why would they have set her leg? The bun gave slightly under Darcy's fingers. When she bit down, she tasted ketchup, the slight sharpness of real mayonnaise. Then the beef—savory, fatty, slightly grainy on her tongue. It tasted better than she thought food should and so she wolfed it fast, like someone might take it away. She looked at the rocking chair and saw that the room was coming back into focus; her vision had been fuzzed and furred with weakness or drugs. She saw a small window up near the ceiling, letting in a chunk of blue sky. She saw the titles of the books on the bookshelf— *The Odyssey, Siddhartha, Merriam-Webster's World Atlas.* Darcy picked up *The Odyssey.* She had never held a book like this before—heavy in her hands, the pages textured like cloth. At school the books were shiny Seafiber, each light as a slice of bread, each shot with bullet points and packed with pictures. She replaced *The Odyssey* and hefted the atlas—three times the size of her *Animal Atlas,* with its title embossed in gold. Tucked inside its front cover was a sheaf of loose-leaf maps, the paper tea-colored, worn at the edges, threadbare in the folds. The first map was of the West Coast and Pacific Ocean, with numbers and notes and a long dotted line written across it in a cramped, spidery hand. The second—just spots scattered across a grid—confused Darcy until she remembered the constellations they'd studied in fourth grade. Then the spots resolved themselves into a hunter, a woman, a dipper, and she understood that the spot circled several times in faded blue ink must be the North Star. She turned the page, and found a sheet torn from another book, badly water-stained but legible, titled "Navigation by Sextant." She'd never heard of a sextant, but from the instructions and the diagrams she could tell it was to help sailors find their way at sea. The papers seemed to buzz in her hands—Tyson must have used them to plot the course from the mainland to the island. Darcy flipped back to the ocean map and traced the dotted line with her finger. It began in Seattle and snaked across the sea, before ending at a spot marked "AP." Darcy stared at the line—a record of her mother's journey, made even before the journey began.

On the second shelf was an oxblood leather binder with the word "Photos" embossed in gold on the spine. It was even heavier than the books; it smelled animal and dark. Alone on the first page, behind a protective film, was a photo of a baby in a maternity ward. The photo was old, turning the odd liverish color of photos from the beginning of the century, and the baby looked pinched and scrawny and not entirely healthy. Darcy turned the page and saw a birthday party for a one-year-old, a fat chocolate cake with a single candle in it, tiny children around the table with their parents rising up out of the photo like trees. The birthday boy was clearly the same one as the newborn, and though a year had plumped him out a little, it had not made him look any better suited to the universe. The other children seemed to be laughing and gurgling at one another; he was staring, faintly cross-eyed, at the cake.

Darcy began flipping pages. She bypassed childhood, and adolescence, and she was about to put the book back on the shelf when she saw the boy, a young man now, standing outside in a graduation cap and a parka. His face was unpleasant—weak-chinned, sallow, prematurely haggard. But it was a familiar face: if you took every part of it and made it stronger, more distinguished and handsome, you'd have the picture of Tyson from the morning flyers. He even held his shoulders strangely, just as Yuka had said—one hitched up higher than the other, the arms unnaturally straight. As though his entry into the world had been some kind of injury.

She looked back at the other photos and saw that in almost all of them, Tyson was alone, if not in fact then in gaze, all those around him seeming to laugh at a joke he was only pretending to get. In his baseball-team photo—nine boys in hats and scarves kneeling on a brownish field—he was slightly apart from the rest, his shoulders in that half hunch, his eyes pointed at the ground. In his high school prom picture, he held his date's elbow like it was a teacup, breakable and hard. Darcy looked at his graduation photo again and saw a misfit boy who had somehow learned relatively late in life that he could influence people. She could see how someone whose childhood snapshots looked like this might want to cancel them out, might want a manly, powerful version of himself plastered on every news flyer. But why, then, the nostalgia? Why the rocking horse? Why build a monument to a time when you were an outcast?

Darcy was confused, and her head still pounded from her recent sedation, but still she felt calmed by the room. She liked its smells, the way it was full without being crowded, the way its furniture was old but not falling apart. She could almost imagine that it was her room after all, that she had grown up here, in another time, without heat or ice or sorrow. She picked another book from the shelf, one called *Kon-Tiki,* and read about sailing until her leg began to hurt again. Then she gave in, took the brown pills, and read some more, until she fell asleep.

Into her dream came an unfamiliar smell. It was thick, greasy, savory, like tiny particles of fat suspended in the air. In the dream it came from the bell of a purple, fleshy-petaled flower. In reality it came from a plate on her nightstand, a plate glistening with red-brown bacon and real, orange-yolked eggs. Marie was sitting on the edge of the bed. Darcy saw that she'd brought a crutch with her; it leaned against the bookshelf, glinting expensively. She wondered where she was supposed to use it.

"You slept like a stone," Marie said.

Darcy didn't like the idea that she'd slept soundly in that place, and she didn't like that Marie knew it.

"I know who you are," she said.

Marie raised an eyebrow in weary amusement.

"Do tell," she said.

"I know Armin Abcarian. He said you had an affair on the mainland. He got you onto a boat so you could be together, but now he thinks you're dead. It sounds to me like you used him."

Marie knit her brows momentarily at the mention of Armin's name, but as Darcy kept talking she shook her head and smiled.

"Armin may not have mentioned his wife to you," she said.

"He did," said Darcy, "but I don't think she's around anymore."

"Maybe not now," Marie said. "Maybe she died, or maybe she found out about another one of his women. But back in Portland, she was very much around. I met her once — she was sweet, kind of impractical. She went on about how much she missed the flowers from her childhood. Anyway, he said he was going to leave her, we were going to go on the second boat together. It was all set up. Then at the last minute he says actually the two of them are going, but it's okay, because I should just wait two years, and he can get me on the next one. I throw a fit, of course, but it turns out his wife is pregnant. He's not budging. He tells me to promise I'm not mad, to promise I'll be with him when I come. He says he has to call in every favor he owes just to get the extra passage, and pay a lot of money, and if I want it I have to promise that I'm not mad, that we can pick up where we left off. So I put on a nice face, and I said of course, sweetheart, I love you, what's two years to our love? In those two years I lost two toes and four teeth and twenty pounds, and in the last six months I lived in an old office building with six thousand other refugees, except by the end it was four thousand, each of us eating one cup of soup a day and so anemic we got bruises turning over in our sleep. And when the time came I took the passage and I was very careful never to run into him again. Maybe I did cheat him, but I don't give a shit about it."

Darcy felt a grudging sympathy. She thought of the cold hotel room she'd conjured up for Armin; it was still easy for her to put herself in Marie's place. It was easy to imagine herself starving in a crowded building, cursing the person who happened to have control over her life. But for her, she reminded herself, that person was Marie herself. Her sympathy withered.

"Where's my mom?" she asked.

Marie sighed.

"The truth is," she said, "I don't know where your mother is. I can find out for you, but it's going to take time."

"Why is it going to take time? You have her, don't you? You kidnapped all of us."

Marie looked up and out the little window with an expression like sadness.

"Look," she said, "why don't you eat your breakfast, and then I'll take you to see Tyson. That'll explain some things."

Darcy was about to demand that they see Tyson immediately, but she remembered the hamburger from the day before, and she decided not to turn down another chance at real meat. She bit into a strip of bacon and let its meaty, greasy crunch—so unlike jelly bacon it almost made her laugh—reverberate in her head. She thought of Snow Rosen, who could eat this way every day but instead let a whole rib roast languish on her counter. People were so stupid.

"Why are you giving me this stuff?" Darcy asked.

"We have it," Marie said. "Why not share?"

The offhandedness of the statement made her angry—why hadn't they shared with her all the nights when she went hungry? But Marie was watching her eat—she seemed to be genuinely enjoying Darcy's enjoyment. Darcy wondered if Armin had been disarmed this way, if Marie had made her face warm and loving when she took her braids down for him at night.

When Darcy finished the eggs, Marie helped her stand, lodge the crutch under her arm, and hobble out the door. The room opened out into a corridor, and the corridor opened onto a square courtyard. The air there was almost cool. In the center a pond lay still and smooth amid bright grass—she'd never seen standing water so clean before, so blue. All around the pond were unfamiliar trees, thick trunked and scaly, with spines instead of fronds. Pines, Darcy realized. Beneath each tree was a bench, but all the benches were empty, and the whole place looked eerie, like it had been recently evacuated.

"What's this place for?" Darcy asked.

Something swift and screaming flew by her head. She crouched behind Marie.

"Relax, it's a marsh hawk. Look."

Darcy followed Marie's finger to the gray shape above the pond. She saw its wings, its pale breast. She heard its mournful, hollow call, like air blown through bone. Then she saw it dive, and scatter the water in shimmering flumes, and come shooting up with a fish writhing in its armored hand.

"The nature preserve was Tyson's idea," Marie explained.

"Originally he wanted to repopulate the island with mainland species. We even used to have a breeding pair of elk, but they got heat stroke a few years ago. Now the whole project's on hold."

Marie led Darcy past the courtyard and up a grassy hill with more trees and a weakly flowing stream. They followed a brick path to a house, a real freestanding house like in the prairie flyers. The house had a front yard with pink and yellow roses; it had curtains on its windows and a wooden door. As Marie selected a key and turned it in the lock, Darcy looked out at the view. At the bottom of the hill was a high wall with guard towers all along its length. Just beyond it were the red roofs of the University buildings—they were ten miles north of Little Los Angeles, and Darcy had seen them only a handful of times before, most memorably on an ill-advised eighth-grade trip when one of her classmates strayed too far from the group and got arrested for loitering. South of the University were the Manhattanville high-rises—the GreenValley Headquarters Tower with its ludicrously hopeful strawberry cutout sticking up out of the roof; the Pacifica Flyers building, ten stories tall, its dome brass-plated, its shiny bravado a relic of the more ambitious time. South of those, through the haze, she could barely make out Upper Chicagoland, its one skyscraper just a Seaboard facade, its real buildings lower and squatter, slumped as though beginning to give in. South of that, the air went black with heaped-up smog, but she knew that Little Los Angeles teemed behind it, full of shouting and cheese food and the smoke of seaweed cigarettes and the messy, reckless freedom of hopes discarded. Darcy felt a twinge of pride—she was behind the wall, at Tyson's headquarters, and no one from her building, no one from her high school, perhaps no one from Little Los Angeles, had ever seen this view.

The front door of the house opened onto a dim hallway. The air smelled like flowers grown old but not rotten. Paintings hung on the walls—a woodland cottage with a snow-covered roof, some sort of red mainland bird. On one side of the hallway was a living room with overstuffed couches and a coffee table made of dark wood. On the other side was a white-tiled bathroom with a claw-foot tub. Ahead of them was another door, this one with a child's drawing taped to it. The drawing was badly foxed and faded and crinkled at its corners. In it a boy was lifting a car. Marie turned to Darcy.

"Keep your voice down." Then she looked toward the closed door and shook her head, smiling ruefully to herself. "Actually, whatever. Yell all you want."

Darcy didn't want to yell. The room behind the door made her stiff with apprehension. She followed Marie inside, into a pinkish gray half light like the inside of a shell, and she saw an animal in the bed, a wolf or dog with a long, grim, wasted snout and a pair of pointed ears. Her breath came unstuck in her chest when her eyes adjusted: lying in the bed was an old man, his hands withered, his shoulders slender as a girl's. What looked like ears were only shadows clinging to his head on the pillow, a head grown long and lupine as though age had stretched and whittled it, but a head that was recognizably Tyson's. The smell of old flowers still hung in the air.

"Go ahead," Marie said, "ask him your questions. Ask him anything you want."

Darcy moved toward him. His face was trapped in a rigid clench; his jaw muscles bulged; even his open eyes seemed locked up against something they didn't want to see. It was obvious that he was beyond hearing or speaking, but he was not slack, not dead. Something vital sparked beneath his frozen skin, tortured, baffled, and afraid. Darcy backed away again.

"What's wrong with him?"

"A stroke," Marie said. "His third."

Darcy looked again at his clenched jaw. Where she had been afraid now she was angry. By lying here mute and incapacitated, he was evading her.

"How long has he been like that?" Darcy asked.

"Like that? A few weeks. It happened just a few days after the Hawaiian attack."

"So you've been in charge since then?"

Marie sat on Tyson's bed. She took a cotton handkerchief from the nightstand and wiped his mouth with it. Next to the handkerchief was something metal with a small lens, like a little telescope—Darcy recognized the sextant from Tyson's papers.

"He gave the order to find the orphans," Marie said. "I let the guards carry it out. But now it's time to stop."

Darcy had been pinning all the pain of the last month on the vague form of Tyson, on his picture in the morning flyers, on the amorphous fact of his power. Now Marie was before her—a real woman, growing old, smaller than Darcy—a physical, fallible being responsible for ruining Darcy's life. Her body told her to attack Marie, to stick her thumbnails in her eyes. Her mind had to remind her that if she did that, she might never find her mother.

"What," she said, "you decided you're tired of kidnapping people? Ready to try something new?"

Marie seemed to grow slightly taller then, to shore up her spine with some emergency reserve of pride.

"Come with me," she said. "Let's let him rest."

She bent over the bed and pulled the comforter up farther over Tyson's chest. He made a strangled sound. Marie seemed to understand—she folded the comforter back again, and then led Darcy from the room.

They sat together on a flowered sofa in Tyson's living room.

Darcy moved so she was as far from Marie as possible. An antique cuckoo clock ticked on the wall. The lamp shade had cutouts of cowboy boots on it—when Marie turned the light on, the boots danced across the floor. The rug was heavy and soft-looking and printed with mainland flowers.

"When I came here," she said, "I had no money. I didn't know anyone except Armin, and I wasn't going back to him. Luckily Chicagoland Hospital still needed nurses, and they gave me a job. That's how I met Tyson. He was visiting a construction site in Manhattanville and a chunk of Seaboard fell on his head. I did a good job sewing him up, but if you look closely you can still see the scar."

Marie seemed to be in a kind of bitter reverie, but still there was something watchful in her face, something careful.

"The thing about Tyson," Marie went on, "is he's not a natural leader. He's not even likable. When I sewed him up, I was repulsed by him. He sweats when he's nervous—his palms and armpits are always sweaty. He has a whiny voice. And most of all, being with him is uncomfortable at first in a way that's hard to describe. When I met him I thought, Why does anyone listen to this guy? And then he started telling me how all the factions on the Board wanted him gone, how they were planning a takeover. He said he was just getting started with all these projects, like the bus system, the jellyfish processing plant. He said the Board wouldn't know how to handle them. I was polite, but I didn't really care much. Then he started listing the people on the Board, saying what was wrong with all of them. I wasn't even listening, until he got to Armin. I made him repeat the name. He said Armin was the front-runner, a lot of people wanted him to take power. And right then, even though I didn't really know him or like him, I told him I'd help in any way I could."

"Don't you think he might have known about you and Armin somehow?" Darcy asked. "He might have used that to get your sympathy."

"Oh," Marie said, "I'm sure he did. But that's not the point. I was just a nurse then, I was living in a shitty apartment in Lower Chicagoland, back when the streets there were still dirt. I had no influence and I was nobody. But Tyson didn't laugh me off. He just asked when I could start.

"I was the one who started publishing the morning flyers. I drew that picture of Tyson. I was the one who invented Founder's Day. I knew that people were confused, and they wanted someone to love, and if they loved Tyson, the Board couldn't just put someone else in power."

"And you did all that just so Armin wouldn't be in charge?"

Marie smiled.

"At first. After a while I got to know Tyson, and I understood why he had to be our leader. See, back on the mainland we were in chaos. We were regressing, we were worse than animals. I saw fathers steal food from children. I saw a woman lock her sister out in the snow so she could take her boat passage. Sometimes someone would try to unite us, get us to share our food or sleep in shifts so we'd have enough blankets. Those people would always fail—once, twenty kids beat a woman to death for suggesting we cut our vitamins in half. They failed because they tried to appeal to the goodness in us, and that goodness was all frozen out. But Tyson knew how to find the bad in people and use it for good. That's how he knew I'd be useful to him, and that's how he always succeeded, even though looking at him you'd think he'd always fail."

"So it's a success when you shoot down a boat full of innocent people and then kidnap more people to cover it up?"

"That was his flaw," Marie said. "He got scared. He'd been a weirdo and an outcast for a long time before he got any power, and he was always afraid it would happen again. Money we should've spent on welfare, public works, he spent on the Sea-guards. He had us build that nursery, and then this whole house, for him, so he could hide away in some kind of childhood he never had. He stopped coming out for Founder's Day. And after the attack, I tried to tell him not to go after the orphans, that it was wrong, that it would get out, but he wouldn't listen. He gave his personal guards their orders. It took me a long time to get them to stop, to gain their trust. I'm still not sure I have it."

"But you kidnapped me," Darcy said.

"I needed to talk to you. I need your help."

A high-pitched, sublinguistic whine came from Tyson's bed-room, and Marie jumped to answer it. All the wariness went out of her face, pushed away by what looked like real concern. She really loved Tyson, Darcy thought. And, shrewd as she was, she had believed in him.

"Help with what?" Darcy said when she came back.

"I'm going to get the guards to tell me where they're holding all those people. I'm going to release them."

Darcy tried to look into her face and see if she was telling the truth. She remembered what it had felt like to play Marie for Armin, to cast herself back into Marie's freezing history. What would the woman who had let her hair down in the decaying hotel rooms of the soon-to-be-abandoned world do now, with a comatose leader and a stash of prisoners? Would she show mercy? But Darcy had not known Marie when she played her part in Armin's medicine-smelling bedroom. And when she looked at her now, she saw only steeliness—Marie's face gave nothing back. It was a private face, a face that communicated only what it wanted to communicate. Darcy thought of Tyson lying in the bedroom, of how quickly Marie had shot up to tend to him. She wondered if this was what your face looked like when you lost the only person you were close to. She wondered if it was what her own face looked like.

"Then what?" Darcy asked.

"I'm going to pick up where Tyson left off. I'm going to do it right. I lived through the refugee camp, and it takes a lot to make me afraid. I think you're the same way. That's why I want you to help me."

"Why me?"

"I've been watching you for a while, ever since the guards took your mother."

Darcy wondered if she'd led them to Yuka and Nathaniel. They might be living peaceful lives now if not for her. Maybe all she'd accomplished was helping the guards clean up loose ends.

"I think you're like me," Marie went on. "People like us get what we want, even if we have nothing to start out with. I'd rather have someone like that with me than against me."

For most of Darcy's life, people had noticed her only to rebuke her. To everyone but her mother, she had been interchangeable with every other Little Los Angeles girl—getting bad grades, dropping out of school, turning one kind of product into another, collecting a paycheck and handing it over to the landlord. Now people kept telling her she was different, and it was becoming hard not to believe it. The kids who did well in school were meant for one kind of greatness, for getting jobs at GreenValley or on the Board and having nice apartments and getting interviewed in the flyers. What if she was meant for setting the bent world straight? The thought filled her with a strange kind of pride, a lightness, a feeling like surprise.

"Let my mom go first," Darcy said. "I want to talk to her. Then I'll consider it."

"I'll talk to the guards," Marie said. "I should have an answer for you by tomorrow."

Darcy still didn't trust Marie—she might easily be lying about her role in the kidnapping. Still, it gave Darcy pleasure to ask for something—not to beg and scrape and sell herself out for it—and to have her request treated like an order.

The next day a man came to see Darcy. He was wearing the gray uniform of Tyson's personal guards.

"I'm Marcus," he said. "I'm here to talk to you about your mother."

Darcy leapt out of bed too fast to think about her leg, and she landed so hard on her cast that the pain took her breath away. But even as she gasped and trembled and blinked away the white hurt-haze, her mind was filling up with sweet disorganized excitement. She thought of her mother's long feet, of the times she would sing to herself so softly that her lips moved but no sound came out, of the private drawings she made with her index finger on the dust of the windowsill, and of how much she had missed these things, and of how every day for the last month had been encircled and underpinned and tainted with fear, and of how that fear was about to be relieved. Then she looked up and saw the guard's face. His skin was ashen.

"First I should tell you," he began, "that she—"

And he paused, and in that pause she heard that he had only bad news for her, news he was afraid to tell, news he knew would fill her with despair or rage, and before he could put the news into words, before she could give words to it in her mind, she let the rage take their place, let it spurt forth before it was called for, hardening her fingers into claws and propelling herself forward with such force that she raked her nails down both his cheeks and left strawberry stripes before he was able to catch her by the wrists, and subdue her, and look down at the floor while still holding her fast, and tell her, "Your mother is dead."

The rage bled away, and Darcy's brain was a box with a slot in it. Words went out the slot; words came back in. The box was tiny. There was nothing else in the box.

"Did you kill her?" Darcy asked.

"No."

"How did she die?"

"We had her in a nice room with a bedside lamp. She took apart the lamp and used a wire to pick the lock. Then she made a run for it. Elvin was guarding her. She was so quiet and well behaved, we never thought she'd try to escape. He didn't know what to do, so he shot her."

"And then?"

"It wasn't in our orders to shoot any of them. We took her to our barracks. We didn't tell anyone. The wound was in her side. We tried to stop the bleeding, and at first we thought it worked, because she stopped crying. Then she said, 'Tell her I'm okay,' and we said we would, even though we didn't know who she was talking about, but she kept saying it over and over, and then the words sort of blended together until she was just making this one long sound like an animal sound, and then she died."

The slot shut and the box filled up. It filled up not with words but with pressure, pressure on all sides of the box, pressure on every point on the inside of Darcy's skull. She held her head together with her hands.

"Would you like me to leave now?" the guard asked.

Darcy nodded without looking up.

When he shut the door and she was alone in the room, Darcy began to feel human again. She felt a surging panic not just in her brain but in her bones and her muscles and her gut, and she wanted to run to a place where the panic was not. She ran in a circle on the floor in front of the bed, ignoring the pain in her foot, and then she took off all her clothes and ran in a circle in the opposite direction, and then she scratched up and down her thighs until she raised dark purple welts all over them. While she was doing all that she kept thinking that her mother would come in the door. In the preceding month she had moved in the world where her mother was less a person than an idea, like the mainland, like the moon. Now every second was the second when her mother reached her hand out toward the door from the outside, the second before she turned the knob. She would hear the turn of the knob and she herself would turn and then she would fall to the floor and she would lie naked on the floor like a baby, and her mother would lift her up by the armpits, but first she would kiss her eyebrows and smooth her hair back and sing her a song. The time in which all this was about to happen was without duration, it was a vast white sheet of time, time like a snowfield, and when the door did open and Darcy felt relief burst painfully all through her body, and when it was Marie touching her forehead and speaking in a quiet voice, the snowfield did not end but went on outside and above normal time, and Darcy felt herself returning to and leaving it all the time she and Marie were speaking.

"Do you want something to eat?"

"No."

"Do you want something to help you sleep?"

Now the pills in Marie's hand were blue.

"No."

"Is there anything I can do for you?"

A calm spot was floating across normal time.

"I want to see her body."

They walked through the courtyard, past a trellis on which a flowering vine was growing, and then down a covered walkway to a large building, and through the silent halls of the building into a room lit with bright, cold bulbs. The walls in the room were full of drawers, and Marie looked at a chart on a table and then pulled out one of the drawers, and Darcy saw her mother's face inside it and then she cried without thinking about anything.

Marie tried to touch her shoulders but she moved away. Her mother's face looked so familiar that it shocked her. It didn't look like her sleeping face—it looked like her face in the morning when she had finished sleeping, when she was leaving her eyes shut and letting the not-yet-hot morning air pass across her eyelids and her shut lips and the smooth loose landscape of her skin. Darcy had often wanted to take her mother's face in both hands at that time of the morning, and to encircle it like a cherished object, a small gem or bead. She had never done it, for fear of disturbing her, but she did it now, and the skin was cold and waxy but her mother's face looked as she always thought it would look, like something contained and boundaried, something that could be treasured and kept safe. Darcy sobbed into the silent room. The engines of the world had failed.

"Do you want me to cut you some of her hair?" Marie asked.

"No," Darcy said.

Then Marie asked again and Darcy realized she hadn't said it out loud.

"No."

"Do you want to go back to your room?"

"It isn't my room."

"It is now."

Darcy allowed herself to be led. She remembered the way back but she let Marie hold her up and guide her down the walkway and back into the room. She sat on the bed and let Marie pull the covers up over her lap, and when Marie left she looked at the wall. Then Marie came back holding a dish of shell noodles with butter on them, and the bland creamy taste made her think of the early evenings when she still had a bedtime, when she held the dishrag while her mother washed the pan. When her mother whispered to her in their private language before she went to sleep. Marie touched Darcy's fingers with her fingers as she took the empty dish away, and that tiny tenderness was enough to make Darcy sob again. Marie sat down on the bed and Darcy clutched at her with her eyes shut, and Marie put her hand on Darcy's back, and the touch was not what Darcy wanted but it was not comfortless, and after a while Darcy let her go and turned away and slept.

10

Darcy did not keep track of the days she spent in bed, ignoring the light from the window, sleeping and waking and taking the two blue pills Marie always left by her bedside and sliding into sleep again. The sleep the pills brought was heavy and solid, and it lay across her for eight or ten black and seamless hours. Only at the end did a few pallid dreams squeak through, dreams of lost objects and broken teeth. Her mother moved through the periphery of these dreams—Darcy found one of her socks, just cast off, the smell of her foot still on it, or saw her hair as she walked out the door. Once she was so sure her mother was calling to her from another room that she hopped to the door and banged on it until Marie came. Her face was cool and sympathetic. That day Darcy began hiding her pills.

She kept them in the bottom drawer of the dresser, in the pocket of a warm-looking gray sweater. She held it up to herself first—it was small, but cut for a man, as were the dark green waterproof jacket and the two white thermal shirts that lay beside it. When she started saving up the pills, she had enough energy to wonder why Tyson would keep those clothes around. Only rich idiots wore sweaters like those, sometimes with the armpits cut out, and sometimes with knit hats that made them pass out in the heat. But these weren't stylish clothes—they probably came from the mainland, Tyson had probably worn them while he watched the winter closing in and hatched his plan for not being a misfit anymore. Darcy liked to think of the mainland now; she liked to imagine walking across the snow forever, the sun always just about to rise behind her back. This was what she hoped death would be like.

She didn't know how many pills she'd need, but she didn't want to underestimate—too few and she might make herself half-dead forever, fry her stomach or cut her legs off from her brain. So she watched her stock grow from two to four to six to eight, all the while scrambling for her bed whenever she heard Marie's footsteps, feigning a drugged stupor when she came into the room. Her new plan lifted the feeling of pointlessness from her days. She fantasized about death the way girls in school had fantasized about boys. Epifanio Beltran from across the hall had died when she was five or six, and later Augusta had told her that just before his eyes went still they danced all around the room, like it was full of people and he couldn't get enough of looking at all of them. Later she had asked her mother about death, and her mother had said that when you die, you see not your life flashing before your eyes like people say, but all the possible lives you could've lived, like a tree growing outward from the root of you, with an infinite number of branches. And then she had asked her whether her father was such a tree now, and Sarah had said no, because death, like life, had many stages, and we only know the first one, from people coming back after bus accidents, or heart attacks, or being pulled from freezing water. Darcy didn't believe any of that anymore, but it excited her, like rumors of a famous person she was just about to meet.

When she had twenty pills, Darcy decided it was enough. She waited until just after Marie came in with her lunch—a turkey sandwich with a round of fresh tomato peeking out between the bread—and then she washed all twenty pills down with a glass of orange juice. She had to do it in two shifts, because she gagged on all twenty and had to spit them, blue-bleeding, into her palm. But once she got them all down, a feeling of limpid calm flowed all around her, like warm water, like hands cradling her body. She lay back in the bed and felt herself being gently carried toward death. First she lost the sense of her body, of all the fingers and toes to manage and keep track of, all the troublesome breaths to take. Then she felt her brain begin to slacken, to go smooth, until the process of living was not a movement from thought to thought but instead a pleasant, static stillness, like a thread lying on the ground. Then she felt her memories begin to melt, so that even the ground fell away, and she was just a thread in space, a thread with no mother and no father and no future, no pain and no joy and no need and no anger.

Then she began to itch. The feeling started where her feet would have been if she still had feet, but since she had moved past all consciousness of her body it was just a burning, niggling field all around the end of the bed, and spreading up, up, up until Darcy was nothing but a bed-length white-hot rod of unbearably itchy air. A human being can scratch, but Darcy was no longer human, and she couldn't mold any part of the air into fingers to scratch any other part. She sizzled. She boiled. A thinking part of her came awake and wondered if this was dying. She wondered if it would last forever, if she had gone to hell and been condemned to spend eternity as an itch. She had no sense of her muscles or limbs, but she managed to gain a kind of purchase on the itch itself, to move it in poorly controlled spasms. She could make the itch writhe, and she could make it buck. When it bucked hard enough, it moved a little toward the edge of the bed. With great effort, she managed to buck three more times, and then the itch was falling, the itch was lower than it had been before, and it was turning inside out, and bucking from the inside, and bucking, and bucking, and then someone's hands were on Darcy's head, and she understood that she had a head, and that she was kneeling on the floor in a pool of blue-green vomit.

"Drink this," said a voice.

The itch was still very strong. It was attached to her skin now, and she was scratching, scratching, scratching, but each scratch seemed to open up a new fissure in her skin for the itch to seep down into.

"Don't scratch," said the voice, "just drink."

Darcy's hand took the glass, and something chalky was in her throat, and then, slowly, the itch began to subside, until it was weak enough that she could breathe and look around and understand that the person with her was Marie.

"They're not lethal," she said. "I wouldn't have given them to you if they were. You're just going to feel uncomfortable for a while."

Darcy rolled herself into a ball. Her skin felt like it had been sanded. It was a great effort to find her lips and make them move.

"Why?" she asked.

"Why what? Why didn't I let you kill yourself?"

Nodding felt like lifting a building.

Marie sighed. "I thought about killing myself once," she said. "But I didn't, and I'm glad. I thought you deserved the same chance."

The words came heavy out of Darcy's throat. "Why didn't you?" she asked. Then she shut her eyes and let her head rest against her knees.

"Unlike you," Marie said, "I never loved my parents. My dad wasn't around and my mom's response to the cold was to drink until she felt warm. I had a brother, six years younger than me. A few days after he was born, he was crying, and Mom was off somewhere, so I stuck my finger in his crib and he closed his whole hand around it, just sealed it in there. And he stopped crying. Up until then nobody had paid attention to me, I hardly ever even heard my name. So I decided, this is what this finger is for, this is what I'm for."

She paused, and put her hand on Darcy's shoulder as if to make sure she was awake.

"I'm listening," Darcy said.

But she didn't lift her head. She liked to imagine she was some-where else—back in her apartment even, listening to a made-up story. She heard Marie take a breath and then go on.

"After that all the things I had to do—I had to kill our cat so we could eat, and starting when I was twelve I had to give our land-lord a hand job every month to keep our heat on—everything was okay to me because I was responsible for my brother, I had to keep him safe. And because of me he didn't know how bad things were. He thought we had plenty of money; he didn't know that the reason people were leaving was because otherwise we were going to die. That was enough for me—because he could sleep at night, I could sleep.

"When I was fifteen I started nurses' training, and I was away from the house every afternoon. My brother didn't have school anymore—they'd canceled everything except nursing and med school and some of the indoor agriculture programs—so I showed him how to manage on his own. Every morning I got out a ramen packet and a vitamin pill, and I showed him what to burn if the heat went out, and I gave him a wristwatch and a rule about playing outside. Five minutes, I said, then he had to go in. I didn't want to make him stay inside all the time—I wanted him to get to be a kid, at least a little. And for a long time it worked. He'd eat his ramen, take a vitamin pill, go outside for five minutes, and then later I'd come home and he'd tell me a silly story about the animals he'd seen, even though we both knew there were no animals left.

"Then I met a boy. He was a nursing student too. He was two years younger than me, and he was missing a couple of teeth, but I was so happy to make out with someone for no reason, not because I needed something from him, that I started staying late at work to be with him. We used to kiss in the corner of the hospital waiting room because it was heated and they wouldn't kick us out. Once I let him put his hand under my shirt and touch my breasts while a kid with frostbite was sobbing right next to us. That's how we all were then—we'd lost all sense of the proper separation of things. That night I got home late; it was already dark. I looked for my brother in the kitchen, and he wasn't there. Then I looked in the bedroom, and he wasn't there. Then I checked Mom's bedroom and the bathroom and by that time I had started to panic, I was running and crying and screaming his name.

"When I got to the backyard I saw him right away. He was lying in the snow with his hands on his chest, like he was playing dead. And maybe he had been. I don't know if he forgot about the time, or if he just lay down in the snow and it felt good to be there, or if I'd made him feel so safe in the world that he didn't take the five-minute rule seriously, but when I touched him he was already so cold he burned my hand.

"After that I wanted to die too. It would've been easy—I could've just lain down beside him. People turned up in snowbanks all the time then, and you never knew if they'd been caught by a blizzard or just decided to give up. The night he died my mom didn't come home, and I just stayed up, thinking about whether I should do it. But in the morning I decided I wouldn't. I decided that trying to protect my brother had made me strong, and that I would get even stronger, and that I should use that strength instead of throwing it away. And I have."

"Use it for what?" Darcy asked.

"For good, believe it or not," Marie said. "I know you think the island's a mess, and it is, but how many civil wars have we had? How many riots? We took twenty thousand starving, desperate people, uprooted them and planted them in a place that was the opposite of everything they knew, and we gave them lots of the comforts of home. Some people said we couldn't have strawberries, or beef, or even electricity anymore—we proved them wrong. We could've done a lot worse."

Darcy thought about the chaos Marie described, about the story Yuka had told her about the food riot at the co-op. She wondered if Marie was right. She looked up at her and saw the steeliness gone from her face. She saw right down to the bottom of her, and she saw need and sorrow and helplessness calcified over time so that an entire life—a life of power and influence—could be built on top of them. But they were quick at their core—warm and soft like marrow—and something in Darcy quickened too, in sympathy. She took Marie's hands and placed them around her head. Marie seemed to understand—she held them there. And Darcy felt, in spite of everything, a tenuous kind of peace.

The next day Darcy woke up early. The pills and Marie's chalky antidote had left a bitter taste in her mouth and a heavy, full-body soreness. But her memory was clear. She remembered clinging to Marie, believing in her. Maybe they could work together, maybe Darcy could help dismantle the Seaguards, use their wages to shore up the food banks so that no one would have to go hungry at the end of the month. It sounded tempting, the idea of living here, with plenty of good food and open space and comfort.

She imagined having her own room, calling this room hers. She got up from the bed, tapped the rocking chair to make it go back and forth on its wooden rocker. She wasn't going to convince herself that she had grown up here, but already she was beginning to get used to real meat, to a soft bed without a valley in the center. Clear, unfetid air smelled normal to her now. In not so long this would feel like her home, and maybe Marie would feel like her family. She didn't know Marie, and she wasn't sure she liked her, but she saw how their lives might line up, and how that might come to feel like kinship.

Of course, it would mean breaking with Ansel and Sunshine. But Darcy had no way of knowing if Ansel's reforms would work—maybe people were too venal to elect their own leaders honestly. In any case, he hadn't shown up, and that in itself meant his plans weren't as good as he thought they were. She had been here at least two weeks, and in the haze of her sorrow she had almost forgotten him. Now it looked like he had forgotten her too.

But accepting Marie's offer would mean accepting if not Tyson himself, then at least his way of governing the island. Would that be like saying that her mother had died for a cause that was essentially wrongheaded? Darcy was angry at her mother, angry at her for not telling her about Daniel, for not telling her everything she had ever known. How was Darcy supposed to know now if Daniel had been right? She tried to imagine her life taking place on the mainland, adapted somehow to the snow. Would she wear a bearskin? Would she eat icicles? Would she have to build up a layer of fat all over her body to hold in the heat? She couldn't picture it—couldn't picture anything but the island, its neighborhoods replicas of the older neighborhoods, its shows reenactments of older lives, its food a mockery of older food. What would it be like to make something that was actually new?

She tried to remember if Sarah ever said anything about how the island should be run. But all she remembered were the games, the songs, a fabric of playacting so thick that by the time she was sixteen Darcy sometimes found her mother frivolous, unacceptably childlike. She remembered shouting at her once, over a cheese-food can filled with hot water, "I'm not going to pretend it's fucking soup!" And that one warning, whenever she asked too many questions: "Don't get stuck in the past." Was that her way of condemning Tyson's nostalgia, his desire to make the island like the mainland, at least for a few people? No matter how many times she played each conversation in her mind, Darcy couldn't extract a philosophy from her mother's life. But her mother had fought, and in the end had died, for something. Whatever that thing was—and she still wasn't entirely sure—Darcy owed it some honor.

When Marie came with her breakfast—strawberries with sugar today, and jiggly poached eggs—Darcy asked to talk to the other prisoners.

"They knew my mom," she said. "I need to talk to them before I decide if I can help you."

Marie looked annoyed.

"You can," she said. "But I'm not sure if it will do much good. They're not exactly the most mentally stable people."

"What does that mean?" Darcy asked.

"Look, I think what Tyson did to those ships was horrible. I told him that at the time. But we can't even be sure Daniel sent them at all. And even if he did, to pin all your hopes for some kind of revolution on someone you knew when you were a child—it just seems a little crazy."

Anger quickened Darcy's blood.

"My mom wasn't crazy," she said.

"Of course she wasn't," Marie said. "I just mean, their plans were impractical. I don't know what you're going to learn from them."

"I want to find out for myself," Darcy said.

"Well," Marie said, "I'm not sure when I can take you to them. I'm not even sure where the guards are holding them right now."

All the doubts that had been ghosts the day before began to take on clarity and substance.

"If you're so close to Tyson, how come the guards don't listen to you? How come they don't at least tell you their plans?"

"They were loyal to him, not me. A lot of them thought of me as an interloper."

"For all those years?" Darcy asked. "When you did all that stuff for him?"

Marie sighed. Then she looked at Darcy with a new fixity.

"Darcy," she said, "you know me. We've had the same life. If you trust yourself, you should trust me."

Darcy thought of her life. She thought of the things she had done to get what she wanted. She thought of Armin, she thought of the circus, she thought of Glock. She knew she would have lied to save her mother's life. Would she have killed? She cast her mind back into the time before she knew of her mother's death, a time whose innocence disgusted her but that was heart-wrenchingly recent and easy to return to. She imagined a choice between her mother's life and someone else's. She found herself wishing that she had that choice.

"If we really have the same life," Darcy said, "that makes me trust you less, not more."

"What are you saying?" Marie asked.

"I can't help you. My answer is no."

Marie's eyes hardened then, and Darcy saw a face she hadn't seen before. It was angry, and thwarted, and grimly determined to push past the thwarting. Darcy was sure she herself had worn this face often enough.

They put her in a hot room with no windows. A woman was in the room already, cuffed to a wrought-iron rack that looked like it had once held gardening equipment, and when she turned her head to look at Darcy, Darcy recognized her little puffy mouth immediately. She was even wearing the same cheap skirt she had on when she came to Darcy's apartment the night before her mother disappeared. Tyson's guards had probably kidnapped her that night. She recognized, too, the family resemblance—the small, shrewd eyes spaced far apart, the round, compact head. Her hands were no longer shaking.

"You're Esther Rosen?" Darcy asked.

"Long time no see," Esther said. The wink she gave Darcy seemed to signal less the survival of humor than the surrender of seriousness.

A guard shoved Darcy down and cuffed her to the rack next to Esther. Behind them was a pile of feed sacks labeled "Deer," "Rabbit," and "Bird." The room smelled like fertilizer and urine. The guard left, locking the door two ways behind him.

Looking at Esther made Darcy cry again. What if she had never come to the apartment at all? It was terrible how easy it was to imagine her mother still in the world, terrible how plausible it seemed.

"Cheer up," Esther said, in a wry voice. "At least you're alive."

"That doesn't cheer me up," Darcy said.

"Yeah, I don't blame you. There's not a lot to do in here. I kept hoping they'd pick me, just to relieve the boredom."

"Pick you?" Darcy asked. Esther's dry voice absorbed some of her sorrow like sand absorbs a spill.

"You know," Esther said. She pointed a finger gun to her head and shot it.

"They said they shot my mom while she was trying to escape," Darcy said.

"If by 'trying to escape' you mean 'sitting on the floor in this room,' then you got it."

Darcy's skin shrank against her flesh.

"Why did they kill her?" she asked. "To keep her quiet?"

"More like to get the rest of us to talk," Esther said. "They wanted us to tell them where Daniel is, so they could send a ship to finish his people off. They kept killing us one by one, hoping to get the rest of us to cave. Now I'm the only one left, and I think they're out of ideas."

"Who's 'they'?" Darcy asked. "The guards?"

"And Marie. With your mom and Cricket, she pulled the trigger herself."

Darcy remembered clinging to Marie's body like a child. She could've reached out and snapped Marie's neck with her hands. She could have gouged her eyes out. She cried again, this time tears of rage that left a sour taste in her mouth.

"What was this all for," she asked finally, "what was the point of it?"

Esther's voice lost some of its cynicism for a moment. "For Daniel," she said.

"What does that even mean?" Darcy asked. "Why did you guys do all this for him?"

"When we were little," Esther said, "we had no one to watch out for us. Your mom, me, my sister"—Darcy caught a hint of bitterness in the word—"a few others. Our parents were dead, or deadbeats, and the grown-ups made sure we got fed, but that was about it. Then Daniel started teaching us. I already liked him— he showed me a type of bark you could chew to be less hungry, and he knew how to go walking outside for a long time without getting too cold. But after we heard about the island he started spending every afternoon with us. He taught us how to read a map, and how to navigate with the sun and the stars. He taught us history, especially the American Revolution. To me it was sad, all these people who thought they were starting a new country, and there we were at the end of it. But Daniel always looked happy, he looked upbeat. And when we were almost ready to go, he said some things none of us understood at the time. He said that Tyson wanted to give us back what we had before the Ice Age, but we couldn't really have it back. He said it would only give us more problems, just like it had the first time around. He said the past was a trap, and we had to break out of it if we wanted to be happy."

"My mom used to say something like that," Darcy said.

"We all did," said Esther. "We got obsessed with it. We came here, and it wasn't anything like what we'd been promised. We couldn't get jobs, we couldn't get apartments, we were pariahs. Now I know it was because Tyson never trusted Daniel, and he wanted to keep anyone who had contact with him from getting too much power. But then we didn't know what to think; we just knew we were getting shat on. Even before things started to go to hell—before the cave-ins, before the sidewalks started to melt, before the last boat came and there wasn't enough food to go around any-more—we were radicals. But we didn't really know what to do. When they finished Manhattanville we protested the ribbon-cutting ceremony—we wanted them to call it New Pacifica Central. When they built the Las Vegas Strip we vandalized a casino—we thought they should make an island theme park instead. We were angry, and we were just casting around. The thing is, Daniel had told us he would send for us. When we left the co-op, he left too. He said he was going south. If he found a place, somewhere we could live and not freeze, he would send a ship from there. We protested, and we made a few crappy little fertilizer bombs, and we waited. We waited for years, and he didn't come."

"Why didn't you try to get rid of Tyson on your own, back then?" Darcy asked.

"We were young, and we didn't really know what we were doing. It had been kind of fun, the whole radical thing, but as we got a little older it wasn't fun anymore. Cricket went to jail and came back with this awful fungal disease in her eye. We had to keep moving to worse and worse places because the island was filling up. We started out squatting in a building under construction in Manhattanville—we had this whole ground floor to our-selves—but by the end we were in the back room of a grocery store in Little Los Angeles owned by a woman Duncan was sleep-ing with. And it used to be easy to scavenge food—mangoes, fish, stuff like that—but the island got more built up and the ocean got more poisonous and we started getting really hungry.

"This whole time Sarah was in charge. We never said it—in principle we were against the idea of having just one leader—but she had this quality that made you want to listen to her. She had always been Daniel's favorite, and it was easy to see why. When you were with her, it felt like you didn't need anyone else and neither did she. And even though all of us felt that way, it seemed absolutely real to each of us. Later I thought it must be some wanting in her that made her that way, some loneliness. But at first it made all of us love her."

It was hard to imagine Sarah a leader, the same person who so often acted like a child instead of a mother. But it was easy to imagine her making everyone she knew feel like the only person in the world. Darcy wondered if it was the same wanting that made her mother seem so far away some evenings, staring off at the apartment wall, or mornings, frozen while brushing her teeth. What did she want?

"When things got bad," Esther went on, "people blamed her. I don't remember who started it, but the flip side of our loving her was feeling really bitter about her. Everybody wanted to be her favorite, and we started to resent the hold she had over us. We called a meeting, and we sat in our little circle like we always did, and we told her she was dragging us down and we needed her to leave the group. She didn't cry, she didn't argue, but I saw all the light go out of her face, and I realized we were all she had, and now she had nothing. I regretted it then, I wanted to take it back, but it was too late. She left in the morning.

"After that there was nothing holding us together. Nobody stepped up, nobody could make us feel like she could. We heard she had a kid, got a job. We kept up the pretense of having meetings for a while, but a lot of us moved out of the grocery store, mostly to worse places. I got hooked on solvent. Duncan lived on the street, Simone was turning tricks. And then, ten years ago, when we were totally broken-down and useless, Daniel finally sent a boat."

Darcy saw why Sarah told her to forget the past—it was Daniel's idea, but it must've been hers too, her way of blocking things out. But Sarah hadn't abandoned the past. Esther had come back that night, the whole thing had begun again. Something must've pulled her back in.

"And then what?" Darcy asked.

"And then nothing, for a while. We all suspected that the Hawaiian story was fake, that the boat had really been Daniel. But none of us knew for sure, and none of us knew what to do. Then, two years ago, Sarah got in touch with me again. She said she'd made a mistake. She said she never should have let us kick her out of the movement. She said life was getting worse all the time — the solvent, the cave-ins, all of it. But she said she didn't care about any of it — all of Hell City could fall into the ocean and she'd let it — but what she couldn't stand was that her daughter had to drop out of school and get a job. She said even we had school, remember? And I did.

"She thought she knew where Daniel was, and she thought he'd try to come again. She thought maybe we could overthrow Tyson and teach everyone to live differently, to adapt. No more buses, she said, no more Seafiber. She thought Daniel could show us how to live on the island like it was an island, not a bad copy of home.

"I didn't really buy it. I didn't think Daniel was coming back. He could have been killed in the first attack, he could've been frozen out. And even if he was still alive, why would he risk another trip? Still, I started getting in touch with some of the other orphans. A lot of us were getting our act together back then — Duncan was working as a janitor, Simone was in the Seafiber plant. We met a few times. And then the second ship really did come."

"How did you know it was him?" Darcy asked. "Your brother said something about a symbol."

Darcy saw Esther stiffen in the dim light. When she spoke, her voice had a new urgency—she sounded more like the woman in the hallway a month ago than the broken-down one who had winked at Darcy.

"You saw my brother?" she asked. "Is he okay?"

"I don't know," Darcy said. "I think they got him too."

The rack vibrated as Esther slammed her cuffed hand against it.

"Fuck," she said. "I thought at least being such an asshole would keep him safe."

"I'm sorry," Darcy said. "I think he thought so too."

A single sound came from Esther's throat, a half-swallowed sob.

"It was so hard for him growing up," she said. "You'd think a bunch of hippie kids would be all kind and gentle. It was bad enough we were orphans, but to act like a boy and pee like a girl—I always thought if I'd protected him better, maybe he wouldn't have cut me off the way he did."

"He told me he felt like shit about that," Darcy said.

"He should," Esther said. "Fucker. Maybe he's okay, though. Maybe they just wanted information from him."

"I hope so," Darcy said.

Esther took a deep breath.

"We didn't have a lot of books in the co-op. A lot of them got torn up for toilet paper or burned to keep warm. By the time Daniel was teaching us, the only kids' book left was called *An Animal Atlas of the West Coast*."

Darcy felt a little pulse of shock.

"I have that book," she said. "I mean, I used to have it. It was my mom's."

"He gave it to her," Esther said. "That was something that used to piss us off, that she was the one who got it. Anyway, we liked the book when we were kids because it had all these animals we'd never seen, animals that were extinct by the time we were born. Ducks, mountain lions, salmon. We had it all memorized, where each of the animals went."

"So do I," Darcy said.

"Well, the ships had mountain lions painted on their sails."

Darcy remembered the mountain lion, its tawny coat, its black eyes. According to the map, it lived in Southern California—below its feet were the words "Los Angeles."

"At least, that's what Sarah said," Esther went on. "She had some Seaguard friend at the docks who told her everything."

"I met him," Darcy said. "I talked to him."

She remembered the Seaguard's young, stupid face, how sweet it had been to hear anything, however slight, about her mother. Now that she had heard so much from Esther, she felt that her mother had been replaced by someone entirely strange to her, someone she would have to get to know all over again. But this stranger was dead, and beyond the reach of her knowledge, and she had only Esther to reconstruct her.

"Why didn't she tell me about any of this?" Darcy asked, hurt.

"Honestly, I don't know," Esther said. "Maybe she was worried you'd tell someone else."

"There was no one else," Darcy said, remembering the days and weeks and years of going to sleep with her mother, and waking up to her, and leaving her and coming home to her, and speaking to her in half sentences, in fragments, as though everything that could be said or known was already shared between them.

"Maybe she wanted to shield you, then. Maybe she thought the less you knew, the less likely Tyson was to come after you. Or maybe she just wanted you to be free to do what you wanted, without thinking about Daniel or Tyson or anybody."

But I was never free, Darcy wanted to say. *Even if we had had money, even if I didn't have to work and I could've gone to the University like the rich kids, I never could have left her.* An alien feeling came over her then, like standing slightly to one side of herself. She wondered if she was free now.

"Was it worth it?" Darcy asked. "Was Daniel worth my mom dying?"

"You know," Esther said, "I don't really know much about Daniel. I couldn't even tell you what he looked like. I remember what he taught us, but after all these years, I could be remembering it wrong. For us, the word 'Daniel' meant 'There is life outside this island.' It meant 'There is life outside Tyson.' It meant 'There is a way of living that is different from this one.' If I were still free, I'd be trying to get to the mainland right now, just on the strength of that."

I I

They were in the room together long enough that time grew shapeless, stretched beyond all its familiar increments. Darcy cried, and slept, and cried again, and once she heard Esther crying, but she stopped when she realized Darcy was awake. At first they were embarrassed by their proximity, but then in the dimness and tedium of the dayless hours, Darcy began to think of Esther the way a rat thinks of its den mates, instinctively, without guilt or courtesy. When neither of them had moved in a long time she scooted a little along the floor, to circulate the air between them. She grew hungry and was surprised at how uncomfortable the feeling could still make her. At one point the guards brought water, but no food. Darcy asked Esther how they were supposed to piss, and Esther suggested that she unbutton her jumpsuit so at least it didn't get wet. By contorting her waist and lifting her hips, she was able to do this with her cuffed right hand.

When the guards brought Nathaniel in, both the women were asleep. Darcy woke to the sound of the door and saw Esther's face turn smooth and vulnerable as a child's. The guards shoved Nathaniel to the floor and then cuffed him to the rack between Darcy and Esther. His chin and cheeks were smeared with blood.

He smelled like shit. He and Esther looked at each other with a terrible wariness. Nathaniel said, "I'm sorry." Nathaniel held Esther's gaze and Esther stared back, blank-eyed, and then she moved her head, awkwardly because she was stiff and constrained by the handcuffs, and laid it against Nathaniel's shoulder.

For a long time they sat like that, wordless, and Darcy felt freshly and piercingly alone. Finally, when she knew she had to either cry or speak, she asked Nathaniel, "Did they get Ansel?"

His voice was muddled, as if some of his teeth were broken or missing, but at the same time there was a strange new steadiness to it.

"I don't think so," he said. "They wanted me to tell them where he was."

"What did you say?" Darcy asked.

"I lied," he said. "I told them he was at a GreenValley processing plant in Lower Chicagoland. They weren't happy when they found out it wasn't true"—he wiped at his face—"but it might have bought Ansel another day."

"Who's Ansel?" Esther asked.

"We hooked up with some revolutionaries," Darcy explained. "Last-boaters. They were going to try to get me out of here."

"That's great," said Esther, animation returning to her face. "Your mom always hoped that would happen, that the last-boaters would rise up too."

"Yeah, well," said Darcy, "don't get your hopes up too much."

"I thought Ansel had a plan," Nathaniel said.

Darcy hated to disappoint him. She saw that he had given deeply of himself to get Ansel that extra day, that he had dredged up a long-disused and nearly forgotten strength. She was worried the guards had humiliated him, that they had not been satisfied with a simple beating.

"Maybe he does," Darcy said. "But I don't know. A while ago I met someone who grew up with Ansel. She said he was a free-loader, that none of his schemes amounted to anything. I didn't believe it then, but now I kind of do."

Nathaniel made a motion that Darcy realized was his attempt to shake his swollen head.

"I don't think so," he said. "I think he's coming for us. All we have to do is wait."

He looked at Esther then, and asked, shyly, as though he had not been able to bring himself to ask before, "How are you?"

"How are you?" Esther asked, and then they both laughed, rueful and also tender, and Darcy thought, These people deserve to get out of here.

"I think we should try to get out," she said out loud. "I think we should try to find a way to escape."

"We did try," said Esther. "We tried leaning over and pulling the rack out of the wall—it won't budge. We tried wearing down the handcuffs on the rack—they won't wear. We tried playing sick and getting the guard to come close, then kicking him in the balls—that's how Duncan died."

"Duncan's dead?" Nathaniel asked.

"All of them are dead," said Esther. Her voice was flat.

"I'm so sorry," Nathaniel said, and Darcy barely nodded—to acknowledge him any more than that would have made her cry again.

"Listen," she said instead, "what if I try to talk to the guards next time they come in? Maybe I can convince them that Marie's crazy, and they'll let us go."

"You can try," Esther said, "but I doubt they'll go for it."

"So that's it?" Darcy asked. "You think we should sit here and wait for them to kill us?"

"I don't think they're going to kill us right now," Esther said. "If I had to guess, I'd say either they'll find your friend and kill him, or if they have too much trouble doing that, they'll come interrogate you. Once they've got him and whatever other information they want, they'll kill you. As for me, they might keep me here my whole life, trying to get Daniel's address out of me."

"Or they'll threaten to kill me," Nathaniel said.

Esther turned her face away.

"That must be why they kept me alive," he said. "Whatever they want from you, they probably think if they hold a gun to my head, you'll tell them."

Esther's voice was small and hard, like a bead.

"I would," she said.

"You can't," Nathaniel said. "I haven't done anything for you my whole life; you can't do that for me."

"Maybe it won't come to that," Darcy said. "They're probably busy with Ansel right now. And they're probably confused about Tyson. The next time a guard comes in, I'm going to try and convince him. Maybe it'll work."

"Yeah," Esther said, "maybe."

Her voice was grim, and grimness fell on all of them for what felt like hours, and Darcy sat and smelled Nathaniel's blood and felt despair. Would it have been better if the pills had worked, if she were dead now? She wished she believed, like the Talking Birds people, that death would reunite her with her mother. She wished anything could. She thought that no pleasure could penetrate that room anymore, but after a while Nathaniel and Esther began speaking again, in quiet voices. They sounded awkward at first, but soon their voices took on an identical rhythm, a rhythm they must have agreed upon in childhood, unconsciously, in a meeting of their half-formed brains.

"You remember when we all got pneumonia?" Esther asked.

"And the baby died?"

"That's right. Unity Ross's baby. She was holding it in the kitchen, next to the stove. Like if she could just warm it up, it would come back to life again."

"I don't remember that part," Nathaniel said.

"Where were you? Everyone was there. We were all coughing and comforting her and trying to get the baby away. It would've been funny if it wasn't so awful."

"I wasn't there that day. I didn't get pneumonia, remember?"

"You didn't?"

"I never did. All the other kids were coughing and wheezing in their sleeping bags all day, but for some reason I never got sick. Then Daniel picked me to go with him on a trip."

"A trip?" Esther asked. "How come you never told me?"

"I think I tried," Nathaniel said, "but you were so sick, and then the baby died, and then not long after that we all left anyway. But he took me to the old baseball field down by the creek. It was only maybe a quarter mile away but he put me in three coats and two balaclavas and goggles. I was scared of freezing but he said I wouldn't if I stuck with him. He said it was good for me to learn how to be in the cold. We had to stop once on the way in an abandoned house, and we lit a little fire in the living room and warmed our hands. The living room had a big TV and a stereo and a fancy lamp, and I asked if we were going to take anything, and he said, 'There's nothing here we need.'

"When we got to the field he let me climb up a snowdrift and hang on the chain-link backstop. The grown-ups used to tell stories about baseball, remember, and I tried to imagine people on the field. I didn't understand how the game worked, so I just assumed all the players would huddle together, like we did, for warmth. Then I saw Daniel in the stands, chopping up the wooden benches with an ax.

" 'What if someone wants to play baseball?' I called to him.

"And he stopped what he was doing, and he came over to me, and he looked almost angry.

" 'It's too late for baseball,' he told me. 'We fucked that up, just like everything else.'

"And then I started to cry a little bit, and the tears were freezing to my cheeks, but he held me to him and I could smell that he was sweating from chopping benches, and it was the first time I realized you could actually get hot living there, you could actually sweat. And then he rubbed my hands between his for a minute, and he said he would teach me a new game.

"He took me to the creek, to a place where a little waterfall had frozen solid. He stood on the ice first, and when it held him, he sat me on top of the waterfall and said, 'Ready?' I said I was, and he gave me a push, and I slid all the way down and onto a flat place in the creek, and I spun around. The waterfall couldn't have been very high, but it felt dangerous, maybe just because I was finally playing outside — anyway, I asked if I could do it again. He said no, it was too cold, but if I took a bath in ice water every day instead of water warmed up on the stove, then I would get a special kind of fat on my back and I could go outside more. He said he'd been doing that for years, and now he could stay outside for an hour or more before he started getting too cold to think straight. He said we should all be doing it, getting used to the cold instead of clinging to the warm stove like babies. I was afraid of him again then, and I didn't understand, and when he brought me back to the house I ran right to the kitchen to get warm.

"I didn't really pay attention when Daniel was teaching us. I didn't really think about anything he said until I was in my thirties and we were trying to make the strawberries at GreenValley. We were burning forty jars of solvent a day just to grow one little twisted strawberry plant, and I thought, maybe it's too late for strawberries. Maybe we need to let that one go."

"It's not just letting go," Esther said. "He wanted us to move on. If he were here now, he'd probably tell us to enjoy the fucking mangoes. And not dissolve our whole island just so some people can pretend they're living like they used to."

"I guess," Nathaniel said. "To be honest, though, I liked the way I was living. It was nice while it lasted."

Then Esther told Nathaniel about her life in the years they were estranged, about breaking into the refinery and stealing solvent directly from the tank, about getting caught and spending six months in jail in the same cell as a woman who had murdered her husband when their child died of parrot fever, about getting out and meeting a nun from Our Lady of the Talking Birds who helped her get clean; and when she paused and she and Nathaniel sat for a moment in the silent satisfaction of their reunion, Darcy spoke up.

"Will you tell me a story about my mom?" she asked. "From the mainland?"

They were quiet, as though it took some time to come back from the private world to which they'd gone. Then Esther said, "I have one.

"One day we snuck out of the co-op," she began. "Sarah and I. One of the older girls was supposed to be watching us but she'd gone off with this man, Simon. Simon always had things to trade— I don't know how he got them. Once he gave me an apple. It was kind of wrinkled but it was still sweet inside, and in return I let him watch me while I ate it. Anyway. We were eight. We had our indoor coats and the indoor coats of two boys we knew, who we bribed with our jerky rations. We were so hot in all those coats we thought it would be easy. We'd been on lockdown six months by then—no one outside except a few of the men to fix the roof when the snow came through—but we thought they were just trying to keep us in line, making rules to make rules.

"They kept the keys in the office, on a big ring. We were on the honor system not to take them, same as with the pantry, but everyone had been stealing from the pantry for months, so we figured we could take the keys too. Nobody saw us. We snuck along the wall like when we played spies. The tool-room door was the easiest. The grown-ups didn't go there much. Still, we were expecting someone to catch us.

"We stood against the rusty lawn mower—it was a joke at that point; sometimes the grown-ups got it out when they had parties and pretended to mow the floor—and we looked back into the house. The tool room was next to the dining room—Emmett and his daughter Rose were rolling sleeping bags up and putting out chairs for dinner. They didn't notice us. Sarah put the key in the lock and then it was like we were sucked out, like the outside wanted us.

"At first we didn't feel the cold. We went jumping and flapping around the yard, shouting, 'This is *nothing! This* is nothing!'

"We made for the trees so they wouldn't see us from the windows. The first line, the old apple orchard the grown-ups talked about—the trees were all dead. They were bare and black with nothing on them to hold snow. It sounds strange, but we made fun of those trees. We had so little to go on then. We made our gloves into claws and stuck out our tongues and bugged our eyes and groaned, 'I can't...I can't take it anymore.'

"We thought we were real tough. We looked up at the sky like we imagined trees would when their souls were going to tree heaven. Then my eyeballs started to burn. The pine trees were twenty feet beyond the apple orchard. By the time we reached them I couldn't feel my hands inside my gloves, and that's when I knew how really cold it was.

"Back when we'd been allowed outside sometimes, we'd learned that with every ten-degree drop, the cold became a new kind of thing. At ten it was brisk and energetic, like splashing your face with water, like having a dog lick your face. Zero is when it got bitter. At minus ten you felt the danger of it, like when you're very sick with a fever and your body feels like it's teetering somehow, even when you're lying down. Minus twenty we'd felt only a handful of times—when it got down that low every day they started locking the doors—but it was almost exciting, like when your fever really crests and you feel yourself splitting from your body. This cold was different from all those. Everything felt bright. My feet squeaked in the snow. The edges of the roof looked like they were glowing. Sarah reached the pine trees before me and cuddled up next to one. I sat against her and felt her body shaking.

"'Can you feel your fingers?' she asked me.

"I realized I couldn't. Then my nose was gone too, and then the skin across my cheeks, and it was like I was abandoning my body and going to another place, where cold was only the smallest, most mundane part of some larger, crystalline thing. I felt Sarah stop shivering.

"'Let's play I'm your mom,' Sarah said.

"This was Sarah's favorite game back then, and maybe because neither of us had a real mom, she was always strict with me. She usually told me to go to the time-out corner or get her some potato meal or stand up straight. That day though, she put her arms around my shoulders and sang a song to me in a low voice. The song said that there was a place for every person in the world, and we were in that place, a hole was cut for us in the earth and air, and now that we were fitted into that hole nothing could harm or bother us, and we would never have to worry again. I started to feel the way you feel when you're falling asleep—my thoughts all floated apart from one another and in between was just the song. As if it had always been there. Pretty soon all I could hear or see or feel was the song, and it was so calm, calmer than I've ever been.

"Then hands were all over us, shaking us, slapping our cheeks, carrying us inside. The warmth burned us. The lights scorched our eyes. We cried like newborns.

"Afterward we had frostbite, Sarah lost her little toe, and we didn't play together so much. When I sang the song again to myself, the words just sounded like gibberish.

"Years later though, when we had moved to the island and were living in the grocery store, Sarah asked me if I remembered that day. I said sure, I said we were lucky we didn't die. And she didn't say anything for a while, just kind of looked past me the way she used to. And then she said maybe we wouldn't have. I said what do you mean, it was minus forty at least; we would have frozen to death if they hadn't found us, and she said she knew, but that sometimes when she thought about that day she imagined us turning into something else, not children anymore, but something that could live in that place, something new. She said she imagined icicles sprouting from our fingers, and under our arms, until we had big wings made of ice, and then we spread our wings and flew away. I gave her a weird look—I didn't understand—and she laughed, but I don't think she meant it to be funny."

A child's whimsy, Darcy thought, like pretending that a cheese-food tin full of water was soup, or a rock with a skirt around it was a doll, or two people were a world. Even dead, her mother hid her real self in songs, in games. Maybe it was the other orphans who had silenced her about the past, had made her think that everyone but Darcy would betray her. But what had driven her so hard to make each of them her best friend and then to reject each so completely, until years later when it was too late for all of them? Was it Daniel? Was it Darcy's grandmother, whoever she was, leaving Sarah in a cold common room at the co-op with a coat she grew out of and a doll that she lost and a silver necklace that she passed on to Darcy?

Darcy imagined her mother on the ocean. She imagined it like it was a story that had been told to her, something sitting safe in its proper place in her brain, something she knew and had always known. She thought of her mother's little pointed face looking out above the guardrails of the ship, her mother stealing jerky or biscuits and curling in around herself to eat them, solitary in a corner of the deck while the gray sea surged around her, while the sky seethed, and then the other orphans, all in a pack, jostling and singing, forming a ring around her, attracted by a light that she turned on each of them, and still, at the center of the center of the circle, at the center of her, a loneliness remaining, her bit of jerky wadded up in her fist, her secret thoughts locked up in her mind. Darcy's heart was empty except for craving. She had one question left.

"Did you know my dad?" she asked.

"Sure," Esther said, "we were friends, casually. I think Alejandro only had casual friends."

"What do you mean?" Darcy asked.

"Oh, I don't know." Esther paused, and Darcy realized she was nervous about what was coming next.

"Your mom," she went on, "she was intense. When she set her mind to something, you couldn't shake her off. The only time I ever saw her give up was when we kicked her out—but even that was only for a while. Alejandro was different. He was into the revolution when he felt like it, he'd come help us paint 'Fascists' on the Board headquarters—but then he'd disappear for weeks, go live on the beach and fish or whatever. He was really funny, he used to do these great impressions, everybody liked him. But nobody was very close to him, even your mom.

"One thing he was good at, though—he could smell a rat a mile away. Your mom was pretty trusting and open—maybe Tyson wouldn't have come after us if she hadn't been asking that Seaguard so many questions. But Alejandro was a good judge of people. I remember one time this guy was going to sell us three barrels of palm wine for ten dollars. Then Alejandro talked to him—"

As she spoke, footsteps clomped in the hallway, and the door swung wide. In the doorway were two guards—the man who had shown Darcy her mother's body, and a woman with the wide, pretty face of a doll. Darcy snapped herself back into the present.

"You can't trust Marie," she yelled at them. "She'll lie to get what she wants. She only cares about herself. I know someone who knew her on the mainland, and he said she's a double-crosser."

The guards ignored her. The man pointed his gun at Darcy while the woman uncuffed her from the rack and pulled her to her feet. Her good leg felt rubbery and out of practice—her bad leg was stiff in its cast.

"Leave her the fuck alone," Esther yelled. "You already got her mom—isn't that enough?"

And Nathaniel: "If you want someone to torture, why don't you just take me? You seemed to enjoy that before."

But the man pointed his gun at them, and the woman pressed hers into the base of Darcy's skull and said, "Let's go," and Darcy went.

They marched her through the courtyard, its cool green beauty now incongruous. The marsh hawk watched her from a pine tree with a reptilian eye. Then they climbed the hill to Tyson's house, now surrounded by guards. Darcy looked down at the wall and saw guards pacing along the top of it as well. Beyond it, black smoke was coming up from Manhattanville. Then the male guard opened the door to Tyson's house and the doll-faced woman shoved her inside.

Marie was sitting on the sofa in the living room. The cowboy light was off, and her face was sunk in dimness, but Darcy saw her hands working, picking at each other. The doll-faced guard pushed Darcy down into the rocking chair and cuffed her arms around the back of it. Then the man moved the end table so it was next to Darcy, removed the cowboy lamp shade, and turned on the lamp so it shone right in her eyes.

"Where is Ansel?" Marie asked.

The guards' big guns looked ridiculous in the quaint little room. Part of Darcy wanted to laugh, but fear made the laughter dry up in her throat.

"I don't know," she said.

The lightbulb was surprisingly bright—the space around it turned a shiny, burned-out black. She shut her eyes. The doll-faced guard jabbed her gun into Darcy's stomach.

"Keep your eyes open," she said.

The center of the lightbulb began to turn an acid bluish green. Darcy wondered if the backs of her eyeballs were burning.

"You're lying," Marie said. "Where is Ansel?"

"I don't know," Darcy said again.

The male guard punched her in the stomach and for a moment her lungs ground against each other, airless. A cold pain pierced her guts.

"I don't care if you kill me," Darcy said.

Only when she heard her own voice aloud did Darcy realize she was lying. Before the kidnapping she had known only work and dirt and bus rides and the alternating closeness and farness of her mother's love. But beneath this was another world, a world larger and older than the island, and in this world were lives Darcy might want to live.

The guard punched her in the face. There the pain was wet and hot, like fuel on fire. Blood seeped out of Darcy's mouth and something felt loose inside her cheek.

"Neither do we," Marie said.

Marie had been wrong about Tyson; he wasn't the only one susceptible to fear. Marie had inherited it along with his power. It crimped the edges of her voice. Darcy squinted. She was trying to see Marie's face.

"I think you care about Nathaniel and Esther," Marie went on. "If you don't tell us, we'll kill them."

Darcy knew they would tell her not to listen, to let them die if she had to. But what if Ansel wasn't really coming, what if they died for a few bags of fertilizer and some half-baked plans? At the edge of the eye-searing light was the ghost of Marie, her dark outline.

"I need water," she said. "I'm going to faint."

Marie ignored her.

"Go get them," she said to the male guard. "Bring them here."

Then she motioned to the doll-faced guard, and the doll-faced guard gave the rocking chair a hard backward shove. The dim room flew sickeningly by, until the floor slammed into Darcy's skull and spine. For a second she couldn't feel or see. Then the pain spread from her head to her hips, a sharp deep shivering bone-hurt. The black cleared off above her eyes and she saw Marie clearly, standing over her, sharp-eyed and imperious and fearful, her hungry guilty lonely self right up against the surface of her skin.

"You don't have much time," Marie said.

Darcy looked at Marie's eyes and she saw that time had stopped behind them. It had stopped long before Tyson went silent in his bed, long before she found him and used her guile and hunger to make him beloved. Long before she set her bitter foot on island soil, before the cold hotel room with the bear rugs and the pot-pourri turning to dust and weak, eager Armin waiting for her to let down her hair. It had stopped in the snow of her once-green backyard in Portland, when her brother's cold skin burned her hand. Everything she did now, she did with that burned hand, that heart casting blindly about for somewhere to lay its strength.

Darcy heard a shot. There was a moment of uncertainty, a silence in her body and the room. A sound escaped Darcy's lips, a shapeless, impotent roar. But Marie and the guard were not look-ing at her. They were looking out the window at something going on outside. Two more shots fired, then three.

"Go out there," Marie told the doll-faced guard. "Tell them we have a hostage. Tell them they have to stop shooting or we'll kill her."

The guard left. Marie lifted her loose tunic and pulled a small gun from her waistband. She knelt by Darcy's head and pressed the gun to her temple. The gun shook against Darcy's skin.

"You think it's going to be different?" she whispered.

Darcy didn't answer.

"You think we wanted to kidnap people? You think we wanted to kill? We were as idealistic as anyone. But you do what you have to do. You become who you swore you'd never be. It'll happen to Ansel, it'll happen to you."

Darcy still didn't answer. She thought of the night Ansel had snapped at Sunshine, his frightening intensity. She thought again of what the whores had said—one that he would never amount to anything, and the other that he would try to amount to too much. Gunfire crackled outside. Below them a wide low noise was rising, a noise like insects, a noise like the air itself.

"You can still call it off," Marie said. "You have more power than you know. If it hadn't been for you, we could've gone on for years. Decades, even, if we found Tyson a good successor—there's no limit to how long. Those people out there need you, and at least for a while they'll remember it. You could be the leader if you wanted to. You don't need Ansel."

A woman called out, close by, was answered by gunfire, and didn't call again. Darcy wondered if Ansel would become another Tyson, and if she could prevent it. What if she could walk outside, put her hands in the air, and declare a cease-fire? Would people really drop their guns? Would they follow her? Then she looked at Marie's face, and saw her fifteen in the snow and screaming, and saw how easily she herself could get stuck like that, and knew that whatever she did in whatever time was left to her, she couldn't take Marie's advice.

"I'm not going out there," Darcy said, and then there was a musical shattering of glass, and another sound so close and loud that Darcy did not immediately give it a name, and then Marie made a face that was almost sweet, a face like giving in, and her body fell across Darcy's body, and Darcy felt the slowing and stopping of her heart.

12

She knew his voice before she saw his face. He was shouting, arrogant and happy, but dangerous too, like a child who has found a gun and knows just what to do with it. He was lifting Marie off her and laying her body on the flowered rug, and there he was, as young and smooth-skinned as ever, flushed from battle as though from vigorous exercise, the guard from the Boat, the guard from her apartment, Glock. He lifted the rocking chair but he made no move to uncuff her.

"I thought I'd see you again," he said. "Where did you go?"

He was insouciant, teasing, but his words had a biting edge. His eyes were wild. Darcy felt her insides clenching.

"What are you doing here?" she asked him.

"Ansel and I have joined forces," he said. "We're the new order, just like I said."

"You and who?" Darcy asked.

"Some of the guards," he said. "I told you not all of us were loyal to Tyson. And some of the gangs, too." He looked out the broken window. "Though not all. We've got some work ahead of us. I hope you're ready for a fight."

Darcy remembered what Ansel had said about excluding the

guards. Obviously he wasn't so interested in taking away their power as long as they could help him. She wondered what he'd told Glock about his plans. She wondered if he made different promises to everyone.

Glock reached into Marie's pocket completely casually, like he was rifling through a pile of trash, and pulled out a ring of keys. Then in one swift movement he holstered his gun, wrapped his arms around Darcy, and fit one of the keys into the cuffs.

"Nope, not this one," he said. "Better try another."

His face was an inch from her face. He wasn't sweating. Incredibly, he still smelled like cologne.

"I missed you, you know," he said. "I came back looking for you. Why did you leave?"

Darcy didn't answer. She made her face and body hard. He tried another key in the lock—Darcy heard it jam.

"It made me feel like you only slept with me to get information. But that isn't true, is it?"

She looked in his eyes. She saw that he knew it was true. He wanted her to deny it, to subordinate herself to him. His breathing was quick. He was used to people giving in. Darcy said nothing.

"Is it?" he asked again.

The next key found its home. She heard the tumblers in the lock begin to give way. She felt the cuffs slide open. Before she could move her hands, he held them fast with his. His eyes were boring into her. Then he put his mouth on hers.

Surely he would stop, she thought. There was a battle going on—surely he was needed outside. If he didn't stop, if he tried to undress her, surely there would come a moment when she could get away. And even if that moment never came, would a second time matter so much? Would it really be so disgusting to do something she had already done? Then a shout sounded outside and

Glock froze for a moment, listening, before kissing her again. He wasn't fearless, she saw — he knew he had enemies outside, people who cared more for her than they did for him. Maybe he would be afraid to hurt her because of what she represented, who she'd become. And even if he did hurt her, she didn't care. She was going to hurt him first. She opened her mouth; he slipped his tongue in; she bit down hard.

He jumped away, and in the moment before she made it to the door and let herself out into the loud day, she saw him reach for his gun, and look at her, and falter, and drop his hand to his side.

Outside the noise was ominous, a hum both human and inhuman, and there was a strange smell in the air. Where once one plume of smoke had risen above the wall, now there were too many to count, and red flames sprang from the windows of the GreenValley building. Guards still stalked along the top of the wall, but they were wearing different uniforms now, green instead of gray. All the guards who had surrounded Tyson's house were dead — Darcy saw the doll-faced guard lying in the flowers, and the guard who had punched her was crumpled with his face in the path. No one seemed to be guarding the house now, but down in the courtyard Darcy saw men with guns, some in green guard uniforms, some in jumpsuits, some in baggy jeans and gang colors. As soon as she reached the bottom of the hill, someone called her name, and she turned to see a man, large and armed. She ducked behind a pine tree.

"Wait," he shouted, coming toward her. "It's okay, it's safe. We're with Ansel. We've been looking for you."

Darcy peeked out from behind the tree. She saw the man's striped shirt, his belly. She recognized Tug, the bouncer from the

Big Top. She was impressed. Ansel's influence was wider than she had thought. She wondered how wide her own influence was.

"Give me your gun," she called out.

He walked up to her, obedient as a boy, and laid his gun in the space between them. Darcy looked to her left and right. She reached down and took the gun. It was very heavy, and just holding it made her feel heavier, like she was wearing armor.

"Are Nathaniel and Esther okay?" she asked.

"Who are they?" Tug asked. "I only just joined up; I don't really know all the—"

"Never mind," Darcy said. She hefted the gun in her hand. "I'm going to need this for a while."

"Ansel wants to see you," Tug said, pointing in the direction of the nursery.

"In a minute," Darcy said. She dashed across to the building where Nathaniel and Esther had been. The guard lay outside the door with blood pooling under his head. Darcy tried the door and found it locked. The guard still wore a key ring on his belt. She remembered Glock rummaging in Marie's pocket, and she made herself hold a hand to the guard's neck and wait until she knew there was no pulse. Then she murmured, "Sorry," and unclasped the key ring and tried keys in the lock until one of them turned and the door swung wide open.

Their faces showed such relief that Darcy felt a lightness, a lifting in her chest—for the first time since she had seen her mother's body, the world seemed to hold the prospect of happiness. She almost cried out with the shock of it, but instead she knelt and unlocked their handcuffs, and when their hands were free they embraced her, and it felt like cold water on scalded skin, almost too much to bear.

"We thought they killed you," Nathaniel finally said.

"Ansel came," Darcy said. "And he has some of the guards with him."

Esther gave a vindictive laugh.

"Turning them against their own," she said. "That's great."

"I don't know," Darcy said. "I need to talk to him. You should come with me until I can get you some guns."

Both of them had trouble getting to their feet. Nathaniel winced in obvious pain, and Esther moved stiffly, like a patient rising from a hospital bed. Darcy averted her eyes from the shit stain down the back of Nathaniel's pants. They leaned on each other, and together they were able to walk out of the room.

Tug was guarding the courtyard, rearmed, along with a stocky man in a Seaguard's uniform. When they saw her, they straightened up and gave her a salute. She was totally mystified by the gesture—she wanted to respond, and to respond in a way that said she deserved this deference, that she had always deserved it, but she had no idea how.

"Thanks," she said, and immediately felt stupid. "Where's Ansel?"

"I'll show you," Tug said, and then he led them down the covered walkway, pointing his gun officiously this way and that, full of purpose. Darcy could walk unsupported if she didn't put too much weight on her cast; she was used to pain by now.

Pine, the girl from the Boat, was standing outside the door to the room where Darcy had spent her long convalescent weeks. The mouth tattooed next to her mouth looked savage and triumphant and she held a machine gun.

"Hello again," she said to Darcy, and Darcy wondered if she caught a hint of irony in her salute. Then she opened the door and Darcy saw Ansel in the rocking chair, a map spread open on his knees. Sunshine was sitting on Darcy's old bed, her spine straight, her face unreadable.

"The heroine returns," said Ansel.

He rose and wrapped his good arm around her. Where his monkey arm had been was a length of metal pipe.

"What's going on?" Darcy asked. "Why are the guards here?"

"We've joined forces," said Ansel, "in a holy alliance. A marriage of love and convenience."

He was in fine form, crowing and gesturing with his good hand. His volubility put Darcy more on edge.

"What did you have to promise them?" she asked.

Sunshine opened her mouth but Ansel spoke first.

"A simple power-sharing arrangement, nothing more. A small price to pay for the achievement of our dreams and the overthrow of our enemies."

Darcy looked back at Pine, who stood in the doorway with one hand on her skinny hip. Nathaniel and Esther flanked her, looking confused. Darcy stepped forward and whispered to Ansel.

"What about the new council? I thought the guards were going to be banned."

Ansel answered her at full volume.

"They've been a big help to us. I think they've earned a role in our brave new world."

He was looking around from face to face, performing. Every word he said was meant not just to answer Darcy but to keep his followers together, to hold them on his side. Darcy remembered the kindred feeling she'd had for him in the shack, when he'd told her that Tyson should fear her. They wouldn't have a moment like that again, she realized, a time that was entirely private, because everything Ansel said now was for an audience, his every word an instrument to consolidate or extend his power. And he had probably always wanted it that way.

"They *are* our enemies," she said. "Glock gets off on danger. I can tell just by looking at him, there's nothing he won't do."

"Is that so bad?" Ansel asked her. His eyes flicked toward Sunshine. "When we stood on principle, we didn't get anywhere. Then you came along and opened everything up. Now here we are—you're a hero and I'm the commander of an army. It's a new island, Darcy, and it's going to be amazing."

Then he made an effort to scrub the glee out of his voice. "Did you find your mother?"

Darcy looked straight at him. "She's dead."

He lowered his eyes and tried to make his expression respectful, but the enduring thrill of his newfound importance was impossible to hide. She thought of his shoeless Hell City childhood, the long sour years of thwarted ambition, and now the triumph, half surprise gift and half entitlement, something he would cling to long after it turned black and septic like a gangrenous limb. Sorrow tugged at her belly—not as strong as the constant gnaw she felt over her mother, but sorrow still. She turned to Pine, pointed at Esther and Nathaniel.

"Get them some food and some clean clothes," she said.

Pine raised her eyebrows and slouched her shoulders, but then she nodded reluctantly and walked off. Darcy turned to Sunshine, still immobile on the bed. A streak of blood ran down her left arm. Her eyes were as haughty and self-contained as ever. Darcy thought of the night in the shack when Sunshine had slapped her face. She probably knew Ansel better than he knew himself, knew what he would do now that he could do anything he wanted.

"Will you come with me for a minute?" Darcy asked her.

Ansel smiled, but he looked nervous.

"When you come back," he said, "we can discuss what to do about the Board."

Sunshine followed Darcy out of the room and up the path to Tyson's house. Darcy stopped when she was high enough to see beyond the wall. The flames in Manhattanville had multiplied, and the noise was louder.

"What's going on out there?" Darcy asked Sunshine.

Sunshine shaded her eyes like an explorer.

"When Glock and his guys came over to our side, it really split the guards," she said. "They're fighting against each other now, and they're not guarding much of anything, so it's a free-for-all for the gangs and anybody else who feels like doing some looting. Once people hear about Tyson, it's going to be even worse. We've got a rough time ahead."

A skinny guard Darcy didn't recognize stood at the door of the house. He saluted. Darcy stared at him until his arm shook; then she nodded to let him relax.

"Is Glock in there?" she asked him.

The guard shook his head; she and Sunshine went inside.

Marie's body was already gone, and a red-black bloodstain lay on the carpet where she had fallen. The living room smelled strongly of dead flowers. In the bedroom a shaft of yellow light threw itself across the covers. Tyson lay in it, unchanged. No one had bothered to kill him. His eyes stared; his mouth hung slightly open; his face remained frozen in impotent fear. Sunshine sat down in the chair next to the bed.

"I used to think if I ever saw him I'd want to kill him," she said, "but now I'd rather let him live."

"I'm afraid this will happen to Ansel," Darcy said. "I mean, not this exactly, but that he'll be like Tyson, and then somebody will come and throw him out, and it'll be exactly the same thing all over again. How can we keep that from happening?"

Sunshine looked at Tyson, and then she looked at Darcy, and

then she began to laugh. Her laugh was cold and shrewd and mirthless and pitying.

"I forgot how young you are," Sunshine said when she was finally finished laughing.

"What's that supposed to mean?"

Sunshine rubbed her eyes and looked wryly at Darcy.

"Look," she said, "I know you think you've had a rough life, and I'm sorry about your mom. But try showing up someplace that's supposed to be your fucking paradise, only to find out you got there too late and you'll never even have a real roof. No matter how hard you work, no matter what you do. Try watching your baby die from a disease they didn't even have when you were growing up, while five miles away other kids get to take medicine and not even miss school. Try being on the very bottom all your life, and see if you don't want to be on top. That's what we've always wanted, and I don't care what Ansel does with it, and I don't care if one day someone comes to kick us out. That's how revolutions work. That's how people work. Anyone who tells you anything else is either lying to you or lying to themselves."

The light from the window had reached Tyson's face. His features seemed to have softened, almost as though he were agreeing. Darcy wondered if it would be a relief to him to realize his life had been just one turn of the cycle, no better or worse than any other, neither success nor failure.

"What about Daniel?" Darcy asked. "What about my mom's plan?"

"If you think there are still people on the mainland, and you can actually contact them, and they'll somehow be better than the people here, go ahead. I'm not standing in your way."

Sunshine stood up.

"You're a hero now," she said. "You can do what you want."

Darcy stayed with Tyson after Sunshine left. She sat in the chair by the bed, and she listened to him breathe, and when a slug of drool crawled down his chin she wiped it away. She watched his unmoving face as the shaft of light crawled up and over it, and when it left him in shadow and his eyes quested momentarily, impotently upward, she looked away.

She rolled up her jumpsuit leg, undid the buckles of her cast, and let it fall open. Her leg was jellyfish pale, and the calf muscle had gone flabby, and when she ran her hands down her shin toward her ankle, she felt a bump that smarted when she pressed it, but the leg felt like hers again. She stood, and put her full weight on it for the first time in weeks, and felt a shifting within herself, a realignment of the bones, but little pain. Her right foot turned slightly inward toward the left one now. She was broken, but she was new. She walked across the room and felt a limp in her step. She thought of Ansel with his monkey arm. She thought of Nathaniel, the savage scar up his thigh that he never regretted. She imagined feathers of ice sprouting beneath her fingernails; she imagined herself flying away.

13

You can't go by yourself," Esther said.

"You want to come with me?" Darcy asked.

Esther looked at Nathaniel. They were sitting on a bench by the pond. Their clothes were clean; Esther was eating an apple. Guards strode back and forth across the courtyard, carrying boxes of ammunition from a storage room to the wall protecting the Northern Zone. The afternoon light had turned an ugly dusky yellow, and the air stung Darcy's eyes.

"Maybe you should give Ansel more credit," Nathaniel said. "You didn't think he could get us out, and he did. Maybe you're underestimating him."

"So you're not coming."

"We would have died if it hadn't been for him," Esther said. "I think we should give him a chance. And also"—she paused, as though embarrassed—"it's been a long time since I had a family. Tyson's gone, Marie's dead, and I want to stop and enjoy it for a while."

Darcy wasn't surprised. Nathaniel and Esther weren't her kin— no one was. She was prepared to go to the mainland alone.

"That's fine," Darcy said. "But I'm going."

"Don't you think you'd be more useful here?" asked Nathaniel. "I mean, if you really think Ansel's corrupt, don't you think you should stay and watch him?"

"If I stay here," Darcy said, "I'm going to end up like Marie. I'm just going to get madder and madder, and maybe eventually I'll do something about it—maybe I'll even get rid of Ansel and take over myself—but it won't stop me from being mad. But if I leave, maybe I'll turn into something else."

"There might not be anyone left in Los Angeles," Esther said. "For all we know that boat was full of refugees."

"Then at least I'll see the mainland before I die," Darcy said. She slung her backpack over her shoulder. She'd filled it with Tyson's things: the atlas with its maps of the sea and sky, *Kon-Tiki,* a little money from his dresser drawer, and the old sextant from the nightstand by his bed.

"How in the world are you going to get there?" Nathaniel asked.

"I'm going to go to the docks and get a boat," Darcy said. "If the guards are busy fighting, they won't be watching them too closely."

"But how are you going to navigate? Have you ever even been in a boat before?"

Darcy patted her backpack.

"I've got a book," she said. "I'll find someone to teach me the rest."

"Be careful," said Esther.

Darcy looked around her. She had penetrated the Northern Zone, she was sitting in its courtyard, she could call any guard to her and he would do her bidding.

"I've come this far," she said. "I think I'll be all right."

"Don't be too sure. Once you're out on your own, you'll be a pretty big target. Remember, you're important now."

Men and women and children were crammed up against the gate in the Zone wall, screaming. At first their voices were a shapeless slurry, their collective body a many-headed monster, but as Darcy drew closer they began to resolve—she saw a man throw a rock at one of the guards, a woman holding up her wailing child, a boy with streaming eyes and a mouth open wide as a melon pushing forward and being elbowed back and shoving his way forward again.

"South Street Snakes!" someone yelled.

And someone else: "Justice for the incarcerated!"

And someone else: "We want real meat!"

And someone else: "Free elections!"

The guards dodged rocks and cheese-food cans and a bottle of what looked like urine, and although each carried a fat gun, Darcy could see the fear in their faces. As she approached the gate, one of them shouted down, "Wait, you can't go through!"

"I'm going through!" Darcy shouted back.

She hoped they didn't storm the Northern Zone. She hoped that Ansel was a fair and gentle leader and that the island would grow to love him, and that he would hold elections and fix the cave-ins and build roofs for everyone in Hell City. But she wasn't counting on it. When she tried to imagine the island in peace and happiness, she imagined the refineries closed down, and the factories silent, and all pretense of the old way of life consigned to memory. And she didn't think Ansel was the person to bring that about. She laid her hands on the gate handles and the guards turned to her indecisively, half-pointing their guns.

"Let me through," she called. "That's an order."

Three of the guards conferred briefly, then descended the ladders on the northern side of the wall and stood flanking Darcy. They pulled the gate open and people rushed forward like water above a dam. A guard on top of the wall fired into the crowd, someone gave a high cry like a kicked dog, and the wave of people closest to the gate stopped advancing, their attention shattered.

"Don't shoot at them!" Darcy yelled.

"Just go," said the guard to her left.

He was in his forties, potbellied and tired-eyed—he looked like he had seen fighting before and was not surprised to see it now. He pointed his gun into the crowd and the crowd, unwillingly, unevenly, cursing and shoving and crying, opened a channel for Darcy. Darcy ran down it, her own gun at her shoulder. The crowd was a block deep, and at the back of it were old women, blind people leaning on canes, and last-boaters so lame and pockmarked and drained of all human power that no revolution would want them, every crowd would push them to its outskirts, and no new order would ever lift them aloft. Darcy saw them try to push their way forward, and she saw the heels and elbows of the crowd push them back, and she felt for them as she had not thought to feel for such people before, but the feeling was impotent and worthless and she ran on, even as they grabbed for her and stuck their faces in her face, and even as she heard the guards at the wall begin shooting.

She walked along Fifth Avenue, coughing and looking for a bus stop. The rains were over, and in their place was a thick black blanket hanging low over the island, a fat layer of bad air much denser than any she could remember. The smog seemed to ooze up from the ground now, pooling around the buildings and sliding into the sky. A smell of seared seaweed and roasting plastic forced its way into her lungs. Then she saw the burning bus.

It looked like a carcass picked clean by wild dogs. The entire hood was gone, exposing an intestinal tangle of plastic pipes. The metal side panels were gone too, and Darcy could see the remains of the seats, their Seaboard covers blistered and cracked. Flames still leapt off the roof deck, but down at street level a boy pried off one of the hubcaps and ran away. Sitting on the sidewalk by the bus-stop sign, two men with tattered clothes and last-boat teeth shared a bottle of expensive wine.

"Are you waiting for the bus?" Darcy asked. "Are some of them still running?"

"Our bus came," said one of the men, holding the bottle high.

"I saw another one burning on First Street," said the other. "Where you headed?"

"The mainland," Darcy said.

"You better start walking then," said the man with the bottle, and then both of them laughed.

Something whizzed past Darcy's head and shattered the window of a furniture store. She tried to run and found she could do it if she favored her left leg and ignored the ghost of pain that hovered around her right. At Second Street she saw two guards with their guns pointed into a fine-foods store. Then a third strode out the door with packages of meat wrapped in Seafiber. The pink juices were seeping out onto his pants. The guards had liverish, suspicious faces and they held the meat close to their bodies like greedy children. The sky looked sick. At Third Street, a woman slammed into Darcy. She was wearing a yellow jumpsuit; she was pregnant; she smelled like fire.

"You better watch where you're going," she yelled in Darcy's ear.

Then she saw the gun. She lifted her hands and her belly spilled out onto the street—coins, not a baby.

At Tenth Street, banners were raining down. People on the

rooftops had sliced them from their moorings, and now Tyson's face, ten times life size, drifted over the crowd and came to rest, crumpled, on the asphalt. A little girl wrapped herself in one and pranced about on the glass-spattered sidewalk, robed in the face of her former leader.

Upper Chicagoland was full of fighting. A pig was roasting in a rusted-out oil drum, surrounded by men and women slugging it out over who got to eat it. A week ago a pig like that would've cost more than Darcy's yearly salary at World Experiences—now any of these scrabbling, screaming people could have it for a well-laid punch, a kick to the balls. Then a gunshot ripped the fight in half. A man fell and a woman bent keening to him; the fighters stilled their fists and looked wildly around, and three gangsters with guns and red bandannas rushed in to take possession of the pig. Another shot was fired and Darcy ducked down an alleyway between two Seaboard processing plants.

The light was dim between the tall buildings, but before her eyes adjusted Darcy could sense the presence of other people. The air inside the alley had a human shape, contoured by dozens of frightened faces pressed against one another, breathing shallow breaths.

"Don't shoot," someone said. "We don't have anything valuable."

The speaker was a man, a little older than Darcy, wearing a jumpsuit and holding a child on his lap. Next to him was an older woman with long black hair, and next to her was another woman, and all down the alley pairs of eyes appeared out of the dark, expectant and fearful. Darcy put her gun in her jumpsuit pocket.

"I'm not going to shoot you," she said. "I'm just passing through."

The woman with long dark hair said, "We keep hearing shots."

"Is anyone in charge?" asked another woman, with a bruise on her face. "Are they going to stop all this?"

"His name is Ansel," said Darcy, "and he'll try."

Before she could say more the alley filled with questions, all blending together into one loud many-throated bellow of confusion and fear.

"Listen!" Darcy shouted. "Ansel took over from Tyson. He's a last-boater and I think he wants to help you, at least for a while."

The bellow started again, but this time Darcy could hear individual bellows within it, each of them asking some variation on *What should we do?*

Darcy wanted to answer them. She owed them an answer, owed them help now that she understood what was happening and they did not. It was strange to have more power than someone else, and unsatisfying, because the only way she could see to really help these people was to stay and fight for their jobs and their homes and their safety, and staying was what she had decided she couldn't do.

"I don't know," she said. "I don't have any advice for you. Like I said, I'm just passing through."

Then a girl from the end of the alley spoke out. She was young, no older than Darcy, but her voice was low and loud.

"Who are you anyway?" she asked.

Darcy knew she should lie. Esther was right—she was a target now. Anyone could decide to hunt her down—gangsters looking for a trophy kill, guards hoping to get to Ansel through her. Glock. He wouldn't have touched her back in the Zone, where he was supposed to be friends with Ansel, but if he found her out here, by herself, he might want revenge for his bitten tongue. But she thought of Daniel, too, the way his name had stayed with her mother long after she should have forgotten it, had made her a rebel when she should have been another disaffected diver. Even if Darcy never came back, maybe her name could be like that, a weapon against complacency, an unexploded bomb.

"I'm Darcy," she said. "And I'm going to the mainland to see if anyone's still alive."

A new sound came up then, not a bellow but a flurry, a mix of questions and speculation that was almost like excitement. They asked her why she thought people were still alive, and if she had heard of such and such a person, and where on the mainland she was headed, and someone said he had heard of Darcy and were the stories true, but Darcy could feel the flurry beginning to hold her back, and so she told them all, "If I find someone, we'll send a ship back."

As she ran down the alley, she heard them repeating her name.

Darcy walked through the rest of the day and some of the night. As she passed through Lower Chicagoland the crowds turned from frenetic to weary, their shouting less joyful and more desperate. Children coughed in the smoky air; drunk men vomited on sidewalks strewn with broken glass. She grew exhausted, but the alleyways looked dangerous, exactly where someone would look for her. Finally she found an abandoned deli in Sonoma Hill, completely looted except for a jar of pickled seaweed rolling back and forth along the uneven floor. She unscrewed it and ate the vinegary strands while she looked among the shelves for a good place to sleep. In the back was a storeroom with a broken padlock. She crept inside and leaned against the door to sleep, and dreamt of rain.

At first she thought the kicks against her back were thunder, and still half-asleep she pressed her palms against her ears, but then she heard a gunshot and drew her own weapon, as fast as if she'd been doing it for years. A man burst in, wild-eyed and shirt-less, a smell of smoke and sweat swirling around him. They stared at each other down the barrels of their guns.

The man spoke first: "Give me your money."

She was relieved that he didn't seem to know who she was. A free agent, then, not someone from the gangs or the guards.

"I don't have any," she lied.

"You're lying. Give it to me."

"Get out." Her voice didn't waver. She was surprised at how angry, how commanding she could sound.

"I'll shoot you," he said. "I will."

In those last two words she thought she heard a crack. She pushed on it.

"Go the fuck ahead," she told him.

He faltered then. He didn't lower his gun but she saw the mus-cles in his forearms loosen.

"I need money," he said. His voice was broken open now; he was almost crying.

"I can't help you." She spoke more softly now but kept her gun trained on him.

"Please," he said. "They want a thousand dollars, or they're going to come and kill me."

"Who does?" Darcy asked. She had a hundred dollars from Tyson's drawer, but she was going to need it later, if not to buy a boat from its owners, then definitely to get enough solvent to cross the ocean.

"The Kings," he said. "They think I have money because I had a store. But the looters took everything—there's nothing left. And nobody will help me."

Darcy told herself he might be scamming her, but the fear in his face looked absolutely real. He dropped his gun to his side and looked at her piteously, whatever pride he'd once had shattered at her feet. If she gave him the money he'd be a hundred dollars closer to safety, but she'd be broke on an island poised for civil war, with no way to get where she needed to go.

"I don't have any money," she said slowly. "Please leave me alone."

He looked at her and he looked at her gun and she saw his whole body shrink with resentment and resignation.

"If you're lying," he said, "I hope you burn in hell."

He said it matter-of-factly, too exhausted from fear even to shout at her, and his words stuck in her brain all the rest of that night and kept her from sleep.

In the morning of the next day she reached Little Los Angeles. Here the guards seemed less established. She saw a few on Figueroa, trying to subdue a crowd outside Carnicería Ortiz. But on the Avenida no dominance was yet decided—empanada stands lay unused and smelling of stale oil, their operators unsure who to pay off, and Darcy saw the faces of women in high windows, looking for patches of safety on the street below. The street itself was nearly empty—there was nothing left to loot, and all the people who thought themselves weak or vulnerable were waiting to see who they should pay allegiance to. All the people who felt strong were jockeying to earn this allegiance, but not in any organized way. Four men in red bandannas were standing on the corner of Fifteenth Street, watching, posturing, and doing cagey, faux-reluctant drug business with a man in an old-style suit. New gangs were forming—the pharmacy had become a kind of headquarters for a loose band of men in jumpsuits, with guns and self-conscious, hard expressions. Two of them were talking to a woman, at first friendly, then harsh, then coming at her from both sides with short barking shouts and guns raised until she sobbed, and pulled from under her shirt two dented cans of beef food and a log of Sealami.

Darcy saw all this, the fear of the woman as she left empty-handed and sniffling, and the different but no less potent fear of the men, workers all their lives, suddenly blessed and saddled with strength, and she let it fill her mind and heart until she sweated and shook with the horror of her home laid waste before her, but she did not stop. Instead she crossed Sixteenth Street and passed Mercado Lucky 7—restocked with stolen goods and restaffed with their thieves—and reached her old building, its ground-floor windows broken and its front door staved in. Above the doorway a spray of blue paint read "Guards Die." A monkey, nervous and patchy-pelted, rolled an empty beef-food can with its hands and licked its metal wall. Darcy paused and was about to keep walking, to let the building molder away in memory. Then she thought of the *Animal Atlas*. It wouldn't help her find the mainland—she had better maps already—but it was something of her mother's, something she could take and hold, and that was enough to make her want it. She turned and entered through the broken door.

The inside of the building had a new sound. Before the air in the stairwell had been thick with unstanched voices, with the clatter of cheap objects breaking, with the squelch and cry of fighting and fucking, but now a cautious, imperfect quiet hung over the stairs. Darcy heard the arrhythmic patchy popping of sounds emitted and then stifled—a scrabble of feet, something metal against something glass, a baby's thin chirruping cough. On the wall at the second-floor landing was the word "Catorce," crossed out and replaced with "Kings." On the wall on the third floor was a brown stain that looked like blood.

The door to Darcy's apartment had been broken down and set back up again, and then sealed into the doorway with several layers of duct tape. Darcy pulled on the knob and the whole door came away with a ripping sound. Feet rushed to the corners of the room. Then someone whispered, "Darcy!"

Pressed against the wall near the window was Dolores Beltran. Her arm was wrapped in a strip of jumpsuit, blood soaking through. Next to her were Augusta and her baby, a rag in his mouth to keep him from crying. More of Darcy's neighbors huddled on the bed— Liberty Ramirez and his sister Luz, the Zargaryans from the first floor. And squatting next to the hot plate was Jorge, the landlord, looking haunted and sleepless and confused.

"You came back," Dolores said. "Is it true you killed Tyson?"

"No," said Darcy. "What are you all doing here?"

Dolores motioned for Darcy to lower her voice.

"This is the only building on the block the gangs haven't taken over yet. Everyone between Sixteenth and Seventeenth tried to pack in here."

"So who's in your apartments?" Darcy asked.

"We don't know them," Dolores said. "They have broken bottles. They made us leave."

"Darcy, you have to help," said Augusta. "Make them give us our apartment back."

They were worse off now than they would have been if she had agreed to help Marie. She hadn't saved her mother, and she had helped drive her neighbors from their homes. Everything she had done seemed worse than a waste. Darcy didn't see her mother's book anywhere, and she knew she couldn't ask for it.

"I can't," Darcy said. "I'm sorry."

"We heard you're in charge now," said Luz.

"You have a gun," said Liberty.

"The baby needs medicine," said Dolores.

And then they were surrounding her, tugging at her clothes, pleading with her, growing increasingly desperate and insistent and angry, and the apartment seemed to shrink around Darcy—a place that had seemed small enough when Darcy was alone and powerless was even tinier now that it was packed full of people who assumed she had power.

"I babysat you when you were little," Dolores said.

"I gave you extra time on your rent," said Jorge.

"Just help us get our apartment back," said Augusta.

"Just help us get something to eat," said Liberty.

Darcy backed toward the door. She felt even weaker now than on the anxious nights she'd spent motherless in this apartment, even more alone. Now more than ever—more than at the wall, where the lame and blind were strangers, more even than in the storeroom with the frightened man—she felt the deep intestinal tug of guilt and duty, and now more than ever she felt the futility of trying to fulfill that duty. She knew she could stay and help them, but she'd have to give up on ever breaking free of the island. And she couldn't bring herself to stay and fester in the memory of her mother's death and the slow attrition of Ansel's ideals. She knew it was selfish—probably she could do something for her neighbors in the short term, and going to the mainland wouldn't help them for a long time. But still, she wanted them to understand her, to know why she was leaving and what she hoped to find.

"I'm not in charge," she said. "The person in charge is named Ansel. He might help you, and he might not. I don't know. But listen—I'm going to the mainland, to Los Angeles. I think there are still people living there, and if I find them, we'll send a ship back. But in the meantime, you could go yourself, if you want to. You could get your own ship together. If you don't like Ansel, if he doesn't help you, you don't have to follow him. You can do something else."

They looked at her silently, their faces flat. Maybe they understood her, maybe they thought she was insane. Dolores looked at her family, then back at Darcy.

"Okay," she said. "Go."

Liberty began to protest. The baby began to cry. Augusta said something vehement to her mother in Spanish. Dolores shook her head.

"No," she said, and then to Darcy, "you should go. And if you see my husband Cristian on the mainland, you tell him we didn't forget him."

Darcy stood for a moment, trying desperately to think of something she could do for them and still escape. Then she remembered the gun. She was still a couple hours' walk from the docks, and once she got there, she'd still need to find a boat and learn how to sail it. If she gave the gun up, she'd be defenseless all that time. And if she didn't, the curse of the man in the storeroom would ring in her brain forever. She drew it out of her pocket, heavy and black, and everyone in the room shrank back against the wall.

"Don't be afraid," Darcy said, holding the gun by its muzzle. "I'm giving it to you."

Liberty reached his hand out, recovering quickly, but Darcy didn't trust him.

"I'm going to walk out the door," she said. "And I'm going to leave it in the doorway."

She began to back away. They could use the gun to defend themselves, she thought. Maybe they could get their apartments back. She reached the doorway, and bent, still watching them, and laid the gun down on the Seaboard floor with a tiny click, and ran. But before she turned away she saw the look in Liberty's eyes, the hunger and excitement, and she wondered if she'd done the right thing after all.

When she reached the ocean it was dusk. The road was deserted; dull orange clouds hung lackluster overhead. The seawall, the barbed wire, the exhausted sky—it looked like a place humans had given up on, a place that had given up on itself. Then she walked through the gate to the docks, and saw the ocean crowded with boats, boats thick as seaweed on the water, and her shriveled heart swelled in her chest, and she charged toward them, barreling through the waves.

They were burned. Darcy smelled it before she saw it, the horrible briny char of flames slowly snuffed by dirty seawater. Their gas tanks were blown out from the inside, the plastic peeling back like the petals of blackened flowers. The lacquered Seaboard of the hulls was blistered and cracked and crinkled—the sea was seeping in, slowly filling the boats with orange water. The sails hung limp and tattered and black from the masts, like the wings of sickly bats. The Seaguards must have set fire to their boats when they heard about Tyson, though whether from a desire to keep them from Ansel or in a spirit of pure chaos Darcy didn't know. Out on the horizon, the big guard ships were smoking too.

Darcy sat in the sand and faced away from the ocean. The solvent in the water had eaten her pant legs threadbare. Halfway up the beach a bony brown dog nosed a pile of fish bones. When it saw Darcy it came toward her with a loping, sidelong gait. She held her hand out; it sniffed at her, tilted its head as though to rub against her open palm, then yipped and took off down the beach.

She imagined her mother shaking her awake. She imagined her mother's lips in her ear whispering a song. She imagined her still astonished after all these years, throwing the window open, shouting, "Feel how warm it is!" They would slurp the dregs of a cheese-food can, and Darcy would put on her jumpsuit and her mother would put on her wet suit, and then they would go to work and come home and maybe buy some hot dogs, and maybe some cookies, and draw funny teeth on Tyson in the morning flyer, and go to sleep, and do it all again. They would be hungry, and sweaty, and Darcy would keep wishing they had more money, but at least their life would be whole.

In her mind, Darcy rolled the days back. The burned boats struggled back out into the water, the black sails whitened, the blown-out gas tanks closed. All the rioters slotted back into their factories, their loot settled back onto the shelves. Tyson's blood unclotted and he sat upright and began giving orders. The rain re-fell; Darcy's leg unbroke itself and her heart healed. Her mother unbreathed her last breath.

Then the islanders piled back into their boats, last ones first, first ones last. They unbuilt the buildings—Manhattanville folded up into neat stacks of scrap, Little Los Angeles melted into a pile of algae and slid into the sea. Finally the founders unpitched their tents, bundled their children up, and unmade their journey.

Why stop? The co-op uncooperated, the roads reopened, crops came back to life and clouds sucked back their snow. Darcy's mother crawled back inside her own mother and was unborn. And somewhere in the retreat of time a switch unflipped, a lamp unlit, a brain went blank, and the whole inevitable slide of the world ceased to be inevitable, so that if time were to start moving forward from that spot, everything would turn out different, fire instead of ice, or plague instead of fire, or somehow, if the clock were stopped and started again just right, the accident of a smooth, safe journey, a straight path to a good place, a present innocent of all possible mistakes. Darcy could not imagine that present, could see only a cool room with books, a hobbyhorse, a rocking chair, someone else's vision, but she knew it existed somewhere in the tree of possible lives, and she ached for it, as for a half-remembered dream.

She stood. The dog was gone. The dark was falling. A bird circled worriedly overhead. Far away on the ocean she could see something white. As it came closer it took on a triangular shape, swelling out away from the wind: a sail. When the sail was the size of a postcard on the sea she saw that it was blank, and when it was the size of a T-shirt she saw three small figures standing in the bow, and when it was the size of a sail the figures jumped out onto the dock and tied the boat up to a cleat.

Darcy ran over. One of the figures was a girl, eleven or twelve years old, with long lank sun-fried hair pushed behind her ears and a watchful brown pointed face like a cat's. The other two were boys — one maybe ten years old, with black hair and a cut beneath his eye, and the other, possibly his brother, younger-looking, but with a much older person's stillness about the eyes and spine. The girl reached into the stern of the boat, pulled out a net with a meager catch of fish inside, and peered at it with a critical eye.

"Is this your boat?" Darcy called to them from the end of the dock.

The girl startled badly and whipped the net behind her back.

"Yeah," she said, "why?"

Darcy walked up the dock; the children eyed her ruined pant legs with mistrust.

"Okay, listen," she said, "I know someone who can help us. Someone who can help everybody on the island. But I need a boat to reach him. Do you think I could borrow this one?"

The boy with the cut looked at Darcy like she was crazy.

"No way," he said. "It's ours now. We found it, and we need it for fishing."

"Can I talk to your mom?" Darcy asked.

"We don't have a mom," the girl said, and her flat eyes hurt Darcy's heart. The smaller boy looked away down the beach.

"Can I talk to your dad then?"

The boy with the cut pushed his hair out of his face. No one had cut it in a long time. The cut looked like it might be infected.

"We don't have a mom, and we don't have a dad," he said to her, in a voice that sounded like he was getting used to commanding. "This is our boat, and you can't have it. Now quit fucking with us before we kick your ass."

Darcy wished she still had the gun. Then she reproached herself. Would she really have threatened children? She had no idea how to talk to them. Her mother had never talked to her the way adults were supposed to talk to children, so that they listened to you and did what you said. She turned away from them, toward the interior of the island. All the smoke from all the fires swirled from the edges of the island into a single plume at its center, like a black funnel turned upside down. The air was thick with half-burned flecks of plastic and Seaboard—it had a burning, chemical sweetness. The roar of the looters and the looted sounded mechanical now, like traffic, like the engine of an enormous, self-operating machine. Darcy turned back to the children.

"Do you know what's happening?" she asked them.

The girl looked withdrawn and upset. The boy with the cut put on a sardonic expression, but he didn't answer. The smaller boy rubbed the soot out of his eyes.

"Someone told us Tyson was dead," he said.

"He isn't dead," Darcy said. "But he might as well be. What else did they tell you?"

The girl spoke up. "They're saying someone named Darcy killed him, and she's a last-boater, and she's going to put all last-boaters in charge."

Darcy shook her head. "I'm Darcy, and I didn't kill anyone, and I'm not going to put anyone in charge."

"You're Darcy?" the smaller boy asked, his eyes wide with fear and fascination. "Is it true you broke into the Pacifica Bank and stole all the money?"

The girl's voice was more cautious but no less curious. "Are you really going to buy everyone in Hell City a house?"

Darcy started to answer, but the boy with the cut interrupted. "I don't believe you're really her," he said.

The girl shot him an annoyed look.

"Think about it," he said. "Why would she be here with us? Why wouldn't she be in the Northern Zone, eating steak and celebrating? That's what I'd do."

The girl's face clouded.

"Can you prove that you're her?" she asked.

Darcy almost laughed. The idea that her identity was now valuable enough to be doubted was hilarious. Instead she said, "I don't think there's anything to celebrate yet. The people in charge now might be just as bad as Tyson, and everybody might be just as bad until we start doing things differently."

The boy with the cut rolled his eyes, but the girl knit her brows together.

"What do you mean, 'differently'?" she asked.

"I need to ask someone on the mainland about that," Darcy told her. "But probably no more refineries. No more cars. No more steak, no more strawberries, no more apples. No more try-ing to make the island like the mainland used to be."

"What's an apple?" the smaller boy asked.

The children were skinny in a stringy, stray-dog sort of way. Their faces had the ashy, grayish cast that Darcy's used to get at the end of the month when she and her mother ran out of food money. They were staring hungrily at the fish in the net. These were children who had never had electricity. They had never been in a car—they probably took the bus only a few times a year. They had never seen a strawberry. If anyone could give up the island way of life for a new one, it would be these kids, who had never tasted its benefits.

"It's a fruit," Darcy said. "Like fruit snacks."

The boy with the cut stood up. All his movements were tense and guarded, like he was used to watching his back.

"Whatever," he said. "We've got to eat now."

The girl turned to Darcy. "You can eat with us, if you want."

They made a fire on the beach out of pieces of ruined boat and some old Seaboard milk containers they found lying in the sand. The smoke rose up, smelling of sick sea, and joined the great cone above the island. It was dark now, and the greenish flames cast shadows on the children's faces, making them look like tiny old people. The girl cooked the fish on an old oar—she had to keep pulling it out of the fire to keep it from catching. The fish were bony and undercooked and tasted like solvent, but Darcy hadn't eaten all day and so she licked the pale meat from the spine, crunched on charred skin. When each of them had eaten a fish there was one left, and Darcy lied and said she wasn't hungry any-more. The girl divided it in three with her fingers and the chil-dren each gulped their pieces down quickly, like seagulls.

When the fire was out, Darcy started making a place in the sand to sleep. The smaller boy watched her for a moment, then said, "You should stay with us."

"We don't have room," said the other boy.

"Yes, we do," said the smaller boy, "if you don't move around so much."

"I don't move around."

"You do. You're always yelling and throwing your arms and legs around like you're fighting."

"How do you know? You're sleeping."

"Sometimes you wake me up."

"Okay," said the girl, silencing them. "There's room. She can stay."

They had a few garbage bags stretched between oars dug into the sand. Underneath was a nest of old jumpsuits and Seafiber bags and a torn blanket with monkeys on it. The smaller boy crawled into the center and fell asleep quickly. The boy with the cut lay down next to him and closed his eyes. Darcy lay at the edge of the nest, her body straight so as not to crowd the boys. The girl took her place on the western side, so that anyone coming from the center of the island would have to go through her first.

Sometime at the night's gray tail end Darcy woke up. The boy with the cut was making a high-pitched keening cry in his sleep, a terrible half-animal noise. The smaller boy was sleeping soundly. Darcy didn't see the girl. She got up and walked out onto the beach. The girl was sitting in the sand, facing away from the surf. The smoke plume showed up harsh black against the lightening sky.

"You couldn't sleep?" Darcy asked.

The girl's face was pinched and drawn inward on itself. She

looked at Darcy like she was trying not to speak, and then she spoke anyway.

"I'm scared," she said.

Darcy sat down next to her.

"What are you scared of?" she asked.

"A week ago we were so hungry we were eating Seafiber. Now we have the boat, so we have fish every night. But pretty soon someone else is going to want it, and they're not going to ask like you did. And we're not going to be able to fight them off."

The girl sat with her hands wrapped around her knees, the habits of her body already hardened into a defensive crouch. Darcy imagined her scavenging along the alleys of her Hell City life, her brain and legs traveling a fixed path from one crisis to the next and the next and the next. She felt a pang of sympathy so strong she almost reached out and touched her. Instead she said, "I know people who can help you. Get to the Northern Zone, find Esther and Nathaniel Rosen. If you tell them I sent you, they'll keep you safe."

The girl looked up at her with hope, and then with suspicion.

"How do I know you won't screw us?" she said. "I'm still not sure you're really Darcy."

Darcy looked out at the ocean. A rim of light was riding the horizon.

"Did they tell you anything else about me?" she asked.

"They said Darcy was six feet tall, and you're not. They said she had a big gun, and you don't have a gun. They said she walked with a limp."

The girl paused, remembering. Darcy's limp was better, but it must still be noticeable. She rolled up her pant leg to expose her ankle.

"Feel," she said.

The girl reached out a tentative hand, pulled it back, and reached out again. She ran her fingers along Darcy's calf, and when she reached the lump above the ankle, her eyes locked with Darcy's.

"Did you get shot there?" she asked.

"No," Darcy said. "I broke it running away from a bear. You can't believe everything you hear, but the limp part's true."

The girl was silent, considering.

"Listen," Darcy went on. "You don't have to believe me. But if you don't, and you just stay here, you're screwed sooner or later anyway. You know that much already."

The girl looked at the sleeping boys and then back at Darcy. Her eyes were very tired but there was resignation in them, and something like relief.

"Do you know how to sail?" she asked.

Darcy and the children went fishing the next morning, and the girl taught her how to hoist the mainsail and raise the jib, and then how to reach and how to run with the wind, and at first Darcy was clumsy and the boat slowed and slid sideways on the sea, and the boy with the cut complained and said she'd never get it, but after two days of sailing she began to understand the boat with her body, and they sailed and caught jellyfish, and that night they put several of the jellyfish on the garbage-bag roof to dry so that Darcy could take them with her.

When she had been with them three days, Darcy and the smaller boy went to Hell City and bought fresh water and solvent from a looter who had set up shop outside the Boat. With what little was left of her money, she bought the children some bread and cheese food, and that night instead of fish they had sandwiches. And when she had been living on the beach a week, Darcy went out in the boat by herself and came back with a big haul of jellyfish and a sunburn on her cheeks and a feeling of the beginning of something new. At night she practiced using the sextant, and she read *Kon-Tiki* to the children, and studied her atlas, and sometimes she told stories about her mother and about Daniel and about the mainland.

But she didn't sleep. The sounds from the rest of the island swelled and slackened—one day it was calm and the smoke seemed to thin and Darcy wondered if Ansel had made peace after all, and the next night the air filled back up with screaming, and a kind of fast, percussive music Darcy had never heard before, and the noxious smell of burning. Sometimes late at night Darcy listened to the mingled din and wondered what part of it came from the Northern Zone, what part from the wall, what part from the compound itself. She wondered if the crowd had ever breached the wall, if the guards inside would be able to fight them off, if Ansel was even still alive. She thought that he was, that probably he would find a way to survive even a direct assault, and she realized this made her glad.

Once Darcy woke from a shallow doze to gunshots so close she ran outside and buried the solvent tanks beneath a layer of sand. No thieves came to the beach that night, but she knew that every hour she spent there made Glock or the gangs or some rebel guards more likely to find her, and to find the children too, and so she made them stay out all day on the water teaching her, until all their arms were rubbery with fatigue and their eyesight blurred from staring at the waves. After a week and a half, when Darcy had learned to maneuver the boat under both wind and solvent power, and they had loaded up the boat with jellyfish and water and solvent and the monkey blanket from their nest, Darcy said good-bye to them on the sand. The boy with the cut still looked distrustful, but there was a brittle hope in the girl's cautious face, and Darcy bent to them and told them, "When you meet people who talk about me, tell them you knew me. And tell them I've gone to the mainland to get help, and that I'm coming back."

14

On the first day the wind was good and she was not afraid. She didn't watch the island as she sailed away; instead she watched the ocean roll forward at her from the horizon, in puckers and eddies and wavelets, not choppy, not still, but each second yielding up a new shape and shade, offering to wipe her mind clean with its green movements. She learned how to feel the direction of the wind in her ears. She turned the sails and tacked windward. She saw how this could become her life, how she could forget she had ever not been on the ocean.

Then she was turning to adjust the mainsail, and she saw the island, the smallest possible glimpse of the island before it passed beyond the range of sight, a brownish patch with smoke coming up, and then a spot so small it was like a bug, a little hairy bug clinging to the horizon. And as she watched, suddenly transfixed, letting the sail go momentarily slack in her hand, it winked out and was gone. And only then did she feel despair like nails driving down into her chest, and she crumpled down into the damp briny space at the bottom of the boat, and she let the boat drift, or rather she forgot that there was a boat, or that she was responsible for it, and she mourned. First she mourned the things she had hated and feared—the sight of a rat creeping across the floor at night or stopping to sniff and leave its fur or shit or the filthy memory of its presence on the only clean shirt she had, the feeling of hunger when they had no food in the fridge, the acrid grating jealousy of seeing someone on the street casually eating something she couldn't afford—an ice cream cone with real chocolate chips, a chicken kebab, a purple smoothie made with berries. A man looking down at her mother as he hitched up his pants. Glock holding his penis in his hand for a moment before putting it inside her. The feeling of being alone in her apartment with nothing to do but think of how alone she was. The smell of rotting jellyfish. The sidewalk melting in the rain. Soot settling on the windowsills when the factory was burning old Seafiber. Monkeys laughing in a dark alley. Mold. The feeling that, no matter how much she hated the island, she could never get away.

Then she mourned the things that were both sweet and ugly, and the ugly things that memory made sweet—the beginning of monsoon season, when a beautiful shining sheet of rainwater would fall down on the island, and stir up all the shit smells, and rot the ceiling out. The first sickening whiff of solvent from a jar, and the way it seemed to tip the world a few degrees off plumb. The number 9 bus back from World Experiences, full of people she saw every day but hardly ever spoke to. The smooth taut scar at Ansel's elbow. Falling asleep face-to-face with her mother and waking up six hours later, still smelling her skin, still breathing her breath, still exhausted, as though no time at all had passed.

And finally, when she had been through all the things that were safer and less dear, she mourned the things she had loved without reservation. She mourned the part of the morning just before the alarm went off, when the air was cool and the sky was gray and she didn't have to be anywhere. She mourned the salty oil slick of cheese food on her tongue when she hadn't eaten all day, and the smell of the churro stand on the Avenida, and mangoes, and the sweet forbidden tang of anything stolen. She mourned the day she got drunk on the unrestricted beach and felt for the one and only time in her whole life that she and the mass of people who lived with her on the island were connected, that when they knocked against her and jostled her and fought her for space on the sand or the last shaved ice from the shaved-ice man, they were actually communicating, in some language that neither they nor she fully understood but that would become clear some day, reveal itself in terms so simple and true and obvious that she would smack her forehead and say she should have known it all along. And she mourned her mother, or not her mother exactly but all the things on the island that carried her memory, that made plain her absence, the hole shaped like her mother in the left-behind world.

And as she knelt in the bottom of the boat, remembering the line of rock dolls under the window, and the imprint in the bed, and the divers coming out of the water, black-suited, slick as seals, and the little girl in Yuka's memory, and the young woman in Nathaniel's, and her own jealousy that these memories could only be stories to her, that she would never know those parts of her mother with her own mind, the sky began to purple, and the wind began to rise, and the boat kicked and made her remember it again, so that she turned the sail and steered the keel through the growing waves with the setting sun behind her.

When it was night, the stars shocked her. She was unprepared for their density, for their number, for the way they crowded so close together that they seemed to form a substance, like the speckled skin of an enormous animal that rounded its belly over her. The fact of a universe outside the island was so suddenly and powerfully before her that she hid from it. She furled the sails and pulled her blanket over her head and pretended that she was back in the apartment again, and that all that mourning had been only a game.

On the second day the wind was still good, and Darcy felt listless and empty, like the ocean had passed through her instead of around her and washed all the sugar out of her blood. Dealing with the sail made her arms sore and her whole body exhausted in a way she'd never known. She thought of her mother dropping limp onto the bed after a day of diving, her mouth loose around her words. She was out of tears, and remembering her mother just made her feel soft and porous all over, like the mast could pass right through her hand.

She ate two of the jellyfish without tasting them and drank some of the water. The ocean was greenish and opaque. Near nightfall she saw a seagull and realized it was the only living thing she had seen all day.

On the third day the wind died down and she had to use the motor. The boat ran slowly against the waves, like someone struggling uphill. The smell of burning solvent in the air was familiar and comforting. The air was cool. It dried the sweat under her arms and made her feel new and clean and awake. For a long time she sat in the bow and let the air float around her. She had never felt so cool outside an air-conditioned room. It seemed impossible that the inhuman world could provide such comfort. The whole ocean was like a cool clean room where she could lie down, just what she had always wanted.

★   ★   ★

On the fourth day the wind picked up again, and she could turn the motor off, but the air had a rancid smell and she had to hold a jellyfish up to her face to mask it. Every few hours she saw things floating on the water, fibrous wads and purplish, rough-edged chunks.

On the fifth day she began to talk to herself, little comforting words and bits of the old songs.

On the sixth day she saw a storm. It was a brownish spot like a sore on the edge of the sea. She steered away from it. She sang, *Have you heard the tale of sweet Betsy from Pike?*

She sang, *Michael, row the boat ashore.*

She got the boat so it was pointing into clear sea, and for the first time in two days the air was clean and had a sweet smell, almost like flowers, and then the rain was all around her like a panic, so constant and inescapable that it might as well have been inside her, and the sky was pus-yellow and then green and then black, and then a strange color that was so dark and changeable and difficult for her brain to describe that it seemed monstrous, as though the benign animal of the starry sky had been devoured by something terrible from outside the universe, or below it, and that thing was now roiling her around in its raw gullet, drenching her with its spit.

She furled the sails, but the boat began to pitch violently from side to side, and a wave slapped her from the right, and filled her mouth with water that tasted like salt and metal and something very bad, like a living rot that would breed and spread inside her. Then another wave broke over her from the left, and the boat made a new and sickening motion, and she saw the sea rise up level with her eyes, and the surface of the sea was pink for some reason, and then the boat fell away in the opposite direction, swaying like a drunk, and her eyes were parallel with the sky and the sky was veiny, and then she felt the boat tip past some critical point, and it was not tipping but falling, and she was ripping through the skin of the water and scrabbling in its rotten guts.

For a long time she swam. She remembered what her mother had taught her; she flapped her arms and kicked her legs, she pretended that she was in air, but she knew she was under water. The water was cold. It was the first time she had ever felt this, cold water all around her. This was a cold that seemed to suck the heat out of her, to pull it from her chest and groin and armpits until there was nothing left there and it pulled on her limbs, slowing them, making her move like an ant in sticky mango juice. She didn't breathe or open her mouth, but still she could feel the smell all around her, the smell that was beyond rot, the smell that was getting inside her through her skin. Soon the stale air began to press against her lungs, and come up her throat and press against the backs of her teeth, and she still had not found the surface of the water; she was moving more and more slowly, and she began to think about breathing. She thought about what would happen if she opened her mouth and let the stale air out and took a big, deep breath. Her mouth would fill with rotten water, and then her lungs would fill with it, and probably she would cough, but what would a cough be under water? Probably she would just breathe in more of the ocean, and then her brain would begin to slow, and she would stop swimming, and then she would die. It came to her that she would see her mother. A door would open muscles in her arm began to burn, she didn't think about dying anymore. She reached the boat and she clung to it, and after a while the rain began to stop.

On the seventh day the air was clear and clean and smelled like pure salt, as though the storm had scrubbed the rot away. After an hour of bobbing and scrambling, she was able to right the boat and crawl back into it. She tried to start the motor but the engine was full of water and it only made a gurgling, coughing noise and then lapsed into silence. The sail was mostly intact except for a few notches on one edge that looked like bite marks, and when she was able to get it strung up it caught the wind and filled out, round as a cheek. For what might have been a minute and might have been an hour, Darcy sat in the bottom of the boat, breathing the cool air, watching the bright green line of the horizon, feeling her muscles mending. Then she remembered the food.

They had tied it down, but the force of the waves had broken the ties, and all of it was gone. Once the shock of this had died down, she realized the water was gone too. All three jugs were sinking through the salt water somewhere, along with her jellyfish and her no doubt sodden and sea-stained blanket. Or would they float? Darcy vaguely remembered a middle school science experiment with salt water and various small toys from GreenValley Meadow Meals. She shielded her eyes and looked out over the ocean, but the sun hit the waves and threw itself back at her, so that all she saw was its white blaze printing itself on her eyeballs, glowing orange when she closed her eyes. She thought of turning about and scouring the sea for her water jugs, but she didn't know how far the storm had taken her. She might backtrack for hours and still find nothing and then be without food and water with even farther to go. She ran her hands all over the boat, feeling for something she could use for a fishhook, but nothing was small or sharp enough, and even if she could knock a shard off one of the motor blades—her best idea—she didn't know what she would use for bait. When she considered her only options, her brain recoiled in disgust. So she kept an eye on the wind, and the sail, and the sun climbed up to its apex in the sky and fell away again. As it was falling she began to feel hungry. It started out as normal hunger, the familiar groan and suck in her belly that no jellyfish fully satiated, but with the knowledge that not even jellyfish were coming, a gray scrim came down before her eyes and her ears rang. Then she saw black at the edges of the gray, like the scrim was charring, and her neck felt boneless, and she let her head fall between her knees.

The ringing in her ears rushed and twisted and became a music. She remembered going hungry as a child, nights near the end of the month when her mother would put hot water in the cheese-food cans. How long had they gone like that? A day? Three? But they hadn't been in the middle of the ocean then, food had been all around them, and she remembered stealing a GreenValley energy bar from the convenience store, begging an empanada from the stall back when she was small enough to suck pity out of people with her gap-toothed smile. They were never really in danger of starving. Still, when the rush in her ears quieted a little, she remembered too how they had made a game of hunger, or rather a game of ignoring it, how the first person to think of food had to pay a penalty, like singing a song in a silly accent or drawing a mustache on her face, how they used the honor system and both cheated a little but it didn't matter, the point was not really to avoid hunger but to make hunger into a kind of joke instead of something to be afraid or ashamed of.

She started a game of flicking herself in the cheek every time she thought about food. The first flick brought her out of her daze a little. The second roused her. She noticed that she had to urinate and of course the bucket she had used for that was gone. She thought of trying to go over the side and then realized that would be wasteful. She unzipped her salt-caked jumpsuit and crouched over her cupped hand. The feeling of revulsion was strong. The wind chilled her bare shoulders. She had the absurd fear that someone might see her. Then she pushed the fear away, pissed into her palms, and lifted them to her lips. It wasn't much, it tasted like jellyfish and undernourishment, and it made her double over with disgust, but she got it down.

Afterward she felt slightly stronger. She thought of GreenValley mint candies, and she flicked herself in the cheek again. When it began to get dark she furled the sail and put out the drag anchor. Then she unhooked the jib and spread it across the width of the boat, loosely, so the fabric dipped at the center. When she was finished the stars were out. For a moment they all looked the same to her, just a white rash on the black, and she was afraid she wouldn't be able to find hers again. But then the sky took shape, the Milky Way seemed to recede into the background, the constellations popped, and there was the North Star, clear as a street sign. She wasn't even too far off course — nothing that couldn't be righted in the morning. It was cold, and there was a new smell on the air, a smell she couldn't put a name to but that was neither bad nor good and that disappeared whenever she really tried to pay attention to it, and she unhitched the mainsail and wrapped herself up in it and went to sleep.

On the eighth day she woke up just before dawn. The sea and sky were slate blue, and the world seemed frozen in hushed preparedness. A light wet wind blew in from the southeast. In the valley of the jib, as she had hoped, lay a shallow layer of dew. She knelt low, pulled the jib in toward her, folded it into a spout, and held her mouth open as a little brackish water trickled down her throat. Then she hitched up the jib, unwound the mainsail from her body and hitched that up, pulled in the drag anchor, and watched the rising sun green the eastern sky.

All day she felt light and strong and fast, like if the sea would hold her she could run across it in an instant. She stared at the surface of the sea and thought about how it would feel beneath her feet—smooth, but not like Seaboard; more like some strong and flexible skin. Time seemed to pass very slowly. When the sun was high in the sky she got very hungry again, and she began thinking of the rib roast she'd had at Snow Rosen's. She thought of ways she could have saved it—sticking it down the front of her jumpsuit, lashing it to her thigh. She had to remind herself that that was weeks ago, that it would surely have rotted against her skin by now. She sucked on her thumb and tasted salt. She looked over the side to see if she could see any fish, but all she saw was her own image, rippled and bent like in a fun house. Then she flicked herself in the cheek and sang herself a song and felt a little better.

On the ninth day she saw a person on the sea. The person was standing exactly on the horizon. She could not tell if it was a man or a woman, but it seemed to spread its arms in welcome. She tried to measure it with her thumb and forefinger, but when she held her hand up it went away. She thought maybe she had reached the mainland, maybe Daniel and his followers had erected a giant statue to greet her, but she sailed all day and it never got any closer. It just stood on the horizon, perfectly still, welcoming. She realized that someone must be walking backward across the ocean, leading her. The wind was good all day, and as night drew near, she felt from the person on the sea a sense of great approval.

On the day she forgot what day it was, there were ice crystals in the jib sail. She crunched them between her teeth. The person on the sea was sending her messages, but she couldn't understand them. It was very cold and the sky was breaking into diamond shapes, and the diamond shapes were falling into the ocean, revealing something behind them. It was a ceiling. It was the ceiling of her apartment. She knew by the leak marks in the shapes of imaginary countries. It was the ceiling of her apartment and she was in her own bed. Outside the rains were starting. She turned over to tell her mother, but her mother was gone. She sat up in bed. Yellow walls came down before her eyes. Just as she was beginning to think that she had seen all this before, she understood the message of the person on the sea. The sails. The person was reminding her about the sails. She got out of bed and the floor rocked underneath her feet, and then she went fumbling about the room looking for the sails. It was hard because her arms and legs were very weak, and because what she saw kept switching back and forth, room boat room boat room boat room, until it got stuck somehow in between and the floor was all patchy where the sea broke through, and the ceiling was spotted with sky, and half the things she tried to grab dissolved like steam in her hands.

Finally she caught something, and held it, and some old muscle memory told her what to do with it, and then there was a mast in the middle of the apartment, with sails on it, and the sails were filling with air, and the apartment was moving on the ocean, and the person was shining through the front wall of the apartment.

Then the boat was moving very fast over the water. The water was screaming past in a green blur. She could hear it screaming. Icebergs began to flash by on both sides, milky green, luminous, shaped like towers, shaped like cows. It got so cold that her breath made a cloud around her head. The water was a new color, cloudy blue-white like a cataract on an aged eye. Its scream was higher. Sheets of ice came and knocked against the boat with a sound like bells ringing. She could see her breath-clouds floating out over the ice. She was weather now.

She saw that this was the final change, that she would become not a bird, but a cloud moving over the ocean. The cloud that she was becoming moved through light, and it moved through darkness. It moved below stars, and it moved below the sun. It saw the water grow thicker and thicker with ice, until the boat slowed down and could barely move. All the while the parts of her that were not cloud were falling away — her hunger, her fingers and toes, her concept of time, her name.

And soon or not soon, when the part of her that was not cloud was almost completely gone, was nothing but a tiny watcher in the middle of the vapor, the boat stopped moving. The ice set up around it, creaking and popping, like a pair of ancient hands closing with her in between. Behind her, before her, to the left of her, to the right of her, everywhere was ice. And then, far in the distance, she saw that the person on the sea had vanished, and in that person's place were three flags waving in the cold wind, and on those flags were mountain lions.

ACKNOWLEDGMENTS

This book and I owe a great debt to my wonderful agent, Julie Barer, whose energy is as infectious as her insights are sharp. I've also been incredibly lucky to work with editors Reagan Arthur and Andrea Walker, who believed in the book and made it better, and with awesome publicist Marlena Bittner.

I am forever grateful to my teachers Rick Barot, Ethan Canin, Nan Cohen, Charles D'Ambrosio, Scott Hutchins, David Mac-Donald, Elizabeth McCracken, Rick Moody, ZZ Packer, Marilynne Robinson, and Malena Watrous. Tobias Wolff has been an invaluable source of knowledge and support. Jonathan Ames provided a key tip early on, and Samantha Chang's smart and sensitive advice made the book what it is today. Seth Lerer has always been a wise friend to me and my writing. Connie Brothers has mysterious powers that should be acknowledged always.

Great thanks are due to all of my classmates at Iowa for their help and friendship. Ian Breen (who read the first chapter four times), Amanda Briggs, and Jim Mattson deserve a special shout-out. Sarah Heyward, Vauhini Vara, and Jenny Zhang have been better friends than I could ever have known to ask for; I miss you every day. Benjamin Hale has heard all the stories that went into this book and many that didn't; thanks for listening. Thanks to Greg Wayne and Darryl Stein for reading the book before it went out into the world. And to Anna Holmes and everyone at *Jezebel* for being inspiring and understanding colleagues. And to Michael Curtis, for all his help with my first published story. Thanks to Meggy Wang for everything—your friendship has been life-sustaining.

Most of all, thanks to my parents and my brother. The seeds of this book were sown in our living room, in front of *Doctor Who*, and all of you were there.

ABOUT THE AUTHOR

Anna North graduated from the Iowa Writers' Workshop in 2009, having received a Teaching-Writing Fellowship and a Michener/Copernicus Society Fellowship. North grew up in Los Angeles and lives in Brooklyn.